ANASTASIIA MARSIZ

THE BIG FELLOW

THE BIG FELLOW

by Anastasiia Marsiz

First published in Russian as *Большой человек* in 2021

Translated from the Russian
by Andrew Sheppard and Michael Pursglove

Proofreading by Richard Coombes

Russian text © Anastasiia Marsiz, 2021

Cover image © Max Mendor, 2023

English translation © Andrew Sheppard and
Michael Pursglove, 2023

© 2023, Glagoslav Publications

Book cover and interior book design by Max Mendor

© 2023, Glagoslav Publications

www.glagoslav.com

ISBN: 978-1-80484-098-6
ISBN: 978-1-80484-099-3

First published in English by Glagoslav Publications in September 2023

A catalogue record for this book is available from the British Library.

ANASTASIIA MARSIZ

THE BIG FELLOW

TRANSLATED FROM THE RUSSIAN
BY ANDREW SHEPPARD AND MICHAEL PURSGLOVE

GLAGOSLAV PUBLICATIONS

CONTENTS

1. CECILIA'S LAST DAY

"My dear," the owner of the vegetable stall politely addressed the elderly woman standing in front of him, "of course, Ernesto is a good man, a trier, but his hands are an absolute disaster. Today, he managed to drop four boxes of produce. Two of them were cherries, and most of them were ruined."

"Oh, Mario, please forgive me," the woman said, going pale. She blushed and looked darkly at her grandson, who was standing in a corner of the shop, smiling vacantly. "I'm so sorry. What can I do? Perhaps I can pay for them."

"No. There is no need for that," Mario replied hastily, lowering his eyes. He wanted to help this unfortunate woman, but how could he? Her grandson was a prize idiot, and clumsy too.

"Ernesto, let's go," the woman said.

The big dark lad, with his huge long hands, dashed up to his grandmother, seized her, and dragged her to the exit.

"Poor Cecilia," mumbled Mario when the door had slammed behind them.

"And where shall we go now, Ceci?" asked Ernesto, smiling joyfully when they had got round the corner of the building.

"To the sea-front, Ernesto," she replied wearily.

"To the sea!" exclaimed the lad. "Maybe I'll run home and get my swimming trunks."

"No, my dear, we're not going to the sea."

"Why not?"

"You must find work, Ernesto."

"And where will we look for it?"

"In the Chalet Martina. I know the lady who owns it. She's strict, but it's worth a try."

Cecilia paused for some moments and gave a deep sigh. Her head was spinning, her feet hurt and her mouth was dry.

"Let's sit down," she said, sinking wearily on to a bench beside a colourful children's roundabout. Opposite them were several restaurants. One of them, Chalet Martina, was about to host a desperate woman's last effort to find employment for her feckless grandson – a hapless orphan, half Gambian, half Italian.

"Ernesto, my dear, go and buy me a bottle of water."

"In a jiffy," he replied delightedly. He dashed off, and immediately collided with a passer-by who was carrying a glass of coffee. The coffee spilled onto the man's trousers, and he gave a yell.

"Pardon me. Please! I didn't see you," said Ernesto. He leaned towards the man and, in trying to help, struck him a direct blow on the chin with his elbow.

"Leave me alone, idiot!" shouted the man, making haste to get away from the whirlwind that was Ernesto.

"Forgive me," mumbled Ernesto, smiling awkwardly.

Cecilia heaved a sigh and looked away. Her face was covered with tell-tale red blotches. Over the past eighteen years she had become used to people insulting Ernesto, looking askance at him, laughing. She did not intercede for him, but merely hid her eyes – fearfully and timidly. Ernesto never noticed either her sighs or her ashamed looks.

"Ernesto," she said quietly.

"Yes, Ceci," he replied, flying to her.

"You forgot to take any money."

Ernesto then set off once again to get the water. Cecilia meanwhile plunged into painful thoughts of the past. Lately, she had been troubled by her memories. Her temples throbbed, burning like fire; her throat was constricted.

Spectral images of the past paraded by her, besieging and devastating her soul and bringing her sick heart pangs of pain. She did not trust doctors, did not get a diagnosis, but felt sure that her last days were upon her.

She remembered the day when Ernesto came home from school, pale and excited, with a still-bleeding wound in the back of his head. He was eight years old.

"Ceci, we had a great time playing in the yard with the kids from my class," he had yelled, delightedly. "A game with text books. You had to hit a target. I was the leader. Dino was happy to let me have it, just here," he said, pointing to his injury. "We drew a spot with chalk! Ceci, I was a human target!"

With a muffled groan, she set about bandaging Ernesto's head, thinking of the cruelty that lies in the hearts of children. In this merciless world, life would be hard for her gormless grandson. Would there be so much as one person who would be kind to him and not turn him away?

She herself had once wanted to be rid of Ernesto. When he was just four years old, she had decided to put him in a children's home. As she had got his things together and dressed him, he had watched her with his trusting eyes and a naïve smile so broad and joyful that she shuddered. She had turned away, ashamed of her intended treachery. When all was ready, she had taken him firmly by the hand and led him to the bus stop, trying not to look at him.

They had walked along the sea-front in silence. It was late autumn. A strong wind got up; it howled like a wild animal, rocked the trees, bent branches to the ground. Waves furiously lashed the shore. Ernesto's small hand, strong for a child of his age, gripped hers, which was enfeebled by her own age. "The hand of a traitor," said the waves.

At the bus stop, Cecilia placed Ernesto on a bench. A bright notice caught his attention. "Ceci, what's that?" he asked, looking his grandmother in the eye.

She had gasped, and even staggered backwards a little. With his clear glance, Ernesto had reminded her of Leah, her beloved daughter. His eyes were exactly the same.

Cecilia had sunk to her knees before her grandson, embraced him, and clasped him firmly to her. Warm tears gushed from her eyes, erasing the remains of her powder along with her treacherous intentions.

So they returned home. Cecilia held Ernesto by the hand as the wind swept her grey locks this way and that; tears ran down her cheeks; her lips quivered and she murmured, "Leah, Leah, my little girl."

She would of course never forget how she had lost her only daughter.

The day on which Leah left the family home had been one of the hottest of the year. Exhausted by her work and the heat, Cecilia had been mighty glad to push open the door of her flat. It was quiet inside, as if everyone were asleep. "Leah. Daughter. I'm home," she had called loudly.

No one answered. In the kitchen, her husband, Roberto, was sitting at the table. He was staring at a sheet of paper with a vacant expression such as she had never before seen in the twenty years she had known him. Moving close enough to get a clear view, she read:

My dear Mum and Dad,
I've fallen in love with a good man. He's called Omar. He comes from Gambia. We want to get married. I know you'll be against the marriage, so I've had to go away. But I'll be back. I'll phone you soon.
Forgive me!
Your Leah.

It was eight months before Cecilia saw her daughter again. Leah came home sad, emaciated, and expecting a baby.

Roberto did not ask Leah where she had been, or look at her outsize belly. He just said, dryly: "Don't go into the street. You'll bring shame on us all."

Leah did indeed stay at home for days on end. At night, repressed sobbing could be heard from her room.

She had changed. She was no longer the vivacious Leah who smiled at the morning sun, took delight in the beauty of the sunset, leapt laughing into the sea, lay on the golden sand and looked at the sky. Her love for life had burned out and cooled. Her eyes no longer gleamed and her voice was weak. She would lie in bed and look at the ceiling with unseeing eyes. Cecilia wondered what had happened to her; wondered where she had been all this time; wondered who this Omar was who had left her in this humiliating situation. In response to Cecilia's questions, Leah just smiled warily and her eyes filled with tears.

So, instead of asking questions, Cecilia would stroke Leah's head, comb her hair and say: "It's all right. Everything will sort itself out somehow. The main thing, Leah, is that you are at home."

One night, Leah whispered to Cecilia: "Mama, I feel bad."

Jumping out of bed, Cecilia saw a huge puddle on the floor. Ten hours later, Ernesto entered the world.

"Signora Bruno, we've done all we can for your daughter, but her body failed…," said a thin young doctor with a thin black moustache. "Your daughter…." The inexperienced doctor crumpled as he tried to speak the words for the first time in his life. "I'm sorry," he said quietly. "My condolences."

A despairing cry tore from Cecilia's chest. Crushed with sorrow, she sank to the floor – life had no meaning for her now. Her pulse struck her head like a hammer; her weak body shivered.

A nurse put something cold on her face; helped her up and settled her on a sofa. She checked her pulse and, leaving briefly, soon returned to give her an injection.

Some time passed. "Signora Bruno, can you hear me?" asked the doctor. "You have a grandson. A healthy, strong infant. Will you take him?"

"What?"

"Your grandson. Will you take him?" the doctor repeated.

"Me?"

"As the closest relatives," began the doctor, running his finger along his thin moustache, "you and Signor Bruno can take your grandson, or you can give him up."

Cecilia was not able to give up her grandson. She lived according to rules which had been instilled in her in childhood: to be an obedient daughter, a faithful and caring wife, and a kind and loving mother – a true Catholic woman.

The only right decision was to bring up her orphaned grandson. It was her Christian duty. When she took his small, wrinkled, dark-skinned body in her arms for the first time, she experienced only a feeling of duty, pain and cruel injustice, which she humbly accepted.

She and Roberto lived modestly. She worked as a maid in a hotel: Roberto caught fish and sold them to local restaurants. They had a two-room flat. There was a small living-room/kitchen, and a bedroom which was divided into two parts by a partition. The furniture was inexpensive: a small sofa, upholstered with a grey, cotton fabric, a simple wooden table, four chairs and an old television. The carpet was worn, and the only wall decoration was a picture of Castle Torregalli.[1] Cecilia had often looked at this picture and said dreamily to Roberto: "We'll save up. I'll buy a proper silk dress, yellow, with blue flowers and a wide-brimmed straw hat. We'll go to Castle Torregalli and walk in the gar-

....

[1] A mediaeval castle (early 14th century), situated not far from Florence, in the foothills between the River Arno and Greve.

den. Leah will run along the avenues catching butterflies. In the evening you and I will drink Pino Grigio and dance."

Drunk on her dreams, Cecilia spun around the room singing:

It is a simple song for two pennies
That is sung on the streets of the suburbs
For those who wait, for those who love, for those who dream,
It is the eternal sweet tale of love.[2]

Cecilia and Roberto never did visit Castle Torregalli.

It was a bright sunny day. Cecilia was cooking lunch, while one-year-old Ernesto played on the carpet. There came an insistent ring at the door of the Brunos' flat. Cecilia gave an involuntary shudder, looked around and opened the door. On the threshold stood her neighbour, Toni. He was crumpling his hat in his hands and shifting from foot to foot. He gave a sigh and, without looking her in the eye, said in a quiet voice: "Cecilia, my dear, Robert is there, at the harbour."

Snatching up little Ernesto, she rushed to the harbour just as she was, wearing her house slippers. There a small knot of fishermen had gathered. The men made a passage for her, shaking their heads. When she got through to the boats, it was to see a pale Roberto with blue lips, lying motionless on a damp board.

He had suffered a heart attack as he came into the harbour.

So Cecilia was left alone with their small grandson.

The years flew by, making of Cecilia the frail, sick old woman who was now sitting on a bench, staring fixedly, sighing, muttering to herself, picking over the threads of bitter memories.

When Ernesto ran up, carrying a bottle of water, she was dozing.

....

[2] *Canzone da due soldi.*

"Here you are, Ceci, I've brought it," he said loudly into her ear.

"Ah, Ernesto," she replied hoarsely. "What took you so long?"

"I was looking for your favourite, in the blue bottle."

Cecilia drank the water greedily.

"All right. Let's go, Ernesto. Let's go." She stood up from the bench and, leaning on Ernesto's arm, headed for the entrance to the Chalet Martina.

Looking around timidly from the threshold of the restaurant, she saw the owner, Signora Marino. She was bending over a young lad who was reluctantly sweeping up the remnants of a broken glass. She stood with hands on hips and was frowning.

"Antonio, how many times do I have to tell you? And how can you make pasta if you can't keep hold of a glass. I give up."

"What sort of a day do you call this?" she further exclaimed, seemingly to the wider world, waving her arms. Then she noticed Cecilia and Ernesto.

"Hello, Cecilia," she said affably.

"Good day to you, my dear Martina. Look, I've brought my grandson. You remember Ernesto, don't you?" She pushed the lad forward.

"Of course I remember Ernesto," exclaimed Martina kindly, surveying him with interest. He was looking her straight in the eye. "Will you come to dinner? Please do. Today, Adriano is cooking his trademark pasta."

"Thank you for the invitation," Cecilia replied, "But we can't do dinner. I'm looking for work for Ernesto. He's a big lad now." She broke off, lowering her eyes. Then, collecting herself, she went on: "Maybe you've got some work for him, Martina?"

"What can he do?" Signora Marino asked, casting an involuntary look at the lad's long, strong hands.

"Since he was a child, he's helped me in the hotel. He's strong and tolerant." Cecilia switched her gaze to her grandson. "He's a quiet boy, kind and honest."

"Antonio! Son!" Martina yelled suddenly. "How long are you going to be clearing up that wretched glass?"

Antonio shot an enquiring look at his mother, shrugged his shoulders and reluctantly continued gathering the fragments on to a tray. Ernesto stooped and began helping Antonio.

"Martina, please give my grandson a job in your restaurant." Cecilia went on, looking beseechingly at Martina. "I can't work in the hotel any more. I'm old already. I can't cope on my own."

"Of course, Ernesto is a fine lad…," drawled Martina.

"I understand," interrupted Cecilia. "You can't take him. I'm sorry," she snapped and, taking Ernesto's hand, made for the exit.

"Why can't I take him?" Martina retorted with a smile.

Cecilia turned and looked unbelievingly at Martina. Her determination to leave the restaurant gave way to perplexity.

"Did I hear you right?" she asked. "You'll find a job for my Ernesto?" The poor woman looked hopefully at Martina.

"Yes, I most certainly will take on the boy in our restaurant," replied Martina, firmly. "Ernesto, my dear, you come along with me."

Smiling broadly, Ernesto followed her.

"Antonio, are you still here?" said Martina, raising her voice again.

Antonio ran to the kitchen. Martina guided Ernesto towards the beach recliners lying folded by the entrance to the Chalet Martina. Cecilia followed them, saying nothing.

"Just here, on this spot," Martina began solemnly, "every evening, at about nine, fold up the recliners. In the morning, at seven, put them out on the beach in even rows. When customers arrive, show them to the places whose numbers I will give you."

The bespectacled Martina fixed a look on Ernesto. "As this is just the second week of the season, I haven't got a security man, so you will also keep an eye on the restaurant at night. Will you cope?"

"Yes, of course, Signora Marino," Ernesto replied, delighted.

Cecilia, her eyes downcast, said nothing.

Martina pointed to the first door of an annex in a narrow passageway between the restaurant's inner courtyard and the beach, where there were chalets for visitors. "You will sleep here," she said. "I will pay you thirty euros a day. Food is on the house."

"Thank you, Signora Marino. I'm very pleased," said Ernesto, smiling broadly.

"Excellent," she replied. "Cecilia, what do you think?"

"I'm very grateful to you, my dear Martina." Cecilia seized Martina firmly by the hand. "What a kind heart you have. May God preserve you."

"Ernesto can start today," said Martina, withdrawing her hand.

"Yes, of course," said Cecilia. "Ernesto will be back here by seven." She took her smiling grandson by the arm and quickly left the restaurant before Martina could change her mind.

Martina followed Cecilia and Ernesto with her eyes and did not notice that her irate husband had arrived at her side.

"What have you taken it into your head to do? That's all we need, that what's-his-name," exclaimed Adriano. Antonio watched from the kitchen, expecting a scene.

"He's called Ernesto," Martina replied calmly. "I've taken him on. He'll be the night watchman, and by day he'll help me on the beach."

"And you're not interested in my opinion?"

"I'm always interested in your opinion, my dear," said Martina, with a smile. She gently patted her flushed husband on the cheek. "Ernesto will work for us, and that has been settled," she said, kissing him. "Come on, let's try the best pasta in the world."

Martina led the smiling Adriano back to the kitchen, of which he was the undisputed master.

Cecilia returned Ernesto to the Chalet Martina at exactly seven o'clock. She once again warmly thanked Martina. Then she embraced her grandson, kissed him tenderly, and set off home with tears in her eyes.

She paused on the promenade and for a long time gazed at the sea. For a moment she thought she saw Roberto in the distance in his boat. He was waving and pointing to a net with a rich catch. Cecilia waved back, but he had already disappeared from view.

She felt a powerful, pulsating pain in her head. A noise in her ears drowned out all else. The muscles in her limbs obeyed her half-heartedly, and only after seeming to delay for as long as possible. She felt tired as never before.

The road home seemed endless. Breathing heavily, she finally reached the staircase to her second-floor flat. Opening the door when she reached it was itself an effort. She stepped into the dark, empty living room. Cruel silence. Solitude.

When the time for sleep came, she found she could not. She stood by the window in her nightdress and for a long time stared into the darkness. An apple tree grew beside her house. Suddenly, it seemed to her that young Leah was standing under the tree. She was wearing a linen dress, white, with red spots; her wavy hair was gathered up in a long pony tail. Looking up at Cecilia, she smiled. With a trembling hand, Cecilia grasped the old window latch and tried to open the window. How many times had she asked Roberto to mend that latch? Finally, she managed to open the window.

"Leah," she cried.

But Leah had vanished.

Tears rolled down Cecilia's cheeks. For a long time, she stood in front of the open window, hoping Leah would re-appear.

When she finally slept, she dreamed that she and Roberto were strolling over the lawn beside Castle Torregalli. Roberto was wearing a light linen suit and a white shirt. Cecilia had on a yellow silk dress with a pattern of blue flowers, and a wide-brimmed straw hat. A little girl – Leah – was running along the path towards them. She was wearing the same dress as in Cecilia's waking vision, with her hair in the same pony tail.

"Mummy, look what a nice butterfly It's got yellow wings with blue spots, just like you have on your dress."

The butterfly continued on its haphazard way. Cecilia and Roberto joined Leah in running after it across the green meadow in front of Castle Torregalli. They were all hand in hand, and they laughed.

The breeze carried the strains of a tune being played somewhere far off:

> It is a simple song for two pennies
> That is sung on the streets of the suburbs
> For those who wait, for those who love, for those who dream,
> It is the eternal sweet tale of love.[3]

The sun rises every morning, illuminating all the inhabitants of earth, with their pain and their joy, their grief and their happiness, with snatches of phrases left unfinished at night. People find each other and lose each other; people are born and people die, and the sun rises again.

....

[3] *Canzone da due soldi.*

ANASTASIIA MARSIZ

That morning Cecilia did not see the rays of the new sun. Neighbours found her lying in bed, a smile frozen on her lips. In her cold and lifeless hands was a photograph in which Cecilia, Roberto and Leah were together, smiling happily.

2. THE YOUNGER CONTE

In a spacious bedroom, which could have accommodated a family of three, in an exquisitely patterned, gold-painted bed, young Calisto Conte was beginning a new day. He opened his eyes and looked at the painted ceiling; an impish Cupid was smiling. The young man grinned at him in reply and winked.

From the lower floor came the clink of cutlery, mingling melodically with animated voices: "Dévi is setting the breakfast," thought the young master Conte.

Throwing off the silk sheet, he lowered his feet to the floor, which was covered with a soft rug. He made for the bathroom, the dimensions of which matched those of the huge bedroom.

"Signor Calisto," came a high-pitched female voice. "Are you awake? Signora Conte is calling you to breakfast."

In Calisto's bedroom a shy girl, Dévi, stood leaning against a door jamb. "I'm having a shower, dear. Come here." said Calisto.

"Why do you joke like that, Signor Calisto?" said Dévi in embarrassment, continuing to hide behind the door. She was ready to shed the light dress of her uniform, to throw herself into the arms of her young boss, but restrained herself.

"Signora Conte asked me to tell you," the girl began, in a serious, almost stern voice, "that if you don't come down in ten minutes, she'll take the keys of your car and you can go off to your 'business' on the bus."

The sound of water stopped, and Calisto threw open the doors. He was irresistible: his clothing consisted merely of crystal droplets. His damp black hair shadowed the pallor of his face, with its fine, regular features. A satisfied smile shone in his eyes. A wave of colour flooded into the girl's face, her breathing became more rapid and her heart fluttered.

"So here I am," he exclaimed, striking a theatrical pose.

"What are you doing, Signor Calisto. You're all wet!" she babbled in embarrassment.

"But I want," he said, lowering his voice, "you to…." His finger touched the girl's heaving breast and undid a button on her dress.

"Signor C…."

"Shh." He put his finger to Dévi's lips and slipped his hand under her dress. "We've got time…. We've got a whole ten minutes," said Calisto with a smile and let her into the bathroom.

Fifteen minutes later, humming merrily, Calisto Conte descended the stairs. He was wearing blue jeans, a bright yellow shirt and green moccasins. Continuing to hum, he went into the dining room.

At the head of the table was a woman, sitting in solemn state. Black silky hair framed a stern face with gentle aristocratic features. In her clear grey eyes was an expression of cold pride. This was the lady of the house, Patricia Conte.

"Good morning, O loveliest of women," exclaimed Calisto in the same passionate tone he had used fifteen minutes previously in his bedroom. He went up to his mother and, taking her hand, kissed it politely.

"Leave your cheap tricks for your stupid girlfriends," replied Patricia coldly, casting an angry look at Dévi, who was running past the dining room. "Son, what do you look like, coming to breakfast like that?"

"What is it in my appearance that displeases you, mother?" asked Calisto with a sly smile. "Please note, I wasn't even late," he said, popping an olive into his mouth.

"How tasteless," said Patricia, pointing at Calisto's yellow shirt. "And don't take food from the table before you sit down." She took a piece of cheese from her son's hands.

Calisto reluctantly sat down beside his mother. "Where's Dad?" he asked.

"Your father is playing tennis with Marcello," Patricia replied, not shifting her gaze from a porcelain cup.

"Why so early? They always play later in the day."

"They've switched to playing in the morning, presumably because of the heat of the past several days. However, I am not involved in your father's business, and he doesn't account for himself to me," said Patricia, a deep furrow cutting across her immaculately smooth forehead. "But what about you, my dear. How do you intend to spend the day?" Her tone was sarcastic.

"As always, cheerfully, enjoying every moment of my youth," replied Calisto, with seeming enthusiasm. "Thanks for breakfast. Now I'm ready to greet the sunny day and…."

"And endless amorous adventures," Patricia interrupted. She compressed her lips in a crooked smile.

"Mum, don't be jealous. For me you are the most wonderful woman in the world," said Calisto. He kissed his mother's hand. For him, this was all a part of wanting to leave as soon as possible.

Patricia jerked her hand away and coldly watched him leave.

Calisto went out of the house into a broad yard. Running past a marble fountain and skirting an age-old row of densely planted cypresses, he reached the garage. Several cars gleamed there. Some of them were collectors' items, objects of special pride for Calisto's father, Alberto. All were polished to perfection.

Calisto opened the door of a yellow sports car and in a matter of no more than a few seconds roared out, raising a cloud of dust as he went.

He followed the winding road of the Ripatransone hills to the town of Grottammare. That was where his friend Giacomo lived. Together, the two of them indulged daily in fun and games. Giacomo took advantage of Calisto's privileged position, and of his propensity to spend money without thinking.

Giacomo had a good mind, but was nothing like so fortunate as the young Conte in his family's social position and wealth. His mother worked in a shoe shop from early morning to late evening, and his father was a waiter in a beach restaurant. Giacomo despised Calisto, and made no attempt to hide that fact. For his part, though, Calisto simply thought that the barbs and sneers addressed to him were the result of peculiarities in his friend's character.

Calisto arrived at their appointed meeting place. "What took you so long?" asked Giacomo sharply. "I've already been waiting ten minutes."

"Giacomo, am I glad to see you. Mama, as usual, with her talk…. You know how it goes…. 'Get a job. I'll take your car keys…,'" said Calisto with a laugh. He did not mention the morning's adventure in the bathroom.

Giacomo looked at him scornfully, but, remembering himself, said: "All right, brother, forget it. Let's go somewhere and sit down. I haven't eaten. My mother left an empty fridge."

He got into the car. Calisto hit the gas and the car shot forward so violently that the driver of an oncoming vehicle nearly drove into a lamp post from fright.

"Where is Orsino?" Calisto asked. "Did you call him?"

"Yes, he will reply when he wakes up. He played video games until morning yesterday. Where are we going?"

"Straight," Calisto laughed, "as always, to Bernie. Or Toto. The girls gather on the beach near Toto. He winked significantly at his comrade.

"I'm fed up with all these samey places. And the girls are all samey too."

"So where will we go?" asked Calisto, disappointed.

"Somewhere, but directly. Listen, let's go to Cupra. We haven't been there for ages. We'll meet some new people."

"I like new people," said Calisto enigmatically, licking his lips and making the car go even faster.

Giacomo thought to himself: "Is he really like that? What a cretin." Out loud, though, he said "Yes" and tried to smile.

Seven minutes later they were already driving down the narrow streets of Cupra Marittima, blasting loud music from inside the car, while the engine roared and the brakes squealed on every corner. Girls who were out walking smiled, hoping that the guys in the yellow sports car would notice them. Elderly women, watching them disappear, shook their heads. Men gave vent to hearty curses.

Calisto parked the car and he and Giacomo headed for the nearest establishment, the Chalet Martina.

A young girl carrying a tray greeted them in the inner courtyard. "Good morning! Welcome to the Chalet Martina," she said.

"Yes, good morning," replied Calisto, bestowing his usual smile on the girl. "Me and my friend want breakfast."

"Of course," said the girl, somewhat embarrassed. "Come through. I'll be with you in a minute."

"We'll wait," replied Calisto quietly and headed for the table.

Giacomo trailed silently behind his friend, eyes fixed on his phone.

The girl who had greeted them was called Federica, known in her family as Féde. She was the eldest of the four children of Martina and Adriano Marino. Except for her hair, which was thick, black and curly, like Adriano's, she took after her mother in appearance, also in sharp-wittedness and strength of character, although they were inexplicably combined with shyness. She was her father's favourite. Signor Marino loved to stroke her head and disentangle her wayward locks. Her judgement, "Perfetto!" on his most creative dishes encouraged him to work in the kitchen with particular enthusiasm.

Féde ran to the bar, found the only mirror, in a corner behind the sink, and examined herself. She adjusted a wisp of hair which had escaped from her pony tail, then abruptly let down all her hair and gathered it up once again.

She then hurried to the table where the young men were sitting. Martina, sitting in a corner, drinking her morning coffee, watched intently.

"I'm ready," said Féde, smiling and breathing heavily.

Calisto looked her in the eyes, but Giacomo gave her a sideways look, puckering his thin lips. "And what is it that you are ready for?" Giacomo growled.

Féde looked highly embarrassed.

"Pay no attention to my friend," said Calisto. "He only has bad manners when he's hungry – otherwise he's politeness itself. That's right, Gia, isn't it?" he asked, winking at his friend. "We'd like coffee and two of your biggest omelettes."

"Right, that would be two coffees and two omelettes with bacon and veg," Féde said, writing in a small notebook. "Any cheese?" she asked.

Her face was reddening, and not because of the baking heat, which had been building since early morning.

"Cheese?" Giacomo queried, irritably.

"Do you want cheese in your omelette? Do you like cheese?" Féde asked, laughing at her own ineptness.

"I like cheese," drawled Calisto.

"No cheese for me," said Giacomo dryly. "Get me some fresh orange juice."

"Orange juice," the girl said as she wrote. "And for you?" she said, giving Calisto a smile. "Would you like orange juice?"

"Oh yes. I'd be very grateful for some," said Calisto delightedly.

"Your order, then, is two coffees…. Oh, sorry, is that coffee with milk?"

"Remember, darling, that in the morning I do like it without milk. So does my friend," replied Calisto playfully.

"Two coffees, two orange juices, two omelettes with bacon and veg, one with cheese, one without. Everything will be ready in five minutes. I'll bring drinks. Thanks for your order." Féde turned and headed for the bar.

"You're here for what you can get," said Giacomo, annoyed.

"What do you mean?"

"About the girl. There's nothing to look at, but you're 'very grateful,' 'in the morning' you 'like it.' Let's just have breakfast."

"Why so worked up? Are you hungry, or what?"

"That's neither here nor there. I'm sick of your tricks. Do you have to?"

"She's simply a nice girl."

"Simply a nice girl? She's nothing. Let her be." Giacomo was yelling now.

"I bet I get off with her in a couple of days. You know, mate, dumb belles like that always turn out very passionate if you press the right buttons. They've got something. They're not like those dolls who know their own worth. In the majority of cases, good-lookers turn out to be air heads; you don't have to do anything: they give themselves with all their charms and lie there like logs. But as for dumb belles – they're passion itself. As if it was the first time in their life when you…."

"Oh, shut up. Can't you think about anything else?"

"Why are you getting so worked up? Listen. My Dévi, by the way…. You remember Dévi don't you?"

"Dévi's your chambermaid. So?"

"So this, my friend. Although Dévi's got a moustache and a huge backside on short legs, how she can…. For now she's my number one. And the main thing is she's always and everywhere ready. And she has…."

"Enough, I get it." Giacomo cut the smiling Calisto short with a baleful look. "If you're so keen on this Dévi, marry her and enjoy her every day if you like."

"You said it," laughed Calisto. "What a face Mama would have." He laughed so loud and so merrily that tears sprang from his eyes. "Marry! Ha-ha! Why should I get married? As it is I get enjoyment every day, and not only with Dévi, but polygamy is forbidden. But to be serious," he said, calming down somewhat, "I'm sure I'll be the first with this waitress."

"As you wish, but I think you'll be lucky if you get a result. It looks like she's the daughter of that woman over there." Giacomo indicated Martina with a look. She was watching them intently. "I think she's Martina, who owns this place," he added in a whisper. "With a mother like that … tee-hee … you'll not get to see the bird."

"We'll see about that," said Calisto. He stood up and made straight for Martina's table.

"Good morning. I'm Calisto Conte." He offered Martina a polite smile. "I must say you have a very nice set-up here, and welcoming staff."

"Thank you. I'm glad to make your acquaintance. I'm Martina Marino," she replied.

Martina had heard a lot about the Conte family, especially about Calisto's father, Alberto, who had a reputation as a provincial philanthropist. "I'll be pleased to see you and your friends as regular visitors to Chalet Martina."

Féde looked on from behind the bar, listening to their conversation. Some unknown power attracted her to Calisto. Without doubt, he was good looking. His face, bearing and ability to communicate bewitched her, giving rise to feelings she had not known before. But with those feelings came extreme embarrassment, and she had no thought that there could be any mutual attraction between them. As befitted a modest girl, she would never have dared even to daydream of a magical love story with a young man like Calisto.

In nineteen years, only one young man had shown an interest in her. His name was Marco. He came to the Chalet Martina almost every day, ordered water with lemon, sometimes pizza. Shy and modest, not at all like Calisto, he would sit and watch her bashfully. He had been in the same class as her at school. He was not at all flashy, but he was clear-minded and kind-hearted. He was in love with Féde. Yes, really in love – forever. That was the sole reason that brought him to the Chalet Martina.

But whatever qualities Marco may have possessed, he had never excited Féde's mind or heart. She regarded him as an everyday occurrence, like a sea breeze which will blow, or not, according to its own whim. All you can do is wait.

"Please, Signora Marino, allow your daughter to come with me on Friday to the Rossini Festival[4] in Pesaro. They send tickets to my father every year."

Féde heard what Calisto was saying to her mother. She was stunned, and did not take her eyes off Martina, awaiting her reply.

"You are talking about my elder daughter, Federica?" asked Martina in surprise, looking at Féde.

"Indeed, I am." Calisto turned his head towards the girl and smiled. "Forgive me, but when did you get to know Federica?" asked Martina. "Eight minutes ago," replied Calisto, looking at his watch.

"Come on!" said Martina indignantly.

"Mama, Calisto is joking. We met at the beginning of summer at the municipal festival in San Benedetto, and now

....

[4]   The Rossini Festival is held every year in July in the Rossini Theatre and Adriatic Arena in Pesaro. Giocchino Antonio Rossini (1792–1868) was the composer of thirty-nine operas, of church music and chamber music.

we've met again here. Can I go to Pesaro? I've always dreamed of going to that concert."

Martina looked at Féde. Her daughter had never before asked such a thing of her, and now she could see how important her agreement was for the girl. Féde's eyes were sparkling, and she wanted to make her day. After all, it was only a concert, nothing more.

"I must ask your father," she said, although this was untrue. "Adriano, dear, come out here a minute!"

After a short delay, Adriano came out from the kitchen.

"This young man, Calisto Conte, has invited our daughter, Federica, to go with him on Friday to Pesaro, to the Rossini Festival. Calisto has promised that Federica will return home in good time." Marina surveyed young Conte intently. He, in his turn, nodded to her and offered his hand to Adriano with a smile.

"Calisto Conte."

"Adriano Marino." Adriano shook the young man's hand. "I have known your parents for a long time. I have cooked charity dinners for them. Those were some evenings. Beautiful, such chic, such glitter."

"Thank you, Signor Marino. I remember those dinners; they were delightful." Calisto lied instinctively.

"So, why not?" Adriano said. "Let the kids go and listen. For me, music is great, and Rossini's music is brilliant."

Féde looked gratefully at her father.

"So, that is decided," Calisto exclaimed. "On Friday, at five o'clock, I will call for your daughter." He kissed Martina's hand and bowed theatrically to Adriano.

Calisto went back to his table. Giacomo smirked derisively.

"Calisto Conte, you've pulled this trick for nothing. The girl has dreamed up heaven knows what fantasies. And you.... Ugh! Who am I saying this to?" Giacomo flared up, waving a hand.

"Give over, Gia." retorted Calisto. "Here's the food." Féde approached the table, carrying a tray.

"Your omelette. I'll bring the drinks. And thanks, Calisto, for the invite to the Rossini Festival. I'll be very happy to go with you."

"I have no doubt about your happiness," hissed Giacomo.

"Thank you for the omelette," Calisto said. "It smells delicious." He touched her hand, tenderly.

His touch made Féde's head spin. This new, unfamiliar feeling, frightened her.

"Mmm…. Thank you, Calisto," she replied, and ran to the bar.

Giacomo said nothing and set about his breakfast, while Calisto, hiding behind a mask of propriety, gazed intently at his new victim.

One man, sitting in an old armchair by the exit to the beach, watched what was going on, heard the conversation between the two friends, and would undoubtedly have influenced the girl's fate if he had been more astute. But this was Ernesto who, on hearing Calisto's words, could not guess his intentions. Only a gut feeling, which he did not fully understand, prompted him to think that the pair were dubious characters.

Calisto sensed that he was being watched, but saw nothing of interest in Ernesto. A black youth in a worn tee-shirt, working on the beach, meant no more to him than the chair in which Ernesto was sitting.

Ernesto thought: if Cecilia had been there, she would have advised him. But Ceci was dead. Attending her funeral and visiting their empty flat had firmly implanted that sad fact in his brain. Now he could lean only on his memories and some yellowing photographs.

Ernesto continued living and working in the Chalet Martina because Ceci had led him there by the hand, telling him that he should be honest, decent and considerate, and that she would pick him up later. He followed her instructions, even though he knew that she could not now come to take him away.

New visitors arrived. Martina called to Ernesto. He jumped up from his armchair and hurried towards her. In passing, he caught a foot under a leg of Giacomo's chair. Giacomo crashed to the floor, fork in hand, and with a piece of omelette in his mouth.

"Excuse me, I…," Ernesto began.

"Cretin!" yelled Giacomo, spitting omelette. "Where are you tearing off to? Are you blind?" Giacomo's face was so red from fury that it matched his scarlet tee-shirt.

Calisto laughed.

Féde rushed over.

Ernesto stood by, utterly dismayed. He tried a smile: "Excuse me," he said again, plaintively.

"Get lost, idiot!" Giacomo barked, as he set about wiping his shorts, spreading a greasy stain.

Martina sighed deeply. "Ernesto, come to me," she called.

He ran to her. "Signora Marino. I did not want…. You must believe me," he blurted out.

"I believe you Ernesto, but you must be more careful," Martina answered calmly. Then, indicating the man and woman who stood beside her, she said: "Now, Ernesto, take our guests to umbrella number fifteen on the first row."

"Certainly," answered Ernesto, smiling, and he set out in the direction of the beach.

Martina apologised to Giacomo for her employee and said it would not be necessary for him to pay for his breakfast. He and Calisto then left the restaurant in good spirits and in search of new experiences.

Ernesto sat on an old sun-lounger on the beach. He was waiting for dinner, which at Chalet Martina was served at exactly three o'clock. He watched Frani, Adriano and Martina's youngest child, as she played with her dolls.

Frani had come into the world at a time when Adriano and Martina were not planning any more little Marinos. A sensible, pretty little girl, clever beyond her years, she met visitors to the restaurant with a radiant smile and looked each of them inquisitively in the eye, making even the grumpiest of people smile involuntarily. She loved the colour red: her dresses, hair bands, bags and bracelets all had to be scarlet. She had a favourite doll, called Jacqueline, from whom she was never parted.

She went up to Ernesto, adjusted her red Panama hat and said: "The heat makes my Jacqueline sad. We forgot to bring her hat today."

"Yes, it's not good to go hatless in this heat," said Ernesto. "Cecilia always told me to put something on my head when it's hot."

"So why haven't you got a hat?" asked Frani, pointing at Ernesto's uncovered head.

He thought for a minute then exclaimed: "Yes. Right now!" and ran off to his cabin.

"Don't worry, Jacqueline," said Frani, turning to her doll. "He's strange, but nice."

When Ernesto returned, he was wearing a yellow cap with the inscription: "Venice."

"That's much better," said Frani. She looked closely at Ernesto. "Why are you so sad?"

"I'm just thinking," he said.

"What about?"

"I do everything wrong. Signora Marino is not pleased with me. Today I bumped into a man and he fell over, then I smashed a glass on my way to the beach, and a man with ice cream…."

"Yes, you are very absent-minded, Jacqueline and I have noticed," said Frani, with a sigh. "But not long after you came to us (I think you had just come back from your granny's funeral), Mummy said to Daddy, "Now he'll be with us." So don't be sad. Mummy is very kind. She loves people, even though she frowns a lot."

"Thank you, Frani."

"What I think," Frani continued, "is that you should learn to be quieter – not make so much noise when you walk."

"You think so?"

"Yes. You're very big and you make a lot of noise. Walk like me." She began to demonstrate, gracefully holding on to her Panama hat. "Like that," she said, pausing, "as if you're as light as a feather and haven't eaten as much ice cream as Jacqueline and me."

Frani continued to teach Ernesto the art of gracefulness until Martina called them to the table.

"We're coming," said the little girl. She took Ernesto by the hand, and together they set off for dinner. "Now, like this … lightly … gently…."

3. AN UNHAPPY MARRIAGE

Immediately after Calisto Conte roared off in his yellow sports car from the family home on Ripatransone Hill, an older man entered the house. Fairly tall, and well-built, he was wearing a white tennis shirt and red shorts. His dark hair, flecked with grey, was combed smooth.

"Signor Conte, good morning!" said Dévi as she met her boss. "Will you be having breakfast?"

"I won't say no," replied Alberto. "And Signora Conte?" he enquired softly.

"Signora Conte is at the table," Dévi replied.

Alberto Conte slowly entered the dining room. Without speaking, his wife, Patricia, cast a contemptuous glance at him. Going up to her, Alberto kissed her on the forehead. On the touch of his lips Patricia shuddered. "Even after tennis he smells of bombast and self-satisfaction," she thought.

"Sit down Alberto. Have some breakfast. I will go to my room."

Patricia stood up and made to leave, but Alberto took her hand and said: "Why, my dearest Patricia.... Will you leave your loving spouse alone? 'One glance of yours such power hath o'er my life....'"[5]

Patricia quickly freed her hand and curled her lips in a smile. She left the room without saying anything more. Being

....

[5] Francesco Petrarch, Sonnet No. 39. The original reads, *Tanta virtute has sol un vostro sguardo.*

left alone did not dismay Alberto: he set about his breakfast with enthusiasm.

Patricia went upstairs to her room (the Contes slept in separate rooms), shut the door behind her and threw herself on the bed. She wrung her hands, contorted her lips, and shivers ran through her body. Tears rose in her eyes.

Patricia had hated her husband from the very first day of their married life. For everyone else, Alberto was a handsome, gallant man, a philanthropist, but for Patricia he was a tyrant and a monster. In truth, even she did not know quite how horrible the dark side of his soul was, or how many base and terrible deeds lurked within it.

She had been born into the family of a well-known winemaker. It was a loving family and she had lacked for nothing. From her earliest days she had known what to talk about and how to behave in society. She learnt English and French and how to play the piano.

Could she have been taught how to live with as dreadful a man as Alberto Conte? Could she have had any inkling of the nightmare her family life would become?

Could she ever have supposed that her own husband would rape her on their wedding night? A day did not pass when she did not recall that fateful night, when all her expectations and daydreams were shattered by the reality of Alberto's cruelty. Alberto … so handsome, so gallant, so educated and so kind.…

That night he had come into the bedroom. Wearing snow-white, lacy underwear, she was sitting on the bed. She observed her young husband with mounting excitement. A shiver ran down her spine. She thought it must have been caused by the intimacy she anticipated with her lawful, though not passionately loved, spouse, the man to whom she would belong all her life.

Alberto stood motionless in the doorway, saying nothing. He looked at his wife fixedly and coldly. There was something dark and insane about his look. The same strange tremor again ran through Patricia's body, but it was a tremor of fear. Alberto approached the bed and slowly undressed. Patricia blushed. Then, as if giving way to an unknown force, Alberto threw himself on his wife, seized her by the hair, pulled her to him and took her, crudely, furiously.

Patricia yelled and tried to break free, but Alberto was holding her firmly. She felt that she was suffocating from lack of air and the sharp pain, which pierced her like a knife point. Alberto stopped, climbed off and headed for the bathroom without speaking. His hapless young wife remained lying on the bed.

That night Patricia realised in full that her marriage was a fatal sham and her husband a cruel man.

Patricia had never told anyone about that first night, or about the other nights when Alberto would come into the bedroom and take her again and again, in spite of her tears, entreaties and even threats. He knew that Patricia valued her status in society too highly to tell anyone else about his cruel "strangenesses." In company, and even in the presence of their domestic staff, Alberto presented a gentle and kind attitude towards his wife.

Patricia resigned herself to her fate. She no longer yelled at or beseeched him, but submitted obediently to the nightly torture. There were not even tears in her eyes, but deep inside her there was sobbing. To deaden the bitter feelings which devastated her, she began to take antidepressants.

Once, after another nocturnal rape, Patricia had to go to the doctor. Soft tissue damage…. Surgery…. More antidepressants.

Patricia dreamed that one day she would be rescued from this hateful marriage; from a man who held such dark and despicable power over her. But she could not face humiliating divorce proceedings, and admitting publicly that her family lived in a state of permanent pretence. So, subject to strange and archaic convictions, she became a slave in her own home – in contradiction of the great name Patricia. With each passing day she became more taciturn, more irritable. When she reached the limit, a state of hopelessness, she would, in her impotent anger, bite her lips until they bled. Sometimes, she felt outbursts of anger during which she cried out wildly, roared, wrung her hands and repeated: "I can't take any more of this! I just can't!" Yes, Patricia loathed Alberto wholeheartedly, but she did not want to take the decisive steps that would end her suffering.

While Patricia struggled with fits of despair, Alberto breakfasted, took a shower, dressed, and settled in his study. That was where he spent most of his time. The room was decorated with fine Gobelin tapestries and reproductions of the works of the great masters. There was Judith killing Holofernes,[6] and the terrifying souls in torment depicted by Bouguereau,[7] and the mysterious, mystical images, filled with phantasmagoria of all kinds, created by the inimitable Hieronymus Bosch.[8] Here the dark world of Alberto Conte's soul was safely concealed.

He would spend many hours reading books, of which he had an enormous collection. It included volumes on history, philosophy and mythology, and the works of the great Italian writers Dante, Boccaccio, Petrarch, and also Virgil, whom Alberto read in the original. He was fascinated by the mythology of ancient Greece, of Rome, of the peoples of Africa, and by Eastern civilisations. He learnt by heart the poetry of the great Italian and English poets. Taking huge pride in that, he never denied himself any opportunity to show off his knowledge.

....

[6]   By Caravaggio (1599).

[7]   *Dante and Virgil in Hell* by William Adolphe Bouguereau (1850).

[8]   *The Garden of Earthly Delights* by Hieronymus Bosch (1490–1510).

He delighted in beauty in all its forms – including beautiful women, stylish clothes and exquisite luxury goods.

And he zealously attended to his personal appearance. He played tennis, went out on morning runs, and used the services of a beautician, a personal hairdresser and a manicurist. He wore bespoke tailored suits and shirts. In all, he looked good for his fifty-two years and was proud of himself.

The Conte family had owned olive groves for more than a hundred years. They were situated twenty kilometres from the current family home. The business was successful and the interest on funds deposited in several European banks by his grandfather enabled Alberto's pleasurable and mostly non-productive life.

In society, Signor Conte had a reputation as a charitable donor and philanthropist. This was richly deserved. He spent a lot of time and money on charitable works and supported talented artists whom nobody had heard of. He founded a fund to help widows and orphans, and made regular visits to a little-known refugee centre.

Every Thursday, after supper, he would leave home in his classic Jaguar, returning after midnight in a relaxed and upbeat mood. He went to the refugee centre, taking food, clothing and money.

At the centre he would choose a young, curvaceous black girl, sometimes the same one in successive weeks, and shut himself in a room with her. There he indulged in debauchery of the worst kind, unbridled sensuality, as he enjoyed every movement of the helpless body of the victim beneath him. A feeling of boundless power took possession of his inflamed reason, and afforded him secret pleasure.

Patricia guessed the nature of his unsavoury adventures. His "distractions" brought with them the expected results, which played a fateful role in her life.

Twenty-two years previously, on a dreary, mid-autumn day, driving out of the Conte homestead, she had noticed a girl standing on the edge of a nearby group of trees. The girl had a pitiful air. She was wearing a long dress of multi-coloured material, such as had been fashionable twenty years earlier. It sat like a sack on her thin figure. Over the dress she wore a shawl with holes in it. She had a pale face, sunken cheeks, and dark circles beneath her eyes.

The following day, Patricia saw the same girl again. She stopped, got out of her car and tried to approach the girl, but she disappeared among the trees.

Patricia did not see the girl again for seven months, and all but forgot about her. Then, as she returned home one evening, there was the girl, once again standing in the shadow of the trees. Patricia stopped and got out of her car. This time, the girl stepped towards her. It was immediately obvious that she was pregnant.

The girl told Patricia that about a year previously her mother had fallen seriously ill, had taken to her bed and not left it. It was at that point that Signor Alberto Conte came into her life. Promising to pay for her mother's treatment, he came to see them, bringing provisions and medicines. One evening, when the girl was showing him out, he threw himself on her, tore her outer clothes off, ripped off her underwear and abused her cruelly in the very doorway of the bedroom where her sick mother lay. The next morning, she had gone to the police.

Weeks passed, but, rather strangely, the "protector" could not be found. However, several months later, she saw her assailant enter the sports club where she earned cash by doing cleaning work. She found out his real name and noted his address. It was on the following day that Patricia had first seen her outside the Conte house. Now that she knew she was with child – Signor Conte's child – she had decided that she must look to Signora Conte for help.

Patricia listened to the girl's story calmly, even indifferently, and asked in a cold voice how much money she was counting on. The girl searched for any sign of humanity in her icy, impassive face; then tears sprang to her eyes, she laughed wildly, and said that Patricia should herself evaluate the cost of humiliation, abuse and the shattered life of a girl who had lost her innocence, her honour and her mother. She would take no money from the hands of the dastardly Contes, but, so that they didn't hope they would be rid of this story: "Let Signor Conte live and remember that he could not escape the judgment of heaven, which cannot be bought for any money." With that, she ran off.

Patricia stood for some moments as gloomy, anxious thoughts took hold of her. She wanted to believe that this story was a lie, an attempt at easy pickings. But an inner voice insisted that the evil done by her husband had begun to spread; that only death could put an end to this horror. She had already felt her own helplessness as the burden of horror and deception became heavier with each passing day. Now the thought that their son, Calisto, might have inherited his father's dark soul brought Patricia to a state of utter despair. Alberto must answer for his deeds – in full. But who, or what, short of the judgement of heaven that the girl had referred to, was capable of punishing the abuser for his sins?

Several more months passed. Every time she left home, Patricia expected to see the still unknown young woman. But she did not reappear. Perhaps she feared the consequences of a lie, but at heart Patricia felt sure the story had been true.

To be certain, she paid a private detective to discover the address of this victim of Alberto's brutality, if indeed that was what she was.

Now she drove up to the house identified by the detective. She looked uneasily at an apparently deserted hovel. Getting out of her car, she skirted the small building, looking into the filthy windows, finding no sign of life.

Perhaps the detective had given her the address of an abandoned house.

She was about to leave when she heard the faint sound of a baby's cry. Looking again through a grimy window, she discerned movement in a far corner. It looked like a small child. Scared, she jumped back from the window. Her instinct was to run away, but something told her that she just had to enter this sinister house.

Barely overcoming her terror, she pushed open the wooden door. The repellent, acrid smell that came out was more than enough to deter almost anyone from entering, but she took a deep, perhaps last, breath of the fresh outdoor air, stepped inside, and looked around.

Scraps of clothing and bits of broken furniture littered the floor. The sharp, nauseating odour asserted itself strongly and was surely the smell of death. Other than from the open door behind her, there was little light. With the exception of one that was hung with a filthy curtain, all the windows were covered by wooden shutters. As her eyes became accustomed to the lack of light, Patricia discerned an internal door, from which the intermittent crying of a baby seemed to be coming.

Self-preservation, of her body and the wholeness of her mind, said: "Run. Run away from this accursed house." She had turned and already taken a decisive step towards the exit when the baby produced a suppressed gurgle. That drew her back towards the inner door, through which she very hesitantly proceeded.

In the small dark room beyond stood a bed. On the bed, furnished only with rags, lay the dead body of the young woman who had visited the Conte homestead. Her lifeless fingers gripped the edge of the filthy mattress; her hair was a formless mass; her dead gaze was fixed on the ceiling. Everything stank.

The baby lay on its back beside its mother's corpse. Its eyes were closed; its mouth vainly sought the mother's breast. Its thin arms twitched convulsively. Patricia tottered across to it. Crying again, the baby wheezed, suggesting an unhealthy chest as well as hunger. Choosing the least soiled of the available strips of fabric, Patricia wrapped the baby in it and ran from the house of death. Daylight revealed that the baby was a girl. She was heavily soiled and her back was covered in sores.

Patricia put the little girl in a family with several other children. Keeping this part of her life a secret from her family and social contacts, she visited regularly, taking with her money, food, clothing and toys. Apart from love and affection, the child lacked for nothing.

When visiting, Patricia scrutinised the infant, the fruit of vice, abuse, debauchery and violence, looking for any resemblance to Alberto. But she was pure and bright – as if her agonizing entry into the world had eliminated all her sinful genes. She aroused tender feelings in Patricia; who thought her so beautiful she gave her the name Mirella ("adored one"). When Mirella looked Patricia in the eye, it seemed that an all-illuminating light poured from her angelic soul.

As she grew, Mirella would put her head on Patricia's knee and firmly embrace her. Patricia caressed the child's soft fluffy hair and quietly sang a lullaby that her grandmother had sung to her when she was little. It was a long time since Patricia had experienced such quiet joy and serenity.

As Mirella grew, Patricia continued to make frequent visits. Often, she was in need of consolation for the distress Alberto caused her. Even when Mirella was asleep, Patricia would sit beside her for a long time.

Once, Patricia arrived very late in the evening, dressed in an evening gown. Her hair was stylishly arranged, and she was wearing a diamond necklace. She lay down next to the sleeping child and tenderly pressed her cheek, wet with tears, against the little girl's plump cheek. Mirella opened her eyes and gave a cry of delight: "I knew that you were a queen!"

Patricia laughed and warmly embraced Mirella. They remained like that all night. Patricia whispered to the sleeping child how happy she would be when she grew up into a beautiful young woman; how Patricia would love her; would take care of her; and allow no one to abuse her. Mirella slept through it all, but smiled as she slept.

When Mirella awoke in the morning, Patricia was no longer there; so she thought it had all been a wonderful dream. She was in no doubt, though, that the signora who had visited her was her mother – and a queen.

When, in the early morning, the queen returned to her gloomy kingdom, her husband, beside himself with rage, threw himself on her, beat her, tore off her dress and took cruel possession of her in the bathroom. Afraid of waking little Calisto, she submitted to her sad fate with gritted teeth. The thought of Mirella's innocence offered such consolation as she was able to summon up at that terrible moment.

Patricia kept the promises she had made to the sleeping child that night. She undertook Mirella's education, sparing neither time nor money. She taught her everything she herself knew, and put her in a good school. She hired tutors of English literature, history, piano and etiquette. Mirella grew into a beautiful, intelligent and educated young woman. At Patricia's insistence, she continued her studies in a private college, and her future seemed to be a wonderful canvas, painted with magic colours.

4. THE DOG

Ernesto's working day started at seven o'clock in the morning and finished after nine in the evening. By night time, he could scarcely stay on his feet from tiredness. He was not able to relax, and he did not have friends. In his free time, he was a lonely guy walking along the seafront. He simply sat down and lowered his feet into the sea where it met the shore. The water receded, uncovering wet sand, then returned, gently touching the ends of his toes.

He enjoyed the play of the mighty element on his toes. He covered his eyes and listened to the tender, calming noise of the waves. From time to time, the voices of people who walked beside the sea would break through. Music and roars of laughter penetrated from nearby restaurants. Together, the sounds merged into a symphony familiar to him from childhood.

He lived well at the Chalet Martina, and he worked hard, trying to please the Marino family, apparently succeeding. Martina was kind to him, and not angry even when he broke crockery or collided with guests. Once, when he bumped into an elderly gentleman, causing the man's cigarette to fall from his mouth, the proprietress grimaced a little, but said nothing. When the time came for him to spend his first night in his small room almost on the beach, Martina sat with him for a whole hour before she went home. She worried that he was there all alone. The next day she brought him clean towels and bed linen that smelled of lavender. She always insisted that he should eat the broccoli, beans and carrots that he left untouched on his plate – just as Ceci had.

Adriano also worried about Ernesto. He treated him to pizza, fresh bread and deserts, and in the evening made fresh tea served with honey. Sometimes, Ernesto noticed that Adriano was sad about something. He sat alone at a table until late in the evening, watching the dark sea and drinking something from a beautiful glass. To Ernesto it seemed that he was thinking about Signora Marino; after all, he loved her so much.

Ernesto had little to do with the Marino sons. Andrea, the elder boy, dreamed of a great career in football, saying that his parents had guaranteed his future by giving him the name of his idol, Andrea Pirlo. He imagined that agents of AC Milan and Juventus would soon be queuing to sign the new star. But while the football agents were moving heaven and earth in search of Andrea, he honed and showcased his skills with the local club, Sambenedettese. Andrea came to Chalet Martina in the mornings, cleaned the floors and set out the chairs and tables. He did not find much to say to Ernesto, but did show him some footballing tricks. Ernesto appreciated this very much, as he did Andrea's beautiful football. But Andrea didn't want to show Ernesto his most prized skills, saying that you need real talent for that. Ernesto knew that he didn't have talent and decided not to ask Andrea to show him his footballing tricks again.

Antonio, the younger boy, did not communicate with Ernesto at all. This may only have been because he was always busy in the kitchen with Adriano. But he was well-pleased when Ernesto praised his prime pasta, the more so because that was the first time he had made it without his father's help.

Federica, the Marinos' eldest daughter, did not like the Chalet Martina's new worker at all. His very presence seemed to agitate her, especially after the day Ernesto bumped into a young guy in a red tee-shirt and collapsed to the floor, dropping the omelette he was carrying. Sometimes Federica was very rude to Ernesto. She said: "Don't get under my feet! Why are you standing there?" Ernesto tried to avoid Federica when she had a tray in her hands.

Ernesto did make one friend at the Chalet Martina, Little Frani. Ernesto played dolls with her. When he did something "completely wrong," Frani pouted, folded her arms crosswise and walked away, leaving him totally dismayed. But she would soon return and say with a serious expression on her childish face: "Ernesto, you don't know how to play at all, but I will teach you." Then she would instruct the huge, shy guy in detail what his doll should say to her doll, and with what intonation. She even arranged something like a rehearsal before the start of a game.

Frani also showed Ernesto how to sit properly at a table; how to hold a fork and use a knife. (Not that Ceci had not also done her best to teach her grandson these things.)

In short, Frani became a friend and mentor to a guy who was twelve years older than she, and twice as tall.

Ernesto enjoyed his new life at the Chalet Martina. Yes, some visitors shouted at him and treated him rudely; one even called him a very bad word. But he had heard such words at school, was not offended, and did not give them the satisfaction of seeing him react. He remembered that grandmother Ceci had taught him that people are only rude to others if they are unhappy and dissatisfied with themselves. So even from childhood he had felt sorry for all those who wronged and insulted him.

Sitting by the sea one day, letting the wavelets wash over his feet, Ernesto was thinking about Ceci. Suddenly, the rustle of paper and the growl of a dog interrupted his thoughts. He turned to where the noise was coming from and saw a large black dog trying to get something out of a bag. He looked beyond the dog, in expectation of seeing the dog's owner. But the beach was empty. Was the dog lost? She was not wearing a collar – so perhaps she was a stray, or had been abandoned. Small wonder she was taking a keen interest in what she might find in a discarded bag.

Ernesto ran to his cabin, where he had stashed some food left over from the restaurant – four slices of bread, a couple of cheese rolls and several slices of pizza. He selected a cheese roll and approached the dog. Hanging on to its paper bag, the dog stared at him with eyes as black as coal, and growled menacingly. But Ernesto was not afraid, and he extended a hand with the roll towards the animal. "Take it," he said. "I mean you no harm." But the dog did not take the food.

Ernesto persevered. He placed the roll right beside the dog's muzzle and stepped back. The dog let go of the bag and sniffed the roll. Keeping a wary eye on Ernesto, she slowly opened her mouth and carefully took the food. While she chewed the roll, Ernesto looked her over. She was quite large, and looked as if she should have a muscular body, but she was emaciated. Drooping ears gave her a gentle air. A piece of skin was missing from her right ear – a new injury, still raw.

She finished the roll and fixed a look on Ernesto – grateful for the snack, perhaps, but wary of what might follow. "Wait, don't go. I'll bring more," Ernesto said, and ran back to his cabin.

The dog followed Ernesto with her eyes, but stayed where she was, her tail between her legs and her massive front paws tucked under her body. When he returned, it was with the second roll, a slice of pizza and the four slices of bread. This time, the dog did not growl as he approached.

Ernesto laid the new supplies on the sand in front of the dog. "Look, this roll is exactly the same as the one you ate, except it's already got a bite taken out of it. This is pizza with mozzarella, tomatoes and chicken. I think you will like it. Now, this one is my favourite pizza, with prosciutto. The meat has already been eaten, but smell it." Ernesto showed the dog a piece of pizza on which there was nothing but a dried tomato. "Can you smell the prosciutto?" He brought the slice of pizza close to his own face, inhaled deeply and made an appreciative noise. The dog watched with definite interest.

"Now, here…." Ernesto showed her a paper bag filled with the four slices of stale bread. "You must try these. Signor Marino bakes the most delicious bread in town; you won't have eaten such good bread ever before."

The dog sniffed the food that Ernesto put in front of her, but she didn't eat. Very likely a human being would have been just as cautious about such a sudden abundance.

The dog knew humans well. A family had taken her home from a shelter. She liked it with them. They had fed her with delicious canned food and pellets that swelled up in her mouth and tasted of meat. She loved meat. She was given a beautiful basket with a soft pink pillow, though had no idea why she needed a basket. At first, she had thought it was a toilet. But the people who had taken her in did not like that and they yelled at her. OK, so it must be a toy, and she started chewing on it. But the people got angry again and even hit her on her muzzle. When she lay down in the basket, resting her head on the pillow – finally she seemed to have done something right – they spoke affectionately to her and even stroked her.

A little girl lived in that house. In the morning, still in her pyjamas, the girl ran to the dog, gently hugged and kissed her, and spoke sweetly to her. The dog liked that. She licked the child's face, making her laugh. But then the big people came, scolded the girl and took her away. Once, the girl took the dog to her room, where there were a lot of toys to play with. The dog began to gnaw on dolls with long golden hair, small pink furniture, plastic bunnies. But when she got to the white teddy bear, the girl tried to take it from her. Holding on to the bear, the dog growled. The girl kept on pulling and the bear's paw tore off. That made the girl cry loudly, and again the large man and woman came running. They began to shout and beat the dog in the face with the white bear and its torn-off paw. She didn't like that. It seemed she had again done something wrong, but what?

The man and woman often scolded and beat her. One evening they didn't come home; the dog patiently waited for them by the door. She got hungry, and wanted to go to the toilet. But they didn't come. When she got desperate, she urinated near the door.

The people never came that night. They only returned the next evening. When the front door opened, the dog wagged her tail happily: her owners had finally returned. The woman crossed the threshold first. Stepping in a huge puddle of pee, she screamed. The man grabbed the dog by the collar and poked her muzzle into the puddle of urine. The dog was in pain.

The woman and the girl shut themselves in their rooms. The man sat motionless at the kitchen table, his head in his hands. The dog didn't know what to do. She wanted to eat and drink; there hadn't been any water in her bowl for a long time. She walked over to the man and sat down at his feet. He ignored her. She put her paw in his lap. He roughly pushed her away.

Then the dog ran to the girl in her room. She had arranged her toys on the floor. The dog took one of the dolls with beautiful golden hair. The girl immediately took it away. The dog chose another. The girl called out: "Mummy! Come and take the dog away, she's bothering me. She's chewing all my toys." She looked the dog in the eyes and said angrily: "Bad dog!"

The woman burst into the girl's room, grabbed the dog by the collar and dragged her to the front door. The dog whimpered, then barked. She was trying to explain to the woman that she was hurting her. The man came and hit the dog hard in the face. She continued to whine. In a rage, the man grabbed the dog; her collar came off in his hand. He opened the front door and pushed her out of the house, kicking her hard in the side as he did so. "You vile dog! Go away! Get lost!" he shouted and slammed the door.

The dog was in pain. She whined plaintively, threw herself at the closed door, scratched, howled. She sat on the doorstep all night, but the people did not come out. In the morning the door opened. The dog thought that they wanted to let her in, and was about to run inside, but the man roughly pushed her back. He went to his car. The dog ran after him, but the car, with a loud screech, quickly pulled away. The dog followed, trying to keep up, but could not.

Soon, she realised that she was in an unfamiliar place. Everyone who passed by, on foot, on a bicycle, or in a car, was a stranger. She darted from side to side, looking for the man, but was unable to find him.

Eventually, among all the unfamiliar smells, she scented food. On the ground, next to some large boxes, were several delicious-smelling packages. She approached them, but a noise from behind the boxes caused her to freeze. Another dog – a huge one, covered in scars and scratches – growled menacingly.

Much more experienced than she as a scavenger and in defending its own interests, the other dog moved speedily from threats to action. Attacking our poor lost dog, it caught her by the ear. She yelped and fled, leaving behind some skin from her ear, but taking with her one of the bags of food.

Running at first, then slowing to a trot, she did not stop until she reached the beach where she met Ernesto.

But was he a trustworthy human, or one of the other sort? Would this excellent meal only bring new misfortunes?

She looked at Ernesto. He moved away and sat near the water. She tried the pizza: it was good. In just a few minutes, all the food Ernesto had offered was gone.

After lying on the sand for a while, she moved closer to the man who had fed her. Ernesto turned and said: "Did you like it?"

ANASTASIIA MARSIZ

The dog remained at a safe distance, so Ernesto gave her a little time before making a move to approach and gently stroke her. The dog lowered her head, clearly not wanting his caress.

"I understand," said Ernesto. "You don't want to talk today. It happens. I also feel sad. I'm glad you've had some food. Good night." He briefly stroked her head once more and went to his cabin.

The dog followed at a safe distance, sniffing his footprints as the two of them proceeded. Reaching the door of his cabin, Ernesto stopped and looked around. The dog took refuge behind a stack of deck chairs. Darkness was falling and her eyes glowed. Smiling, the young man opened the cabin door and went inside. The dog stayed in the same place.

After a couple of minutes, the door opened and Ernesto reappeared with a large towel. He placed it on the wooden boards beside the cabin door. "You can sleep here," he said, pointing to the towel. Then he again disappeared into the cabin, closing the door behind him.

Some minutes more, and he came out again, this time with a bowl of water. "You must be thirsty," he said, placing the bowl next to the towel. The dog didn't move.

"You don't want it? Goodnight, then. I'll see you tomorrow." Ernesto waved his hand as he closed the door, and this time the door remained closed.

In a dream that night, Ernesto was a child running to the sea. Cecilia followed him. Wearing a white dress with a small brooch in the shape of a yellow butterfly with blue spots, she smiled. Ernesto ran to the sea and put his hands in the water. Gentle ripples caressed his fingers. The boy felt the heat from the water soaking into his body – this was happiness. He looked at his grandmother and said to her: "Ceci, I have a dog now. She is my friend forever." Cecilia smiled, but did not speak. Her gaze reminded Ernesto of the dog's gaze. He was surprised, perplexed….

Ernesto awoke. The clock showed five in the morning. Daylight was already penetrating the windows of his cabin. Opening the door, he looked out. The beach was shrouded in the cool of the dawn and the golden glow of the rising sun. The sea was calm, the sky cloudless. He looked down at the towel he had provided as a bed for his new friend, and there, curled up in a ball, lay the dog. She opened her eyes and looked carefully at Ernesto. "Just as in the dream," he thought. He leaned over the dog and stroked her gently. The dog did not withdraw her head, but licked his hand with a warm, wet tongue. He felt comfortable and happy, as in his dream. The realisation came to him that he loved this dog; more than that, he had always loved her.

Briefly going back inside his cabin, he took a blanket, wrapped himself in it and sat down outside near the dog, leaning his back against the wall. He stroked the sleeping dog and stared at the water in the distance, feeling the even beat of his happy heart. The orphan was at peace sitting next to his new friend. He sat like that until Andrea arrived to begin his day's work.

Around seven o'clock, Ernesto took the dog into the cabin and, to ensure that the secret of her presence remained safe, asked her to sit quietly.

Andrea waved to Ernesto. He began to clean up, dancing to the music provided by his small earphones. By nine o'clock, the whole Marino family had gathered at the Chalet Martina, and the working day was well underway. Everyone knew their job well and went about it as usual. Only Ernesto departed from his normal routine. He took his breakfast of omelette and toast back to his sleeping quarters. An hour later, he took a bucket and a rag to the cabin and shut himself in for a further ten minutes.

When lunchtime arrived, he took that to the cabin, plus the bucket and rag again. Having seen all this, Martina asked Ernesto if he was unwell. Avoiding her eyes, he replied that he felt fine, and expressed surprise that she had asked such a question.

Of the Marinos, Frani was the first to meet the Chalet's mystery guest. The next time Ernesto paid a visit to his cabin, she silently followed and slipped through the door behind him.

"You have a dog here!" she exclaimed with delight. "How beautiful she is. And big." Frani went up to the dog, sat down on the floor beside her and placed her face close to the dog's muzzle, radiating delight and joy. "What's her name?" she asked, stroking the adorable creature.

"Dog," Ernesto answered, experiencing mixed feelings of fear and pride in his new pet.

"Dog?" The dear animal was already licking Frani's fingers. "How sweet you are, Dog," Frani exclaimed.

The dog and child were happy; Ernesto too. Smiling broadly, he stood in the middle of his small room. Suddenly, though, a disturbing thought came to him, and a deep wrinkle creased his broad forehead.

"Hey, Frani, you won't tell anyone that I have a dog living here, will you?"

"Of course not," Frani replied. "This is our secret. I love secrets so much, and I've never had a real secret." She sprang up and joyfully jumped up and down on the spot, clapping her hands. The dog also stood up and raised its head with interest, realising that it was participating in something special.

"I'll get Dog something to eat," Frani whispered, as if there was a danger that someone would overhear them. Together, they tiptoed out of the cabin.

Anyone observing their furtive behaviour would immediately have begun to wonder what was going on. At that moment, however, the courtyard of the Chalet Martina was deserted. Frani went to the kitchen and asked Adriano for cheese and prosciutto. "Jacqueline doll and I are hungry."

"Anything for my little sweetheart and her friend," Adriano answered tenderly, placing a large piece of cheese and slices of prosciutto on a plate.

Coming out of the kitchen, Frani stopped, looked around, took a deep breath and was about to go down to Ernesto's cabin when Féde suddenly appeared. "Where are you going with all that food?" she asked in surprise.

"Nowhere in particular. Isn't it possible for a young lady to have a bite to eat in peace?" Frani pouted angrily. "I'm human too."

"Human?" said Féde, laughing. She disappeared behind the kitchen door.

"That was close: I almost got caught," Frani reflected. She stood where she was for a couple of minutes before deciding that all was now clear and striding purposefully towards Ernesto's cabin.

An hour later, Frani asked her father for some "delicious sausage and cheese," returning, not long afterwards, for more cheese. Adriano decided to follow the little glutton. He saw her entering Ernesto's cabin. Ernesto was working on the beach at that time, so definitely not at home.

After waiting a few minutes, Adriano entered the cabin. "Wow!" he exclaimed, seeing the dog. "So Jacqueline is not the only hungry one!"

"Daddy, dear, please don't say anything to Mama," begged Frani, running up to her father. "Mama won't let the dog stay here, and she has nowhere else to go. And she's so cute." The little girl was on the verge of tears.

"Don't worry, my little kitten, I won't tell mama," Adriano said, very quietly. Then he went up to the dog, sat down beside her, and extended his hand to pet her. The dog sniffed his hand and licked it.

"Yes, she is very sweet," he agreed. "Let's go see what we can find for her to eat." Adriano was about to leave, but stopped and asked: "What's her name?"

"Dog," Frani replied.

"Oh, that's unusual." Adriano shrugged his shoulders and hurried to the kitchen.

When Ernesto returned to his cabin, he was astonished to find Frani, Adriano and Antonio sitting on the floor, tenderly watching Dog chew on a piece of meat.

"Is that you, Ernesto? Come in, just be quiet," said Adriano, turning back to Dog.

Whatever Ernesto might have expected to find on returning to Dog, this was certainly not it. Perplexed, he decided the best – the only – thing he could do was to join the company watching Dog eat her dinner.

Standing in the courtyard, Martina wondered where the rest of the Marinos were. Neither Adriano nor Antonio was in the kitchen; Frani had also disappeared somewhere. Ernesto wasn't around either.

"What a strange day it's been," she thought to herself.

Then she saw that the door to Ernesto's cabin was open and that all the missing Marinos were filing out with ecstatic looks on their faces.

"What's got into them? Did they find treasure or something?" Martina approached the cabin.

"Ah, Martina, dear," Adriano said, blocking the door with his back, "We were…." He didn't have time to finish, as Martina, frowning, pushed her way into Ernesto's dwelling.

"Now we're for it," Antonio said.

"Mama won't be happy," Frani whispered.

Ernesto didn't say anything. He thought Signora Marino would expel not only Dog from the Chalet Martina, but himself too. He had no one left except the Marino family, and had no idea where he would go. He stood with folded arms and bowed his head dejectedly.

The few minutes spent waiting for Martina to emerge from the cabin seemed to last for hours. Ernesto, nervously bit his lip; beads of sweat formed on his broad forehead.

Finally, Martina came out, Dog obediently following her.

"What on earth is going on?" Martina demanded to know. Ernesto winced, took a step forward and said timidly: "It's me…. I brought the dog. Forgive me, Signora Marino."

"What I am asking is, why is the animal locked up, and why am I the last to know about it?"

"I only brought her here tonight…. That is, she turned up last night … on the beach. She was hungry. I just … I … I'm sorry." Ernesto was on the verge of tears. Frani was already crying.

"All right, all right," Martina said, softening her tone. "So, what do we do with her now?"

Dog, sitting with her tail between her legs, stared into Martina's eyes. Her canine mind understood that this woman was leader of the pack.

"I'll take her, and I'll leave," Ernesto said quietly. He had made up this mind that he wouldn't part with Dog, even if that meant leaving the Chalet Martina, starving and living on the streets.

"And where do you think you would go?"

From the expression on his wife's face, it was clear to Adriano that Dog would be staying. He smiled, Antonio too. Frani wiped away her tears.

"I guess she'd better stay," Martina said. "What is her name?"

"Dog!" everyone cried out, breaking into a laugh.

"Dog? You could at least have come up with a nickname for her. Oh, well, Dog, let's go, I'll feed you." She turned affectionately to the happy animal, which had finally found a loving family. They all laughed, and Dog licked Martina's hand.

5. GRASSO'S
MIRACULOUS RESCUE

Rino Grasso lived at Number 9, … Street in the town of Cupra Marittima. By reputation, Rino was sullen and highly irritable. Nothing pleased him. He found something to criticise in everything Maria, his poor wife, did. He found fault in whatever she cooked: either she overcooked the fish, or over-salted it; boiled the rice into a soggy mush; put too little pepper in the food, or too much; or there wasn't enough cold beer. And his endless complaints were accompanied by angry shouts and deep sighs.

If his children were late for school, Rino got so cross that red blotches would cover his plump face. Then he would be annoyed when they came back home. The very sight of his neighbour's dog made him angry; its constant barking drove up his blood pressure.

He also worked himself into a state of extreme rage when he saw people with dark skin. His strongly-held opinion was that Africans should remain in their homeland. It was completely unacceptable to him that some lived in his beautiful Italy and breathed the same air as he did. He also believed that all African men were thieves, rapists and cold-blooded murderers, and that their desire to commit crime was passed down from generation to generation in their genes.

To illustrate the full force of Rino's hostility to dark-skinned people, it is worth mentioning an incident that occurred many years ago. The young Rino Grasso was lounging in an armchair watching television one evening, slowly eating some oversalted pasta, when the news of a murder in the neighbouring town of Offida caught his attention. Three Italians had attacked a Gambian who was walking with his pregnant Italian girlfriend in the groves of an olive farm. They beat up the young man because he, as they put it, had "desecrated an Italian girl." Severely injured, the Gambian was taken to hospital, but his life could not be saved.

The news of this lynching raised Rino's blood pressure, but this time not because of rage or anger.

"Maria, dear, come quickly!" he shouted, jumping from his chair.

Maria, shocked that for the first time in five years of marriage her husband had called her "dear," dropped a frying pan. For once, that usually-certain cause of irritation did not register with Rino.

"Leave the housework, come and see. Finally, one of these blacks has got what he deserved. Our guys did him good." Rino was ecstatic. Pasta spilled from his mouth, making greasy marks on the chair.

"But the man died," Maria said.

"Yes, they may have overdone it a bit, but he still got what he deserved. Don't touch our girls!"

"Unbelievable," Maria muttered under her breath. Shaking her head, she returned to the kitchen to wash the dishes.

The killing was soon forgotten by all except the few most closely affected. Nevertheless, it was destined to play a pivotal role in the events eighteen years later that unfold in this, our present tale.

One Saturday afternoon, Rino and his family went to the beach as usual. Rino carried a heavy bag stuffed with towels, creams and all the other things needed for a day at the seaside. Rino cursed, grumbled and spat all the way. When his youngest daughter, Marisa, asked to take her inflatable ring along, he said no, adding sharply: "We've got no room, or time, to drag any more rubbish around. You're a big girl now – learn to swim!"

Marisa was four years old, and she couldn't swim because no one was willing to make the time to teach her. Her mother was always busy with household chores; her father was tired after work; her older sister, Pina, spent her entire time on "engagements" with her friends; and her brother took any and every opportunity to disappear into the yard to play football.

The Grasso family arrived at the Chalet Martina's beach. Ernesto approached them and was about to point them toward some available sun loungers when Rino burst out: "Where the hell did you come from? Don't touch our stuff! Don't you dare come near my daughters!" He shielded the astonished girls with his fat body.

Ernesto stood in the middle of the beach, not knowing what to do. Fortunately, Signora Marino arrived in time to help him.

Turning to her, Rino asked: "Martina, what is this Kenyan, or whatever he is, doing on your beach?"

"Ernesto is Italian," Martina said calmly.

"Since when do Italians look like Kenyan monkeys?" Rino yelled, his face turning purple.

Maria Grasso lowered her eyes and looked embarrassed.

"Ernesto is our new worker," Martina said, evenly, leaving as little room as possible for argument. "His work is on the beach." She looked kindly at Ernesto.

"Let him work where he wants to," Rino raised a fat finger, "but make very sure he doesn't come within a metre of my family. You never know what to expect from his kind.… I have two daughters – two young flowers."

Thinking that anything he had left out of his argument would now speak for itself, Rino pursed his lips and looked at his girls with as much tenderness as he could muster.

Maria Grasso stood silently, her eyes still lowered. Pina, the elder daughter, stared at her phone, loudly chewing something. Marisa, the younger daughter, gave the huge, dark boy a sweet smile.

Ernesto also smiled as he regarded the Grasso family.

"Why is he smiling like that?" Rino asked. "Is he a fool?"

"I heard you, Rino," Martina answered dryly, barely reining in her anger. "Come with me, I will help you." She led the Grasso family to the sun loungers.

At lunch time, Rino sat at a table in the restaurant. He ordered pasta and a large glass of cold beer, announcing that Maria would not have any lunch because she could barely fit through the doorway as it was. Pina ran off to meet a friend, and Marisa stayed by the water because she loved the sea more than pasta.

Rino was finishing his lunch and was about to order a second glass of beer when he heard a desperate cry from the beach: "Help! Help my little girl! Someone help my girl!"

Rino jumped from his chair, knocking the remaining pasta over his belly, and ran to the sea. Marisa was fifty metres from the shore, floundering and choking in the water, Maria stood at the water's edge, sobbing and shouting incoherently. A male figure with dark skin and huge hands was cutting swiftly through the water towards the drowning girl. It was Ernesto.

Playing in the shallows, Marisa had gone further and further into the sea. Eventually, she had realised that her feet could no longer touch the bottom. Frightened, she screamed, took in a mouthful of salt water and began to flounder helplessly. Her head went underwater; she surfaced and tried to gulp in some air, but immediately sank back beneath the water.

Ernesto heard Marisa's scream from where he was sitting. Without hesitation, he jumped out of his chair, raced across the beach, plunged into the sea and swam with all speed to the place where she had disappeared beneath the waves. He then dived into the murky water, grasped the little girl and raised her to the surface.

A minute or two later, Marisa was lying on the dry sand. Adriano and Martina came running. Onlookers gathered from all over the beach, all excitedly chattering with their own version of what they had seen – or not even noticed until it was almost over. Dog came too, clearly as alarmed by the turn of events as any of the humans.

Pina Grasso made her way through the crowd. Seeing her little sister lying on the sand, she rushed to her. Rino stood with his legs wide, his arms hanging helplessly, tomato sauce decorating his huge belly. A grimace of horror distorted his face, tears frosted in his eyes. He was experiencing fear and despair such as never before in his life. Maria, mad with grief, shouted in a voice that was not her own: "Oh Lord! Almighty and Almighty! Save my girl! I beg you!"

Ernesto remembered the first aid training he had received at school and set about trying to resuscitate the child.

The siren of an ambulance called by Martina was already getting close when Marisa coughed and opened her eyes. The first person she saw was Ernesto, still bending over her. She looked frightened, then caught sight of her mother and stretched out her thin arms towards her. Maria rushed to kiss and hug her daughter – and, overflowing with gratitude, she did her best to find words adequate to thank Ernesto from the very bottom of her heart.

The crowd cheered and clapped. Martina and Adriano breathed a sigh of relief and embraced. Pina smiled as she wiped away her tears. Dog, who had been lying beside Marisa, jumped up and wagged her tail.

Rino trembled all over and slowly sank to his knees. He gently stroked his daughter's little legs, his dry lips whispered a prayer of gratitude to the Almighty for this miracle; tears flowed down his fat cheeks.

Ernesto stood by, smiling. He was happy that he had managed to do what was necessary at the decisive moment, and that the outcome was so good – the little girl's life was saved.

The crowd parted as the paramedics ran up. They knelt beside Marisa to examine her, then put her on a stretcher and took her to hospital, assuring everyone that she was in no danger. Maria went with her, determined now not to leave her alone for a second.

Getting up from his knees, Rino stared intently at Ernesto. What was he thinking? Suddenly, he grabbed Ernesto's hands and with deep emotion said: "You saved her. You … You saved her life. Thank you – son!" He hugged Ernesto tight; the same Ernesto, to whom, not long before, he would never have extended a hand, or allowed within a metre of his family.

"So," Rino declared, releasing Ernesto from his strong embrace, "I'm throwing a celebratory dinner in honour of the hero who saved my daughter!"

Adriano and Martina exchanged glances, and looked at Rino with great surprise, astonished by the miraculous transformation of the grouchy Grasso.

"Everyone, and I mean everyone, is invited to the Chalet Martina. Right now," Rino announced, holding up a fat finger. That was his favourite gesture, one that he used to convey a multitude of different meanings. "Martina, dear, can I arrange dinner at your place?"

"Rino, where else?" said Adriano, butting in quickly before his wife could answer. Then, taking Rino by the arm, he led him to the restaurant.

"I'll cook my signature pasta. M-ma! Just fantastic. At the establishment's expense."

"No, no!" Rino objected. "Dinner's on me – the happy father of a miraculously saved daughter."

The voices of the departing comrades faded into the distance with: "No, I still insist.…"

Ernesto stood, surrounded by an admiring crowd. Many wanted to shake his hand, others patted him on the shoulder. For him, though, that was by the way; the most important words were uttered by Martina: "You acted bravely and nobly. If only Cecilia could know, she would be so proud of you."

Later on, after darkness fell, the tables of the Chalet Martina were filled with dishes and drinks of all kinds. People rejoiced, had fun, laughed. Little Marisa, wearing a smart blue dress, played with Frani, seemingly without a care in the world. Frani had put on her favourite red polka dot dress, and Frani's doll, Jacqueline, was also dressed for the occasion.

Féde fluttered between the tables with a tray: in her case it was not Marisa's miraculous rescue that made her steps so light. Antonio peeked through the kitchen door. His father, taking a seat at table with Rino, had left him alone in there. Martina busied herself taking care of the guests. She kept an eye on Ernesto too. He sat in a place of honour, handsome, bewildered, and with his eyes radiating a light brighter than all the lamps illuminating the Chalet Martina's courtyard. Martina had given him a white shirt. It was too small for him, but it highlighted his bronzed skin in a most pleasing way.

Rino repeatedly called Marisa to him, lifting her onto his knees, hugging her, kissing her cheeks. He laughed and shouted with joy. Maria wholeheartedly welcomed her husband's transformation, fervently hoping that it would prove long-lasting.

Adriano's delicious food was eaten, carefully chosen wines were drunk, the women were led home shouting "just a little bit longer," whilst children and grown men alike fell asleep at their tables. In short, the party was a big success.

Rino was seen holding a glass of whisky in one hand and with his other arm firmly around Ernesto. With the whisky hand, he gestured towards Ernesto's chest: "Ernesto, son, I want you to know that you … are a member of my family. Yes, I swear it."

He paused to take a deep breath. Perhaps that would help unknot his alcohol-addled tongue. He looked at Adriano, who nodded to show he was paying attention.

"I am Rino Grasso," Rino continued, raising a finger. "I give you the word of an Italian that never…. You hear? Never…." He patted Ernesto on the shoulder. "I will never forget what you did for me today … and I will always be your friend."

Rino paused to sip his whisky. Adriano also raised his glass to his lips.

Ernesto, deeply moved, stared at Rino. Their eyes met.

Suddenly, Rino jumped up from his chair, spilling his whisky.

"Wait! I understand now." He examined Ernesto closely, then shifted his gaze to Adriano, who was also having trouble focussing his tired eyes. "I thought you looked familiar."

"Who?" Adriano asked.

"This guy…." Rino paused, hunting for the right word. "That poor guy from the news." He clapped his hands and, expecting Ernesto and Adriano to understand him, stared at them knowingly.

But understand they did not. Ernesto looked at Adriano, searching for some sort of clue. Adriano clicked his tongue, narrowed his eyes, and again nodded his head as if he understood something – although he really had no idea what Rino was talking about.

"Ernesto, you look exactly like him. Years ago, I was watching the evening news. Maria had boiled and over-salted the pasta again. Ugh!" He grimaced and spat. "I was sitting in front of the TV, and there you were. I saw you."

Rino sat down beside Ernesto and leaned towards him. Adriano pulled a chair closer to Rino, the better to hear.

"I don't understand," Adriano said. "Many years ago, you were watching the news…."

"Yes, I was watching the news, eating Maria's over-salted pasta…."

"I'm not asking about the pasta. You said that many years ago, you were eating and watching the TV news…."

"Don't you get it, Adriano?" Rino was getting agitated. "How many times do I have to tell you? I was watching the news, eating pasta, it was very salty…."

Adriano could take no more of this. He rose to his feet as if elevated by his own words: "Rino, what are you banging on about? I'm simply asking how, all those years ago, you could have seen him." He pointed at the frightened Ernesto. "I mean, how many years are we talking about here?"

"How long ago? Well, let's see. Neither Marisa nor Pina had been born, and my eldest, Stefano, would have been five, but Maria always cooked badly…." Rino grimaced again.

"There you are. How could you have seen Ernesto on TV when he is only…?" Adriano turned to Ernesto: "How old are you?"

"Eighteen," Ernesto said.

"Eighteen. So, he'd just been born. Was it a baby you saw?" Adriano was triumphant: his logic had won the day – or so he thought.

"Did I say I saw him?" Rino pointed at Ernesto.

Sensing that matters were getting out of hand, Martina moved closer.

"That's exactly what you said. You said, 'I saw you,' and you pointed at Ernesto." Adriano said at the top of his voice.

"I said, 'I thought you looked familiar,'" Rino insisted. "He looks like his father, the one who was killed."

Now it was Ernesto's turn to jump from his chair. "What? You said my father … was killed? Did you know my father?"

"How would I have known your father?" Rino demanded, indignantly. "I know you. You are a good guy, a hero. I didn't know your father."

Martina ran up to their table. "What's going on? What are you all shouting about? Sit down, all of you."

They all obediently sat.

Martina continued: "Now, Rino, calm down and tell us exactly what you mean."

"I said," Rino began again, "that twenty years ago I was sat watching the news, eating pasta that Maria...."

"Let's skip the pasta," Martina snapped. "Tell us about Ernesto's father."

Finally, Rino managed to explain that the news on TV that evening was about an immigrant from Gambia, or Kenya, or wherever it was, murdered by three Italians; that he died in the hospital; and about the pregnant Italian woman; also, that the murdered man looked like Ernesto – like two peas in a pod!

Adriano and Martina looked at each other in concern. Ernesto sat silent, his face motionless, like a mask.

"Are you sure he looked like Ernesto?" Martina asked softly, as if afraid that Ernesto would hear.

"I am certain; as certain as that forty-eight years ago Bella-Rosina Grasso gave birth and brought me into this world!"

Ernesto's face remained motionless. He had never known either of his parents. Cecilia had told him a lot about Leah, and in his mind's eye he had a bright, flawless image of a tender and loving mother. The only thing he thought he knew about his father was that he was a bad person who had abandoned them both. Even so, he had dreamed that one day his father would return and provide answers to his many questions. But now, this revelation that his father had been murdered changed almost everything. A reunion and reconciliation were impossible and, it now transpired, always had been. Cold despair seized him: he was filled with loneliness and a sense of helplessness.

Again in a quiet voice, Martina said: "Ernesto, can I make you some mint tea?"

Seeming not to have heard Martina, Ernesto asked Rino: "Who killed my father?"

"Who knows? Three guys ... Italians – that's all they said." Rino felt guilty. He hadn't meant to upset the poor guy, especially on a day when he had rightly been feted for heroism.

"I need to find them," Ernesto said – out loud, but mainly to himself.

Burning thoughts swept through his head. His life had been aimless and empty until now. When Cecilia had been around, he had done whatever she told him. Since her death, he had looked to Martina, Adriano, and even little Frani for direction. But now a real purpose had presented itself. Now he knew that every step he made, every breath he took must be dedicated to finding those who had deprived him of the love of his parents. How many tender words his mother and father could have said to him; how many kisses, hugs they could have given him. And all this not due to a terrible accident, but the consequence of the brutal actions of three human beings who had callously ended his father's life. They – he assumed – had gone on to live and love, while his tender mother and strong father lay in the ground, robbed of the chance to bring up their son.

The desire for revenge coiled in Ernesto's head like a black snake, poisoning his thoughts with its destructive venom.

Martina touched his hand. "Ernesto, you're burning up," she said. "Water, Adriano. Water, quick!"

"I'm going right now. I'll be back in a moment." The past few minutes seemed to have sobered Adriano up, although he stumbled as he ran to the bar.

"Rino, Rino…," said Martina, shaking her head disapprovingly.

"Why are you treating him like a child?" Rino asked, indignantly. "Ernesto, you are my hero." Rino hugged Ernesto and pulled him close to himself. "That's what I wanted to tell you."

"You've already said enough," Martina interrupted him angrily. She took the glass of water brought by Adriano and handed it to Ernesto.

"Rino, will you help me find them?" Ernesto asked.

"I…." Rino hesitated a little and thought. "Yes, I will help you," he said, adding, "That's a promise. For Rino Grasso, there are no unsolvable questions."

Ernesto looked at Rino with gratitude. Martina sighed loudly.

"I'll start by taking you to Bitto Leone," Grasso announced enthusiastically.

"And what's he going to do with Bitto?" Adriano was taken aback. "Ernesto is a quiet, decent lad."

"What's he going to do?" Rino laughed. "Boxing, of course. How about it, Ernesto?"

"Will I be able to do it?" Ernesto asked, his voice reflecting the doubt he felt.

"Are you kidding?" Rino replied. "Look at the size of your hands."

"I thought that too," Martina murmured. "So, it's time to finish up here – before you come up with some other bright idea."

"Martina, my little olive," Adriano said, "we'll just sit here for a little longer." He tried to fix an expression of cheerfulness and resolve on his face.

"Yes, Martina, just a little longer," Rino said. "We will be gone soon." He poured more whisky into his own and Adriano's glasses.

"As you wish, Adriano. I'm going home. Frani is already fast asleep. Close everything as you leave, and don't dilly-dally!"

Martina then turned to the hero of the day. "Ernesto, you have a good rest. Tomorrow, you can start work at nine." She patted his cheek, cast a withering look at Adriano, and left.

The men sat at the table for a long time. Rino kept talking about boxing: about the world of the strong and hardy to which Ernesto would soon belong. Adriano shared memories of his youth when he would chase hooligans out of the yard. For as long as this continued, Ernesto listened to the amazing anecdotes, all the while making plans for some daring exploits of his own. Dog slept peacefully at his feet, already well into her night.

6. FÉDE'S DATE

The day of Féde's assignation with Calisto had arrived.

Her excitement seemed to transmit itself throughout the Marino family. Even Ernesto understood that this day was special. Martina was dissatisfied with everyone. She scolded Andrea for poor cleaning, Antonio for laziness, and Adriano for a burnt omelette. Ernesto caught it for his sluggishness. Frani managed to avoid her mother's eye and wrath by escaping with her faithful friend Jacqueline to the playground on the beach.

Towards the end of a long, hot afternoon, Féde wafted into the Chalet Martina like a fresh breeze, surrounded by an aura of ethereal beauty.

She was gorgeous. The lilac silk dress she wore emphasised her slender figure and brought out her mysterious, dark-coloured eyes. Her hair fell over her shoulders in soft waves. A joyful smile played on her face. Féde had never before appeared so beautiful. Who could know whether the transformation was due to her falling in love, the thirty-Euro hair-styling, or the dress on which she had spent all her remaining money.

"My little olive!" exclaimed Adriano, running out to meet his beloved daughter. "You are so beautiful." Tears welled up in his eyes – and not because of the onion he was chopping.

"Féde, are you ready?" Martina asked, pretending to be calm. "You look nice today. I hope your *fidanzato* is worth it. But why are you already here? You are early. That's not the way to go about it: girls should be late," she said, shaking her head.

"What are you doing, dear?" Adriano interjected. "Don't embarrass the girl. Poor Féde is trembling all over, Martina. Just look at her." Féde really was shaking and on the verge of tears.

Adriano hugged his daughter. "Let's go, my darling. I'll make you dinner. You probably didn't have time to eat breakfast." He winked at Féde, letting her know that he was on her side.

"No, Daddy, I'm not hungry," Féde answered quietly. "I'll just sit here." She pointed to a table in a corner under the awning. It was Martina's usual place. "If I'm allowed?" she added, looking timidly at her mother.

"What kind of question is that?" exclaimed Adriano, waving his hands. "You're just not yourself today, sweetheart. I'd better go to my kitchen…." He frowned a little, then, smiling broadly at his daughter, he added: "What a beauty you are." He put two fingers together and kissed them: "M-ma!"

Féde smiled back at her father, checked her appearance in the mirror, and sat down at the table. There was still more than an hour before Calisto was due. She leaned back and began to dream.

Calisto spent only twenty minutes getting ready. He slept well, caressed Dévi, sauntered downstairs and strolled into his father's office.

Alberto Conte was reading a history of the Etruscans. He was looking for evidence to support his pet theory that everything in the world moves in cycles. In particular, he sought affirmation that the same set of vices that consume people today also prevailed in ancient times. He was looking for assurance that the evil so comfortably lodged in his own soul had been around for over two thousand years; that countless "brothers" just like him had always marched through the pages of history. That being proven, there would be no need for him to stop indulging his own vices – or feel any guilt about them.

It might be added, though, that he was only interested in "brothers" of a certain class: those from noble families, or who possessed riches and fame.

As Calisto walked into his father's office, Alberto looked up from his book and smiled benevolently. If Alberto Conte was capable of loving, Calisto alone could bring it out. Alberto's feelings were deep and tender: he firmly believed that his son was the only beautiful and good thing in his existence. Calisto could lift him from the world of corruption to the world of purity. There, love and compassion ruled – but, in truth, for Alberto that world no longer existed.

He got up from the table and hugged his son tightly, as if they were reuniting after a long separation. Alberto always hugged Calisto like that. It was as if he was afraid that this vicious world would finally consume him; as if his son was his last thread of connection with kindness and mercy. He felt immense joy every time he breathed in his son's unique scent.

"How are you, Papa?" Calisto asked affectionately. He truly loved and admired his father. "Are you still burying your head in all these dusty books?"

"Yes, my boy. A book is an inexhaustible source of wisdom and knowledge. It opens endless worlds to us. Sit down, I'll tell you something very interesting. Do you know that…."

"Papa, please don't be offended, but that will have to wait for another day. I came to tell you that I've taken your advice to go to the Rossini Festival today."

"Excellent, my boy, excellent! Art is magical…."

"Yes, yes," Calisto interrupted, curtailing what he knew would be an excruciatingly tedious lecture on the miraculous healing power of art. "I will definitely expand my horizons tonight and discover something beautiful, new and sublime."

"I see, Calisto, and what exactly are you after?" Alberto smiled. "Why did you suddenly decide to listen to 'Demetrius and Polybius?"[9] Last year, nothing and no one could persuade you to go to the festival."

"Well, Papa dear, the older I get, the stronger I feel the desire to partake of the eternal and beautiful. After all, I have to find something to inspire me. I can't just waste my time idling in bars and cafes."

"And who's the lady?" Alberto asked, laughing.

"Papa, why do you think I'm going with a lady? Maybe I'll go alone, or with Giacomo." Calisto's facial expression was the same as when, as a child, he had been accused of taking an extra helping of ice cream.

"You definitely won't go alone. And there's no chance you'll go with Giacomo. He wouldn't know the difference between a cavatina[10] and an intermezzo.[11] So, tell me who this trip is for – and none of your nonsense about love of art." Alberto smiled cheerfully as he said this.

"My, aren't you perceptive?" Calisto sighed. "Yes, I confess, there is a girl, and I would like to spend a romantic evening with her in Pesaro, especially as you said you would not go this year, but that you had tickets and even hinted I should take Dévi," Calisto rambled on, unconvincingly.

"Don't drag Dévi into this," Alberto laughed. "And who is the girl for whom you willingly agreed to spend the evening in the company of Jessica Pratt and Ricardo Fassi?"[12]

"Who?"

"Oh, don't worry about them," Alberto replied indulgently. "But who is the girl? What is her name?"

....

[9]   Italian composer Gioacchino Rossini's first opera.

[10]   A small lyrical opera aria.

[11]   A small independent instrumental piece or part of an instrumental cycle.

[12]   Jessica Pratt and Ricardo Fassi are, respectively, soprano and bass opera singers.

"Her name is Federica, and…." Calisto broke off. He did not want to tell his father the truth about his argument with Giacomo, although Alberto would have completely understood and would have appreciated the game.

"So, Papa can I go?" Calisto's face took on a childlike, pleading expression.

"I'm not forbidding you," Alberto smiled.

"I also wanted to ask…." Calisto hesitated.

"About money, most likely." Alberto laughed.

"How do you know everything?" Calisto exclaimed joyfully and hugged his father. "I don't have a lot of cash, but you know, I'll go…."

"Oh, don't go on," interrupted his father. "I'll give you the money. If there are no more questions, go. And don't forget that tomorrow you and I are playing golf."

"I'm offended, Papa. I always look forward to our Saturdays," Calisto said as he made for the door.

Alberto returned to his reading, and continued smiling for a long time.

Calisto entered the Chalet Martina at exactly five o'clock. He held two huge bouquets of roses. The first, he presented to Martina, bringing a slight smile to her face. She ran her grey eyes over the young man, noting his regular, beautiful features; glossy hair; expensive, fine linen suit; and confident air.

Féde accepted her bouquet with trembling hands and gave Calisto a shy smile, trying to disguise her excitement. To his wife's surprise, Adriano had changed out of his work clothes and into a clean blue shirt, playing the role of the proud father. Frani looked with interest into the face of her older sister's *fidanzato*, a word she really liked.

"Federica, you are beautiful! What a blessing that you agreed to accompany me tonight," Calisto said, kissing Féde's hand.

"Thank you for the invitation," Féde replied.

"It's time for us to go," said Calisto.

"Have a nice evening," said an emotional Adriano.

"Don't be late!" Martina added, sternly.

Féde and Calisto walked hand-in-hand to his gleaming car. Martina followed them with an unbending gaze until the car slipped out of sight.

Féde felt infinitely happy all the way to Pesaro, enjoying Calisto's closeness, the smell of his aftershave, and the soft timbre of his voice. She admired the way he drove: observing how his small hands held the steering wheel; how the muscles tensed when the car skirted an obstacle or entered a sharp turn, and relaxed when the road straightened.

When they arrived in Pesaro, Calisto suggested to Féde that they dine at the Nostrano restaurant. She agreed. The restaurant proved to be very cosy. The restrained interior was simply furnished with wooden tables, and a glass veranda overlooked the sea. Everything was designed to encourage relaxed conversation. Féde felt special and mature. She allowed Calisto to order, completely trusting his taste. They feasted on tuna tartare and fried mullet. And the dish with shrimp, white truffles and fennel was simply amazing.

Calisto suggested they order wine. Féde agreed. She was not used to drinking alcohol, but wanted to be a real adult this evening. The wine went straight to her head and she relaxed. It felt as if she went to restaurants such as this every day. And Calisto was so close.

When Calisto decided that they had eaten and drunk sufficient, the young couple left the restaurant to immerse themselves in art.

As they strolled along the quiet streets of Pesaro, Calisto told Féde entertaining stories about his friends Giacomo and Orsino. He represented them as educated and reserved, the exact opposite of reality.

Féde listened spellbound. She offered no matching stories about her life, because it seemed so humdrum; like a boring movie mapped out by a lazy director.

They approached the Rossini Theatre. The audience had already gathered in the square in front of the building, waiting for the performance to begin. Some were sitting in pairs on the steps of the fountain opposite the entrance.

Calisto put his arm around Féde's waist and they ascended to their seats in a box. The red velvet that dominated the interior contrasted exquisitely with the blue-grey curtain and artistic wall paintings. Féde had never attended an opera before – this amazing, magical world of high art. Calisto gave her a printed program, which she diligently studied. Then the curtain rose, revealing a richly decorated stage.

Féde kept glancing at Calisto. He sat with an expression of obvious boredom on his face. Catching her gaze, he tried to put on the air of a passionate opera-goer, making brief remarks from time to time that exactly repeated comments made by his father several years before in this very box. Féde listened attentively to his learnt discourse, fully persuaded that he was a connoisseur of the operatic arts. He stroked her hands, whispering passionate words into her ear. And, then, as if by chance, he touched her thigh. Féde was so taken aback by the surge of heat she felt at his touch that her lips went dry.

Féde began to look around at the audience to distract herself from her burning thoughts and desires. Her attention was drawn to a girl in a dark dress with a white collar. She looked about twelve. The girl was sitting between a man wearing small pince-nez glasses and a woman wearing the same dress but without the white collar. They were completely absorbed in the action taking place on the stage, so still that they seemed like dolls.

She then noticed a woman she had first seen as they entered the theatre. She was wearing a leopard print dress so open that it seemed her magnificent breasts were about to fall into her hands. Her hairstyle could best be described as "unique." The bouffant rose so high that the spectators behind her couldn't see the stage. Her brightly painted eyes and fiery red lips would have put the performers on stage to shame.

Eventually, the final chord of the opera sounded out. There was a thunder of applause and many cries of "bravo." Féde clapped so hard her palms reddened and ached. After the applause subsided, the young couple headed for the exit. They walked slowly to the car, Féde joyfully shared her impressions, and Calisto either nodded his head or smiled tightly, inserting: "Hmmm…. I think so too…. Did you understand that?"

When they were once again travelling along the motorway, Calisto asked Féde a pre-rehearsed question: "Féde, tell me, would you, like Lisinga,[13] risk your life for the one you love?"

"I…," Féde began, then hesitated. If Calisto had looked at her at that moment, and if it hadn't been dark, he would have seen that she was blushing. "I would do anything for the person I love," she finished softly.

Calisto was waiting for her to say the word "love," and had hoped for just that answer.

"Do you love somebody, Féde?" he asked, lowering his voice and emphasising his prey's name, as he habitually did. He well understood the power and significance of using a person's name.

"I love you," Féde answered quietly. "I think," she added, shyly.

Calisto went in for the kill: "Can there be any doubt about love?"

---

[13] The daughter of Polybius (King of Parthia) is the protagonist of Gioacchino Antonio Rossini's opera *Demetrius and Polybius* (1812).

"No," Féde whispered.

The interrogation was over, the necessary evidence gathered.

Calisto stopped the car near the Marinos' house, got out and offered his hand to his companion. He led her to the door and kissed her on the lips. He made her promise to meet him the next evening.

Martina observed them closely from behind a curtain.

The next morning, Féde flitted between the tables at Chalet Martina with a tray in her hands. That much was as usual, but the idea that such a noble young man as Calisto might be in love with her had brought a transformation in other ways. She reacted to Martina's remarks with unusual restraint. She managed to serve more than three tables at the same time without dropping a fork, a spoon, or a tray laden with glasses. She even apologised to Ernesto when they bumped into each other, smiling affably and astonishing him by saying: "It's nothing, it was my fault."

Only one person was not fortunate enough to earn Féde's favour on this sunny day. When Marco made his customary visit to the Chalet Martina to drink a glass of water and bask in the presence of his beloved, Féde did not have a good-natured smile for him, no kind words, not even simple politeness.

"Water?" she asked curtly, without any greeting and with a slight edge of mockery.

"Hello, Federica! What a wonderful morning! The heat is just unbearable. So … I was passing by and … I decided to stop by to say hello and yes … to drink a glass of refreshing water." Marco spoke with mock swagger, but stammered nervously nevertheless.

"I'll bring it right away," Féde said, dryly.

She was about to leave Marco's table when he added: "You are so beautiful today, Federica. And this hairstyle really suits your face."

Féde gave Marco a contemptuous look and grimaced. "Thank you," she snapped, and quickly left him.

Martina noticed the lad and went to his table. "Marco! Good morning!" She smiled cheerfully.

"Signora Marino, hello!" Marco answered, jumping up from his chair and bowing his head.

"How are you doing, my dear?" Martina asked.

"Very well. I've been writing a little. This week I sent an article to *La Gazzetta dello Sport*,[14] and they bought it. Of course, it wasn't much money, but still," Marco answered proudly.

Martina liked this shy, intelligent and hard-working young man. It was precisely such a person that she wanted for her daughter. She knew well that nothing good would come from Féde spending time with the young Conte.

"I always said you'd do well," Martina said good-naturedly.

Féde returned with a glass of water. Marco blushed again.

Martina turned to her daughter and smiled enigmatically: "Féde, I was just telling Marco that he might become the next Furio Colombo."[15]

Féde gave her mother a sideways look, snorted disdainfully, and asked Marco: "Do you want anything more, Signor Colombo?"

Before Marco could reply, Martina interjected: "Of course, he does. Get Marco a glass of lemonade and a serving of strawberry sorbet."

Marco tried to speak again. "On the house!" Martina added.

"I'll bring it right away, Signora Marino," Féde said with mock obedience, and headed for the bar.

....

[14] An Italian sports newspaper, published daily.

[15] Italian journalist, writer, political commentator and lecturer at Columbia University's School of Journalism.

"Thank you, Signora Marino," Marco said quietly. He looked gratefully at Martina, again bowing his head.

"No problem," Martina replied. "Good luck, my dear." She extended a hand to him, and Marco shook it warmly.

"Come to us more often," said Martina, smiling and winking.

"Thank you, Signora Marino. I will."

That evening, Federica, wearing a pale blue dress, ran toward what she believed was true love. From the moment she and Calisto had said goodbye the previous evening, she had thought only of their next date. She could smell his cologne everywhere; she remembered his pleasant voice, the warmth of his hands. Intoxicated by these feelings, she had no idea that she was falling into the young Conte's devious trap. All she could do was dream of the happiness she believed she could find only with him.

Calisto greeted her with a kiss on the cheek. The kiss was somehow both passionate and innocent. She smelled once again the heady scent of his aftershave. Calisto was dazzling, and nothing about him revealed his true intentions.

"How do you feel about going to my father's olive grove? It's not far, about twenty kilometres towards Offida," Calisto said, helping Féde into the car.

Féde was confused as well as flattered that Calisto was asking her to decide.

"Yes, let's go. I think … I'm sure it will be very interesting. I would love to go with you."

"Believe me, you will like it," Calisto said, with affection – and a wink.

On the way to Offida, he entertained Féde with his deep knowledge of the grove, which had been in the possession of the Conte family for decades. He explained the complex process of growing Ascolana Tenera olives. And he did not neglect to inform the besotted Féde that he was the only heir to his parents' fortune.

She listened to Calisto and dreamed of the future. Her fantasies transported her from the mundane present to a bright and exciting future, where she, the young Signora Conte, would labour heart and soul for the good of the family business.

As they turned off the motorway, the sight of the beautiful hills looming ahead distracted her from her dreams. A huge grove of olive trees was revealed. The setting sun illuminated the branches to perfection.

They stopped and Calisto took a large wicker basket and a blanket from the rear of the car.

"Picnic!" he announced.

"You do know how to surprise a young lady," Féde said in the tone of an experienced coquette. She clapped her hands.

"Yes, I do." Calisto winked. "Come with me," he then said, and he led the way down a path leading into the olive grove.

They settled under the crown of a large tree and together enjoyed pecorino cheese,[16] veal carpaccio with black truffle seasoning, Ascolana olives, and wine. They exchanged entertaining stories and anecdotes, laughed together, and Calisto again kissed Féde. This time, his kiss was unexpected and salaciously sweet.

Silently, she stared into Calisto's eyes. Shy by nature, she could not find anything to say, but she felt there was no need for words because both of them understood everything anyway. She glowed with serene happiness.

After they had eaten, Calisto took Féde by the hand and invited her to stroll through the grove with him. The hot, windless day had eased into the cool of the evening. Féde stepped lightly, her head in the clouds. Calisto told her about new technologies for growing olives, explained a few clever harvesting tricks, listed the names of fertilizers. But she was

---

[16]   A hard cheese made from sheep's milk.

inattentive: she was again dreaming of the future. She found it hard to believe that fate had bestowed such happiness on her.

They approached a small rectangular building with boarded-up windows.

"What's the building for?" Féde asked.

"Temporary housing for the workers we hire for the harvest in November. But no one has lived here for a long time," Calisto answered.

"Interesting," Féde said thoughtfully, and took a few steps closer to the building.

"There is nothing interesting about it at all," Calisto snapped.

Féde was looking at a drawing under one of the windows. She examined it intently. Composed of dark grey strokes, the picture was of a girl, seen in profile. Her curly hair cascaded down to a bare shoulder. Féde found it tender and touching. Beneath, was an inscription in English:

My L. — my pier of hope O. 2001

"What a beautiful picture. Who is the artist?"

"One of the workers who lived here. They love to damage other people's property."

"I think it's very nice," Féde said.

"I don't know." Calisto cast a bored glance at the drawing. "For some reason, my father did not want to paint over it. 'Let these walls keep their history,' he said. I don't know what he meant by that … and I'm really not interested."

Turning away, Calisto then said: "It's getting dark. Let's go."

"As you say."

While she still could, Féde glanced back at the house a couple of times, feeling uneasy. There was a bleakness about the place. Or maybe it was just the twilight….

After the date in the olive grove, there were more assignations. Féde and Calisto visited San Benedetto del Tronto;

dined at the Puerto Baloo restaurant; watched a film at a cinema; and took evening walks along the Grottammare coast. Féde was happy, as only a young woman who has fallen in love for the first time can be happy. Then suddenly, Calisto disappeared. He didn't call, he didn't come, he didn't answer calls. Her boundless happiness was replaced by minutes, hours and days of doubt, torment and despair.

Two weeks later, Calisto reappeared at the Chalet Martina and invited Féde to his home for a dinner that he said he was preparing especially for her. This was to be the final act in his play, "The Seduction of Féde."

The next evening, Féde sat in a huge room at a large table, intimidated by the Contes' luxurious home. Only the thought that she was an acquaintance, and had been invited by one of the owners of this chic house, calmed her a little.

There was no one in the house except herself and Calisto. Patricia and Alberto had gone to a charity evening and would not return until very late; Dévi had been made to take a day off.

The dinner went well, but there was more wine than there should have been. Féde felt dizzy, and it cannot be said with complete certainty that love was the reason for it.

When Calisto took her hand and led her up the stairs to his bedroom, she refused to face up to what was happening and gave herself up to desire. Her timidity was replaced in turn by passion, a feeling of shame, then again unbridled passion, pain … again timidity, deep shame, and in the end there was confusion and an awareness of something new.

Calisto got out of bed. Féde expected him to say that he was hers for life, but he only patted her hair and gave her an unfamiliar, unsettling smile. A part of her knew what that smile meant, but she drove the thought away, refusing to believe it.

Calisto went to his marble bathroom and remained in there for a long time, loudly singing cheerful songs. Still lying on his bed, one thought tormented Féde: "Why does he have Cupid painted on his ceiling? And why is Cupid mocking me?" Her thoughts again flitted over Calisto and her future, but then she decided it was better to look at the ceiling and its leering Cupid.

Meanwhile, Frani and Ernesto, at the Chalet Martina, were discussing the meaning of love. Frani sat on the swing in a corner of the restaurant, Ernesto on the sand near her feet. Dog slept contentedly beside the two of them.

"Love is like a flower that needs to be watered and nourished," Frani declared wisely. "Otherwise – and don't say later that I didn't warn you – this flower will wither and die in a desert of callousness and irresponsibility." Frani had taken this basic truth from a popular soap opera.

"I think," Ernesto said, "that if love is real, it doesn't need to be watered."

"What are you saying?" Frani produced the response her heroine in the soap would have made. "And where have you come across love that does not need to be watered and nourished?" That was her own line.

"My parents had such a love," Ernesto replied.

"You think so?" Frani was genuinely curious to know more.

"I know it, because only true love could die so tragically."

"Your parents died?" Frani was horrified.

"They were killed."

"Killed? Who…?" Deeply shocked, Frani tightly hugged herself.

"I don't yet know, but I will find out. Those who did it will answer for everything."

Frani was unusually restless that night. She dreamed of a desert. A man and a woman, dressed in white, hand in hand, were running away from three men who were chasing them. The pursuers had huge daggers in their hands. The woman held a scarlet flower that radiated light, illuminating the entire desert. Waking, Frani thought: "I hope they got away."

7. BITTO LEONE

One evening, when Ernesto was stacking the Chalet Martina sun loungers, Rino Grasso approached him.

"Lugging the deck chairs around again," Rino said loudly, with a laugh.

"Signor Grasso, good evening." Ernesto was glad to see Rino again.

"As you see, I have come for you. I left all my affairs – and, believe me, I have a lot of them – and here you are, messing around on the beach."

"I don't understand, Signor Grasso." Ernesto put down the chair he had been holding.

"He doesn't understand," said Rino, waving his hands. "And who am I taking to meet Bitto Leone today?"

"Bitto Leone," Ernesto repeated. "Who's he?"

"He still doesn't understand; and he asks: 'Who is Bitto Leone?'" Rino's hand gestures became more extravagant.

"My slow-witted boy, Bitto is my old friend, a good man, and the best boxing coach I know. That's who Bitto Leone is."

"Ah, now I remember," Ernesto exclaimed happily, "you wanted to introduce me to your friend, Bitto Leone, the boxing coach."

"Boy, if you keep repeating what I say, I'll get angry, despite what you did for me." Rino raised a fat finger, indicating something between a desire to emphasise the significance of his words and extreme displeasure. "Come on, hurry up! Bitto is waiting for us."

"I … now. I'll finish folding the sun loungers and…."

"You are really testing my patience. Forget about the sun loungers!"

Martina came to Ernesto's rescue: "Rino, why are you shouting?"

"Ah, Martina, dear. Can you believe that I've dropped everything and, by the way, dear Martina, haven't had a bite to eat all day, and come to take Ernesto to Bitto Leone, and all he can say is: 'Who is Bitto Leone?'"

Rino mentioned his lack of food in the hope that Martina would treat him to something.

Martina quickly saw a way through the problem that Rino presented. "Rino, it's good that you came. Why don't we let Ernesto finish his work, while you and I and Adriano have a chat and a bit of supper?"

"Well, I don't know…," Rino began, but before Martina could withdraw the invitation he quickly added: "Okay, let's go!" Then he turned to Ernesto and, raising a finger, said: "Don't take too long. I don't have all night."

"I'll be just one minute." Ernesto then set about grabbing the deck chairs with his big hands and stacking them, one on top of another.

"No need to rush, lad, we've got time," Rino said; a remarkable about-face that made Martina smile. Rino then turned towards the kitchen, his nose following the aromas of Adriano's culinary masterpieces. "Let's go, Martina, let's go."

Fifteen minutes later, after Rino Grasso had consumed three salmon bruschetta, half a salami pizza and a large beer, Ernesto stood next to Rino. He had changed into a fresh polo shirt and was grinning from ear to ear.

"Ah, Ernesto, are you ready?" Rino's tone conveyed a hint of disappointment. "Let's go! I am Rino Grasso, I always keep my word. I said that we would go to Bitto, and go we will." He looked at Adriano with an apologetic air and reluctantly got up from the table.

"Adriano, my friend, it's been so good to see you. Thanks for dinner. At least you know how to feed poor old Rino. My Maria doesn't much care for me." His face fell as he remembered the spaghetti Bolognese waiting for him at home.

"Rino, buddy, come to us again," Adriano replied. "We are always glad to see you. And you, Ernesto, have a good workout." Adriano made jagging and jerking movements with his arms that were apparently meant to be boxing punches.

"Thank you, Signor Marino," Ernesto said. "I will try – if the coach takes me on, of course." That last thought brought some concern to his voice.

"Take you on?" exclaimed Adriano. "Why wouldn't he take on such a huge guy, and with such enormous hands?" Adriano looked to Rino for support.

"Yes, yes…." Rino's response was a little sluggish. He was feeling sleepy after his impromptu meal and beer.

Recovering a little, he turned to Ernesto and said: "Of course, you will have to work hard, but I think that my relationship with Bitto, our old friendship, so to speak, will help. We will make you a great champion." After a short pause, he added: "Or at least a good boxer." Another pause, and then: "OK, it's time for us to go."

Rino hugged Adriano, said goodbye to Martina and, with Ernesto as his passenger, drove to Bitto Leone's boxing gym.

Grasso's car soon stopped outside a long, two-storey building. Ernesto looked with particular interest at its three large windows and a big sign that read, in English: "Bitto's Boxing Club."

Getting out of the car, Rino said: "Let's go, boy. You won't learn anything in the car." He then headed for the boxing club's entrance. Ernesto followed.

They passed through a dark, narrow corridor that led to a rectangular hall. The large hall was made to seem even more spacious by the three windows that Ernesto had seen from the outside. Despite the hall's size, however, the stale, sweat-soaked air made breathing difficult.

Placed centrally in the hall was a ring, the usual "squared circle" for boxing, in which two big guys in boxer shorts and black leather helmets were sparring. Elsewhere, large punching bags wound in thick tape and small pear-shaped bags hung from the ceiling. Men of various ages were engaged in perfecting their punches on them. Opposite the entrance, there was a large mirror. A lad stood in front of it shuffling his feet as if he were dancing, while he jabbed out first one arm, then the other.

Ernesto, who had never been in a boxing gym before, was struck by the way the men's voices, the muffled sounds of punches striking the bags, and the trainer's cries all merged into a continuous rumble.

"This is what I was talking about, Ernesto," Rino said in a voice trembling with excitement. "This is where you will become a real man."

Rino then pointed a finger towards a tall, elderly man with thick, combed-back grey hair who was leaning with both arms on the ringside ropes, shouting instructions at the two boxers. "This guy," he said, "is the one who will be your coach, friend, and father." He gave the matter a few moments' thought, then added: "Well, I hope so anyway."

Grasping Ernesto's hand, Rino pulled him towards the ring. They moved closer to the coach, but Rino did not distract him from his work.

"Idiot! You missed with the cross again!"[17] Bitto Leone yelled at the big guy in the red shorts, who took a powerful blow to the head, staggered, but did not fall. Determined to continue, he raised his gloves to his chin and rushed at his opponent.

....

[17] In boxing, a cross is a straight counterpunch.

ANASTASIIA MARSIZ

"Duck and weave! Yes, to the right, I tell you!" shouted the trainer in a hoarse voice, bluish veins bulging in his muscular neck.

Suddenly, the guy in red shorts, dodging a side blow from his opponent, dived under his arm and delivered a powerful uppercut[18] right to the jaw. The opponent, staggering, threw his head back and collapsed to the canvas floor of the ring.

"Hey you! Take it easy there! This is just a workout. That's enough for today." Bitto then turned to Rino, who was standing beside him.

"Bitto! Old man!" Rino greeted Bitto and embraced his comrade.

"Ah, hello Rino," Bitto said wearily. "I haven't seen you for ages. What's up? How is Maria?"

"Nothing new. I'm rushing around from morning to evening: there are so many mouths to feed in my house. And Maria? She's not getting any taller, but she is getting wider." Rino laughed merrily.

"Here, look, I've brought this lad to you." Rino turned to Ernesto, who had moved away from the ring and was looking with interest at the other people in the hall. They, in turn, were looking at him – a strong black guy in a bright green polo shirt that was too small for him.

"Ernesto!" Rino called out. "Come here!"

"Yes, Signor Grasso." Ernesto smiled amiably. Bitto looked him over.

"This is my friend, Signor Bitto Leone, the owner of this gym." Rino solemnly gestured around the hall. "And the best coach in Italy."

"Good evening, Signor Leone," Ernesto said, offering his hand to Bitto.

....

[18]   A vertical blow going upwards to the chin or torso.

Bitto growled, "Hello," and, taking Ernesto's huge hand, glanced at Rino in surprise.

Bitto knew that Rino had a strong dislike for dark-skinned people. Seeing Rino lead a huge black guy into the hall, treating him like a son, puzzled him no end.

Rino fully understood the reason for his friend's surprise, and smiled. Two weeks ago, he would have spat in the face of any insolent person who so much as suggested that he, the offspring of Signora Perlita-Luisa Grasso, would associate himself with a black kid.

"Bitto, my friend," Rino began to explain, "something you don't yet know is what this young and brave boy," he gripped Ernesto by the shoulders, "did for old Grasso." Bitto looked at Ernesto with interest. "He saved my little Marisa!" choked Rino, his eyes glistening.

Then Rino related in detail and, as always, with dramatic gestures, the story of the miraculous rescue of his youngest daughter. To enhance the dramatic effect, he blew his nose into a handkerchief, wiped away his tears with the same handkerchief, blushed, and finally turned pale. On finishing his amazing tale, Rino hugged his friend, begging him to take this kind, big-hearted lad into his club and make a boxer of him, perhaps even a champion.

"Just look at his hands. What a broad back. What muscular legs. And all this even though he doesn't do any sport."

Bitto had shown no emotion during all this, only gripping one hand with the other occasionally, to suppress an embarrassing tremor.

"Well, Bitto, old man, will you take him on?" Rino asked.

"How could I not take on a hero with such physical virtues," Bitto replied. His lips shaped something like a smile, although it could have been mistaken for a scowl. "And you, lad," he turned to Ernesto, "do you want to learn to box?"

"I really want to learn," Ernesto said, somewhat timidly. Then he added, with much greater force: "I need it!"

Bitto was intrigued: "What for?"

"I just do…." Ernesto fell silent, pursing his lips.

"All right, so be it," said Bitto. He turned to Rino: "I'll take on your hero."

Rino turned to Ernesto: "Go on, get changed."

"I don't have any gear," Ernesto answered.

"How were you expecting to do any training?" Rino shouted at Ernesto, thinking to himself that perhaps he should have told him to bring a change of clothes.

Laughter filled the hall. Bitto looked around angrily. The laughter stopped, and the boxers continued their training.

"Hey, Tony, get him shorts, boots and a tee-shirt. Lively, now!" said Bitto to the nearest youth. The lad ran to the locker room.

"I've got a tee-shirt," Ernesto suddenly said, lifting his green polo shirt to reveal it. "Ceci said always to wear a vest in the evening."

"Well, at least you brought something," Bitto said, chuckling mentally at the young man's naivety.

Rino, on the other hand, vaguely thought this wasn't the way a hero should be, but couldn't think of anything better than to ask who Ceci was.

"She was my grandmother, Cecilia Bruno. She raised me." After a brief pause, Ernesto added: "She died thirty-four days ago."

The awkward silence that followed was broken by the arrival of Tony, with shorts in one hand, boxing boots in the other.

"You didn't say what size, Signor Leone, so I brought the largest."

Handing the boots to Ernesto, Bitto said: "Go with Tony to the locker room and try these on. When you've changed, come back and we'll have a talk."

Ernesto took the boots and shorts and followed Tony.

When he and Bitto were alone, Rino said: "That guy with the uppercut is pretty good."

"That's Cenzo Rossi," Bitto said, "a promising boxer. I will try to get him a bout in Milan in December."

"Yes…," Rino murmured, as if knowledgeable about such matters.

Ernesto emerged from the locker room. He looked rather comical in his shorts, battered boots and grey tee-shirt. But his muscular body and long arms, broad back and strong legs were definitely impressive. "Yes, he really is a big lad," Bitto said thoughtfully.

"What did I tell you!" Rino exclaimed.

"Take this skipping rope to warm up a bit," Bitto said.

"I don't know how," Ernesto confessed.

"So learn," said Bitto, frowning. There was more laughter in the hall. Bitto called over one of those laughing and told him to show Ernesto how to skip.

Ernesto tried very hard that first evening: he skipped for a long time, then attacked the punchbag in the way that the coach showed him, following that with more use of the skipping rope. Two hours later, tired, but pleased with himself, he went to get changed.

The other lads in the locker room grinned mockingly when Ernesto walked in, then returned to talking among themselves. Ernesto looked around at them and smiled broadly. He wanted to make friends with everyone, but did not know how.

One joker mimicked Ernesto's skipping technique, causing the rest of the youths to burst into laughter. Then Cenzo Rossi, the boxer with the formidable uppercut, entered the room.

"You really know how to punch," Ernesto said, as Cenzo walked past him. "I would like to learn how to fight like that."

That statement brought renewed laughter to the locker room. Perplexed, Ernesto joined in the laughter.

Cenzo stared at Ernesto, then at his comrades and, smiling, said: "Thanks. I'm Cenzo Rossi." He held out his hand to Ernesto. All those who had been laughing fell silent.

"I'm Ernesto Bruno. I'm pleased to meet you. Let's be friends," Ernesto said happily, and he shook hands with Cenzo.

This brought another explosion of laughter to the locker room.

"We'll see," Cenzo replied, casting a displeased look at everyone else in the changing room.

Rino stood near his car, smoking

"Well done!" he said approvingly and patted Ernesto on the shoulder. "Good effort!"

"Thank you, Signor Grasso," Ernesto replied. "I really enjoyed it. So interesting. Signor Leone is very strict," he added. "If I train hard and well, will I become strong?"

"Of course, son. You will not just become strong, you will be a champion. After all, you are an Italian … although dark. Okay, let's go, I'm hungry!"

"I've made a friend. His name is Cenzo Rossi."

"Did you say Cenzo Rossi?"

"Yes. Do you know him, Signor Grasso?"

"Yes…. He really knows how to punch." Rino laughed at that thought, and Ernesto joined in.

Rino drove Ernesto back to the Chalet Martina. Before they parted, Ernesto offered Rino renewed and heartfelt thanks. Rino promised that he would visit his hero again, embraced him, and wished him a good night.

"Signor Grasso? You haven't forgotten my request, have you?"

"What was that?" Rino asked, his mind already sitting at table at home, ready to eat.

"You promised me you'd find out who killed my father."

"Ah, that…," Rino mused. "I'll find out…."

"Is that a promise?" Ernesto asked, looking into Rino's eyes.

"It's a promise. I always keep my word." With that, Rino drove off.

The next morning, everyone at the Chalet Martina wanted to know how things had gone with Bitto Leone. Ernesto detailed his conversation with him several times. He described the boxing gym; his new friend Cenzo Rossi's fighting skills; and showed them the exercises he had done. The Marino brothers asked Ernesto to teach them some boxing moves.

Martina allowed the aspiring boxer to attend his evening training sessions. Adriano gave him the gloves he had bought for Andrea in the hope of turning him into Rocky Marciano. Unfortunately, his son had said that he wanted to become Andrea Pirlo instead, so the gloves were useless to him. Ernesto was glad that he now had his own gloves, and thanked Signor Marino for the gift.

Féde wondered why Ernesto was receiving so much attention, and why there was such a stir because this oddball had suddenly decided to take up boxing.

Frani pouted and announced solemnly to Ernesto that his new activities must in no way interfere with their games, and she demanded a vow that he would never stop being friends with her. The promise was made, and Frani calmed down a bit. Even so, she continued to complain to her doll, Jacqueline, about how changeable men's hobbies are, and how tired she was of their nonsense, especially as making a game of hitting each other was beyond stupid – the most incomprehensible activity imaginable.

Just as his coach had instructed him, Ernesto ran along the beach each morning and evening, punching the air with his fists. Dog ran beside him. He thought about his grandmother Ceci, and about his father. He wanted Ceci to know that Omar was a decent person, loved Leah, his mother, and would never have left them if not for…. There was so much he wanted to tell Ceci, but could not.

A particular dream repeated itself over and over again. He was standing in the middle of a boxing ring. Spectators were yelling: "Hit him!" "Give him a right hook!" "Jab him with the left!" "Come on!" "Don't stop!" The guys who laughed at him in the locker room were shouting his name. In a corner of the ring, behind the ropes, Cenzo Rossi stood, shaking his head disapprovingly. Coach Bitto Leone leaned on the ropes, watching intently.

Ernesto could not see his opponent's face, only a vague outline. No matter how he moved in the ring, no matter which way he turned, the bright lights dazzled him and he could not discern his opponent's features. He raised his glove, tried to strike, but something restrained his hand, prevented him from completing the blow. He tried to break free from the invisible force, strove with all his might, but all was in vain: his hand would go no further.

His opponent circled around the ring, not closing the distance, for he had seen that Ernesto could not get to him. Then he abruptly went on the attack, inflicting a powerful blow to Ernesto's head. Still without having seen the face of his adversary, Ernesto fell to the floor. The noise faded and everything turned dark.

Someone wiped his face with a wet sponge – he felt better. The darkness dissipated. He awoke and realised that Dog was licking his face. "A dream," he thought. "It's only a dream. But who was my opponent, and why couldn't I hit him?"

8. LITTLE ALBERTO

The golden rays of the morning sun illuminated Ernesto's path as he ran along the shoreline. The sea was calm, and only the seagulls flying over the water in search of breakfast rippled its surface. The freshness of the cool morning breeze energised him as he inhaled the aroma that had been familiar to him all his life. He ran in the sea, parallel to the beach, for some distance, then back on the sand. Dog ran alongside, never falling behind. Her ears flared like two black sails as she "chased the wind." She had found a home and a friend-owner with whom she was more than happy to run wherever he wanted, follow all his commands, anticipate all his desires, and even give up her life for him, should it come to that.

When Ernesto finally collapsed on the sand to rest, he lay on his back and looked at the sky. Dog was pleased to lick his face, hands and legs, and when that was done she lay down too, resting her muzzle on his hand. Man and dog were both serenely happy.

The long, hot day passed, finally yielding to the welcome cool of evening. Dog then accompanied Ernesto to Bitto Leone's gym. Ernesto had been going there daily for several weeks, but still he was so tired after each session that he barely had the strength to get home again. Bitto did not praise Ernesto, but the new trainee's perseverance did not go unnoticed. Indeed, tired as Ernesto might be at the end of each day, Bitto was impressed by his stamina.

That evening, Bitto called to Ernesto and told him to bring a twenty-kilogram barbell to him. Bitto laid a towel on Ernesto's broad shoulders, and placed the barbell on top.

"Hold it like this, with both hands." Ernesto gripped the bar firmly.

"Good. Now dance until you drop."

"Dance? How?"

"Any way you like."

"What about the music?"

"Why don't you get yourself a cocktail while you're at it?" There were limits to Bitto Leone's patience. "What's your favourite song?"

"I don't have a favourite song," Ernesto replied.

"Then I'll sing my own favourite: Perché."[19] In a hoarse voice, Bitto began to sing: "*e capì di aver vissuto troppo in fretta, adesso che stava stretto nell'imbuto dei perché perché, perché, perché...*"[20]

Bitto then showed Ernesto some simple dance moves.

"You get the idea," Bitto growled. "Dance until you drop." Bitto then left the hall. Ernesto hummed the song and danced, trying to repeat the coach's moves.

An hour later, Bitto reappeared. He was much surprised to see a sweat-soaked Ernesto still dancing with the barbell on his shoulders. Ernesto's face was twisted, his mouth gaped open, he could barely stand, the veins bulged on his neck, but he was still going.

Everyone in the gym had gathered around Ernesto and there was some betting on how much longer he could hold out.

"Get on with your training, you loafers," Bitto barked. Turning to Ernesto, not hiding his surprise and admiration,

....

[19] Fausto Leali's song, "Why."

[20] "and realised that he lived too fast, and suddenly found himself in a whirlpool of why, why, why, why...." (Italian).

he said: "That's enough, son. You've been dancing for an hour."

"You said to dance until I dropped, and I haven't yet," Ernesto replied. A peal of laughter rang round the hall.

"I didn't mean it literally," Bitto said, a little embarrassed. "Come on. Let's get this off you." He carefully removed the bar from Ernesto's shoulders.

The stern old coach had not expected such endurance and fortitude from his new student. Neither had he anticipated that he would feel such affection when he looked at this hulking, good-natured lad.

"Thank you, Signor Leone." Ernesto turned to Bitto and grinned. "Now I've got a bit of lightness in the legs." Laughing, he began to dance and spin on the spot.

"Crazy," Bitto muttered, barely audibly. He then sent Ernesto to the locker room.

As he ran back to the Chalet Martina, Dog at his side, Ernesto hummed Bitto Leone's favourite song. He now rather liked the song himself. He was interrupted by Dog barking.

Beside them, a black Mercedes had stopped at a red traffic light. The driver of the car was a man in a white polo shirt, his greying black hair neatly styled. Dog growled angrily and rushed at the car, barking loudly. Afraid of what could follow, Ernesto ran after her.

"Signor, please excuse my dog," Ernesto said to the driver. "She doesn't usually behave like this."

The man looked at Ernesto, winced, and suddenly turned pale, as if he had caught sight of something terrible.

"I'm so sorry," Ernesto said quickly, and without waiting for an answer he grabbed the growling Dog by the collar and dragged her away from the car. The driver continued to glare silently at Ernesto.

After running on a little, Ernesto looked back. The Mercedes still stood behind the traffic lights, even though the signal had changed to green. The stranger maintained his intense gaze. Unsettled, Ernesto turned away and ran on.

The driver was none other than Alberto Conte. He was stupefied when he saw Ernesto run up to his car to get the dog. Ernesto was the spitting image of someone Alberto had for long done his best to forget. "This can't be," he thought as he stared. "He…." Alberto trembled; felt paralysed; a terrible image moved to the forefront in his head. He tried to drive it back, but failed utterly. It took some loud beeping from the car behind his to bring him back to the needs of the moment and move his car onward.

He arrived at the tennis club a very different person from the Alberto Conte his friends were used to. His friend and tennis partner, Marcello, found his agitated and distracted behaviour utterly baffling. Usually, Alberto won masterfully every time. Tonight, he lost two sets in a row, threw his racket on the ground, snapped at Marcello that he had business to attend to, and sped home.

On arrival, he locked himself in his study. He sat at the table for a long time, his head in his hands. Then he suddenly jumped up. In a frenzy, he took books from the bookshelf, opened them, flipped through them, shook them, and threw them on the floor; one after another. Soon the whole floor was littered with books. Finally, he retrieved a photograph from the floor and stared at it long and hard.

The photograph was of a young woman, Alberto's mother – Alberta Grazia Conte. She was beautiful, with a chiselled forehead, a straight nose and perfectly shaped lips, all framed by dark, wavy hair. Her eyes, however, had an unmistakably evil gleam. Although of the most noble origin, she was evil by nature. Alberto had feared her. And it was she who had destroyed his kind and honest father, Sergio Conte.

Alberto remembered a particular day of his childhood when she had inflicted fear, disappointment and pain on him.

"Finish it off!" Alberta Grazia ordered, pointing with a riding crop to a bird with a broken wing that was dragging itself towards a large rose bush.

"Mama, why? She's hurt," seven-year-old Alberto protested.

"I said finish it off!" his mother insisted, handing him the riding crop. Alberto stared at her in horror. He wanted to say something, but no words would come out. He felt sorry for the unfortunate bird; was angry that he was unable to fulfil his mother's command; and unsettled by the unrelenting, mocking gaze of the huge black Jamaican, Gian, standing behind his mother. As a small child, faced with all this, he burst into tears.

The Jamaican's real name was Bob. His mother had brought him from South America, and since then Gian-Bob had been her constant companion. Little Alberto was afraid of Gian-Bob and his malicious and constantly mocking gaze. Alberto did not understand why this vile man had such enormous power over his mother, and why she was so supportive of him.

"You are just like your father. Weak and spineless," said Alberta Grazia contemptuously. She signalled to Gian, who took the crop from her, swung it, and with a single blow decapitated the unfortunate bird.

Alberto screamed and covered his eyes with his hands. He heard the laughter of the terrible Gian-Bob and the receding steps of his cruel mother. When they were out of sight, he carefully picked up the remains of what had been a vibrant living creature adding its physical beauty and joyful song to the pleasures of their garden.

He wanted to save it, but there was nothing to be done. So he found a biscuit box and placed the almost-weightless broken body inside. He buried it beneath the rose bush where, just minutes before, it had been seeking refuge. Afterwards, he sat for a long time next to the bush, weeping for the lost life, and on account of the emotions relating to his failed relationship with his mother that he could not have expressed in words.

On another occasion, when his father, Sergio Conte, was away in Rome for some days, a noise woke Alberto in the middle of the night. He ran to his mother. The door to her bedroom was standing open. Strange sounds were coming from the room. He went to the door and saw a picture that burned into his memory for the rest of his life. Naked Gian was lying on the bed and Alberto's mother was sitting astride him, moving rhythmically. At that moment, Gian-Bob turned his head towards the door, and stared straight at him. He smiled. Alberto was terrified, and felt hot streams of shame and horror flow through his body. Fearing that he had been discovered, he covered his mouth with his hand and rushed to his room. There he hid under the covers and burst into tears. He never revealed to anyone what he had seen that night.

Alberta Grazia Conte died after giving birth to her second child. They said it was a long and painful labour, and all through it she kept calling for Gian. Sergio Conte left the hospital and drank all night. Gian took his place and seemed to enter a state of insanity, constantly mumbling something in a language unknown to those who overheard him. Finally, Alberta Grazia gave birth to a healthy, dark-skinned girl and, without saying goodbye to her first child, died the next day. A week later, Gian-Bob disappeared with his daughter in his arms, and Alberto never again saw or heard anything more of the vile Svengali. The mark left on Alberto's soul by the relationship between Gian-Bob and his mother nevertheless proved indelible.

These painful memories exhausted Alberto. He went to his bedroom, collapsed on the bed and fell asleep. Waking in the night, he discerned a man with a cruelly disfigured, bludgeoned face bending over him. The man's parched, black lips moved ominously and muttered something incoherent. The bloodied ghost was Omar. Alberto cried out. The spectre stretched its long arms towards Alberto's neck. Terrified, Alberto groped for the light switch. The room filled with warm light and Omar was nowhere to be seen. "It was just a dream," Alberto tried hard to tell himself. His hands were trembling, his mouth dry, and cold sweat ran down his body. "This can't be…. He's gone…. It was a dream, … no more…. Just a bad dream. He's dead!"

He jumped out of bed and ran to his wife's room. When Alberto burst into her room, Patricia was already sitting-up in bed. Alberto's cry of horror on seeing Omar had woken her.

"Not tonight," she said quickly.

But Alberto rushed to her, fell on his knees and whispered hoarsely: "Patricia, dear, help me!" He turned to the door, as if looking for something, then turned back to his wife and hissed in a voice that none who knew him would have thought was his: "Help me. He is here. He has come for me!"

"Alberto, what is the matter with you?" Patricia demanded. He was frightening her.

"Shh!" Alberto again shot a glance at the door.

"Is someone in the house?"

"You must help me! He…." Alberto stopped, took a deep breath and said quietly: "It can't be him. It can't be!" Alberto's face was pale, his eyes burned feverishly, his hands trembled.

"Who are you talking about, Alberto?"

"No, it can't be him," Alberto repeated several times. "But I saw him. How is that possible?" Staring wildly, he tugged on a handful of his hair, as if to pull it out.

"Calm down," Patricia said. She said this soothingly and held out a hand to him.

"Patricia," he moaned, taking the hand she offered.

Patricia hugged him tightly, as if he were a child. "It's nothing, Alberto. Hush. Calm down…. I'm here." She continued to comfort him, cradling his fallen soul, until sleep overcame them both.

As the morning arrived, Alberto shifted and straightened up in the bed. Patricia squeezed her eyelids tight, pretending to be asleep. She felt only disgust, contempt and hatred for her husband. She berated herself for having been weak enough to feel concern for this terrible man. She winced as she felt his hand on her back and his breath on her neck. The odious stench of his sin-poisoned breath overwhelmed the notes of amber, musk and sandalwood of his expensive cologne.

After he finally left her bedroom, she hastened to the bathroom to wash his touch from her body. It took some time.

When the couple met again at breakfast, nothing in the cold expressions on their faces betrayed anything of what had happened in the night. Alberto expressed no gratitude to Patricia for rescuing him from insanity, neither did he feel any. The contemptuous glances of two people who hated each other were the same as usual, the surface politeness just that, no more.

Alberto recalled his hysteria, and despised himself for giving in to his terror. He hated Patricia for her mercy. How stupid she was. He glared at her once-beautiful face with disdain. Wrinkles were forming around her eyes, disgusting tokens of the withering of her youthful femininity. The freshness and purity of virgin beauty still appealed to him powerfully; but he no longer found any in Patricia.

9. LADY IN RED

A young girl in a red dress walked with a cheerful, confident step along the San Benedetto waterfront. Bathed in the rays of the midday sun, she basked in the thought of her own irresistible beauty – wondrous, angelic, captivating. Now and then, she felt the longing glances of men playing over her body. This nourished her inner feminine strength and gave her a feeling of unlimited power. She smiled and, shaking her hips, continued on her way. She knew that men found the curves of her body seductive, and her face captivating. Her crowning glory, though, was her thick, long hair, in the golden strands of which, as if playing, the sun's rays were entangled. This enchanting girl was Mirella, the girl who Patricia Conte had saved from starvation. Mirella had been in her hometown for two days and was hurrying to meet Patricia, who, to hide her real identity, represented herself to Mirella as Signora Ricci.

Mirella entered the restaurant at which they had agreed to meet. Several men turned to look at her; one winked. Mimi turned up her nose and blushed.

Beautiful and proud, like a queen, loving and tender, like a mother, Patricia was sitting at a table on the terrace overlooking the sea. "How beautiful she is," Mimi thought. She quietly approached Patricia from behind and hugged her tenderly.

"Mirella, dear!" Signora Ricci-Conte hugged her back. "You're late," she added, with gentle reproach, her eyes glowing affectionately.

"Signora Ricci, forgive me. I was walking around the town and got distracted by the sights."

"I forgive you. Come, sit, Mirella." Patricia smiled. "I've already ordered food for us."

"I'm not hungry, Signora Ricci." Despite the depth of their relationship, Mimi never used Patricia's first name.

"What do you mean, not hungry? I ordered *vongole*[21] in white sauce, a seafood salad, and your favourite *frittura mista*."[22]

"You are so kind to me, Signora Ricci," Mimi said with a cheeky smile.

"Oh, you! How was your flight?" Patricia's caring tone and gentle voice warmed Mirella's soul. "Did you take the sleeping pills I sent you?"

"Yes, Signora Ricci, thank you. I slept so soundly that the steward had to wake me in Ancona. You are beautiful as always," she added.

Patricia surveyed Mirella affectionately, then adopted a stern voice: "Mirella, I'm glad you had a good rest, but the school year is coming up and last semester you got a low score in science. I hope you won't disappoint me again? Do you remember what we talked about last time?"

"Of course I remember. Don't worry: I'm a good student, I don't drink alcohol, I don't use drugs, I don't accept expensive gifts, and I only meet young men in public places where there are surveillance cameras. And, most importantly, I never date older men." With a serious expression on her lovely face, Mimi finished listing Patricia's rules. At the mention of men, Signora Conte shuddered. "And as for my studies – my dear Signora Ricci, I got the highest score in Philosophy!"

....

21 Clams.

22 Deep-fried pieces of fish or vegetables.

"That's wonderful, Mimi. Well done for remembering my advice, and I am so pleased with your academic progress. I'm proud of you." Tears welled up in Patricia's eyes.

As they ate their meal, Mimi amused Patricia with funny stories about her summer holiday in England. Patricia looked at her with motherly tenderness, smiled, and felt a deep sense of contentment.

After a long conversation, the two beautiful women embraced and said goodbye. Patricia Ricci-Conte left, while Mimi sat a little longer on the terrace and enjoyed a lemon sorbet and the view of the sea. Her journey into adulthood was beginning. Despite her own early experience of the reality of life, she felt that it would be like an eternal holiday filled with light, laughter and new encounters.

As a little girl, Mirella would stand in front of a mirror, examining her body, face and hair, and try to guess what she would look like when she grew up. Her wish was to transform from the thin, sickly child staring out of the mirror into a beautiful woman – a queen. She dreamed of becoming as beautiful and majestic as Signora Ricci. Her chosen husband would not be an ordinary man, but a knight; a brave and strong prince.

As she now sat on the terrace overlooking the sea, she still held to her dream of a fairy tale life, her prince, wealth and love. As she gazed at the slow movement of the jade green waves, and into the sea itself, she made a wish. She always did that when she stared into the sea. It was a secret she and Patricia shared.

When Mirella was six years old, Patricia had taken her to a remote, deserted shore. Mimi came to think of the small bay, surrounded by rocks, as "theirs." Only Queen Patricia and Princess Mimi knew about this secret place. Mimi imagined that huge quantities of treasure had been hidden in the rocks by an unknown king. She didn't know what kind of treasure was there, or why it had been hidden, but the thought that the rocks kept a great king's secret added to the magic of this secret and very special bay.

"Mirella, come here," Patricia called. "I've got a secret to share with you."

"A secret? I love secrets." Mimi laughed, and her face shone with the happiness that could be found only in "their" bay.

"Tell me the secret! Tell me the secret!" Mimi demanded, jumping up and down on the sand.

"To find out the secret, you have to be attentive and obedient," Patricia answered kindly, as she sat down next to the little girl.

"I am! I am!" Mimi cried. She squeezed her lips, trying to restrain her delight.

"Look at the sea," said Patricia, hugging the child. "Remember, my beautiful girl, that you can dream about anything and make any wish."

"Any wish?" Mimi asked in a whisper.

"Yes, any wish." Patricia herself peered into the clear waters, wishing for her own cherished desire to come true. A deep sadness came to her eyes.

"How will my wish come true?" Mimi asked.

"Because the sea, the sky and everything you see," Patricia pressed Mimi closer to her, "is the work of the Great Creator, and you are making a wish through one of His creations."

"And the Creator will hear me?" Mimi asked, uncertain.

"Certainly! If you are good. He hears all those who love Him and are pure in heart."

Sitting now on the terrace overlooking the sea, Mirella gazed into the far distance and remembered "their" special bay. She thought about Patricia. Intelligent and beautiful as she was, she was not always able to hide the monster that dug into her with sharpened claws, tormenting her soul.

When Patricia's suffering was reflected in her beautiful face, Mimi felt an urge to help. But what could she do without revealing that Signora Ricci's inner torment was not hidden from her?

As Mimi was thinking on these matters, three young men entered the restaurant and took a table opposite her. They were behaving rowdily, talking loudly and laughing. Two of them, each in his own way, immediately showed signs of being attracted to her. One covered his face with a hand and looked at her furtively. The other, noticeable in a red shirt and green moccasins, gazed intently into her beautiful face, as if that was all that was needed to win her. Amused, Mimi smiled.

The three young men were of course Calisto, Giacomo and Orsino. This was one of the restaurants they visited almost daily. Calisto had missed finding his mother there by just a few minutes.

Mimi was about to leave when the lad in green moccasins walked up to her table. "Good evening, beautiful stranger. Calisto Conte, at your service."

Calisto produced a smile, expecting his irresistible introduction to quickly open the way to the next stage of his campaign. Setting aside his caution, the second young man removed his hand from his face, the better to see what would follow.

Mirella grimaced in displeasure, raised an eyebrow and sternly answered her smooth-talking suitor: "I do not require your service."

Then she stood, and with a confident step walked away from the crestfallen Calisto. Mimi's withering response had left him temporarily rooted to the spot.

When he recovered himself sufficiently to return to his friends, he did his best to put on a nonchalant expression and said: "Try to get your heads around that, guys."

"Do you really think that every chick will come running to you every time?" chuckled Giacomo. "It didn't work for you that time, did it?"

"What didn't work? I just asked her for the time."

"Oh, yes, we believe you!" said Giacomo, laughing in Calisto's face.

Calisto had already opened his mouth to answer Giacomo, but the waiter came up and interrupted him: "Have you decided on your order, Signor Conte?"

"What?" Calisto asked confused.

"Would you like the prawns in white wine sauce, or the usual?" By "the usual," the waiter meant a bottle of white *fritta mista*, three pastas and, of course, a triple portion of *vongole*.

"No. I'm not hungry. Bring me some whisky," Calisto muttered, frowning.

"Whisky? At five p.m.?" Giacomo asked mockingly. "Anyway, I'm hungry, and Orsino too, probably. Orsino, are you going to have dinner?"

"No, I'll have what he's having," Orsino said, pointing a finger at Calisto.

"Order whatever you want. I'm having whisky with ice and that's it." Calisto yelped.

"That's it, brother, you just asked for the time!" Giacomo laughed and ordered two bowls of seafood pasta, two green salads and an iced whisky. He never missed an opportunity to fill his stomach at Conte's expense. "Who was that girl?" he asked.

"How would I know?" Calisto responded in irritation, nursing his wounded pride.

"Well, I think she's beautiful … and has character," Giacomo continued. "Orsino, did you like the girl in the red dress?"

"What girl? Loads of girls wear red."

"There you have the very essence of Orsino," Giacomo laughed. "Loads of girls wear red," he mimicked his comrade.

"It's true, he doesn't care," Calisto waved his hand at Orsino and laughed. "He's only interested in his games. All he ever talks about are witches, knights and other such nonsense."

"But I think she's an extraordinary girl," Giacomo said thoughtfully. "There is something about her."

"She's certainly good-looking." Calisto looked at the table where Mimi had been sitting. "I'll find her. And then…."

"Stop it," Giacomo interrupted. "Why are you so sure that every girl is crazy for you? Are you the only guy on the whole coast?"

"Are you talking about yourself?" Calisto chuckled.

"Yes, I…," began Giacomo. But he stopped and, after a pause, quietly continued: "I'm not talking about myself, but about you, mate. Just calm down and let this one go."

"I'll find this lady in red, then I'll calm down," Calisto said. "Maybe she's the one I've been looking for all this time."

"Yeah, you've only ever been looking for one…," Giacomo answered, and tried to laugh, but it came out sounding edgy.

"Laugh all you like," Calisto said, cheering up. "You'll see – she will be mine."

"First, find out her name," said Giacomo, smiling nervously.

"I know … and not only her name," Calisto said. Dreamily, he stared towards the sea: some kind of feeling still unknown to him was emerging in his soul.

The waiter served the dishes, and the conversation among the three friends moved on to other topics.

At about nine in the evening, just as the daylight faded, Calisto's phone rang. Quite tipsy, he looked at the screen, grimaced in disgust and cancelled the call. It rang again. Again, he disconnected the call. After this happened several more times, he screamed into the phone: "What? I'm busy!" and slammed it down on the table.

The calls were from Féde. She had not seen or heard from Calisto for two weeks. After that night in his bedroom, he had not called, written, or visited her. She waited, and came up with various reasons for his silence. She thought that he must be busy with family affairs, working with his father at the olive grove, or that he had fallen sick. She had terrible visions of him lying unconscious in a hospital ward.

Finally, her torment became unbearable and she decided to call him. First, she sent him a dozen messages, moving from the innocent "Hi. How are you?" through the hysterical "Why don't you answer?! Call me back immediately!" to the desperate "Calisto, my love, what's wrong?"

At last, her face pale, Féde called Calisto's number. As she listened to the ringing tone, she bit her lips until they bled. She kept being cut off, but she repeated the call again and again until Calisto answered. She understood immediately that his rude "I'm busy!" could only mean that there was no place in his life for her.

She sat for a long time with the phone in her hands, unable to move. How could such a caring, gentle and affectionate gentleman treat her so shabbily? Could there be an explanation for his strange behaviour? Deep down, however, she knew the answer. Tears rolled silently down her cheeks.

10. FRIDAY DISAPPOINTMENTS

After that first encounter, Calisto searched everywhere for "the lady in red." Neither her refusal of his advances nor his argument with Giacomo had anything to do with the way he was drawn to her. He was gripped by a burning passion that was new to him. He could not forget the disdainful way she had stared at him, as if he were a clown. He wanted to show her his real self, without any masks.

But first he had to find her. He went to restaurants, wandered along the beach, walked along the streets of San Benedetto, and visited the morning market in the central square. But all his searches were in vain.

Then, on a sunny morning on the first Friday of September, he suddenly got lucky. He was again strolling around the morning market. He scanned the crowd hoping to glimpse Mimi's lovely features; he listened to the chatter of the crowd in the hope of hearing her voice. He meandered along the rows of colourful stalls with their toys, watches and bags. Then he spotted her. She was standing next to a sweet stall. There could be no doubt that shock of wavy golden-brown hair belonged to the lady in red.

Calisto hastened towards her. He passed three stalls, fought off importunate sellers of Chinese watches, and there she was, in front of him. She did not notice him. He followed her, admiring her beautiful profile and the way she smiled at two traders selling silk shawls, telling them she was "just looking." One of the vendors showed her one shawl after another. He offered her a wrap the colour of white porcelain, saying: "Look at this one, it really suits you." Looking into the mirror held by the other trader, she spotted Calisto standing behind her. He held her eyes with an honest and direct gaze that bore no hint of the arrogance and narcissism she had seen in him before.

"This one is almost worthy of your beauty," Calisto said as he placed a silk shawl of delightful craftmanship across her shoulders. It seemed to him that he could feel the warmth of her naked shoulders pass through the shawl to his hands.

One of the vendors smiled, revealing crooked yellow teeth. "Here's a man who knows what he's talking about. It's handmade. I will offer a discount just for you."

Mirella ran from the stall. Calisto grabbed the discarded shawl, threw a hundred Euros to the merchant, and chased after her. Mirella moved quickly through the crowd, Calisto following. He smiled: he wouldn't be letting her slip away again.

Mirella ran past the last stalls, their smiling merchants calling out to her to "have a peek" at their wares. She slipped into a long alley, Calisto still in pursuit. Looking back, she saw that he was still a short distance behind her. She quickened her pace, and so did he. Then she stopped abruptly, turned to him, took a pepper spray can from her handbag, and warned in a trembling voice: "If you continue to hound me, I will be forced to take action."

"I have no choice," Calisto answered with calm confidence. He plunged his hands into his trouser pockets.

Mirella was outraged: "What do you mean?" How beautiful she was in that moment of fear and anger.

Calisto smiled disarmingly and, bowing his head meekly, said: "I can't help it."

"Are you one of those … psychos?" Mirella tightened her grip on the pepper spray and, remembering Patricia's advice, quickly looked around hoping to spot some security cameras.

Calisto said softly: "Over there, on the next building, there is a camera. So now I've been spotted and I'm left with no other option than…."

A terrible thought flashed through Mirella's head. Calisto smiled and completed his sentence: "…to marry you."

Mirella was completely taken aback. She flushed. In truth, there definitely was something she liked about this young man. "And he doesn't look like a psycho," she thought, "although he's wearing those strange moccasins again." Today, the ones he wore were bright yellow.

"I have been looking for you everywhere these past few days," he said in a serious tone. "I wanted to apologise."

"There was no need for that. And was it worth the effort?" Mirella asked, lowering the canister.

"I wanted to apologise for being such an idiot the last time," he said softly. He came closer, his eyes warm. She looked at him, considering.

He continued: "True, I confess that to all the other gir…," Calisto stammered, "people," he corrected himself, "I don't seem like an idiot. I'm not really like that at all. Not when it comes to you," his voice dropped as it usually did when he spoke to a girl, but for the first time in his life he sincerely emphasised the word "you." "I have to say, I am finding this awkward." He laughed, nervously.

"Go on." Mirella offered a reassuring smile.

"Let me open up to you. Let me show you what I really am," said Calisto, taking her hand. She did not resist, but her other hand still firmly held the pepper spray behind her back.

"What's your name?" Calisto asked.

"Mirella, but many people call me Mimi."

"Calisto Conte," he said, delicately kissing her hand.

"What about the shawl?" Mimi asked, playfully. She pointed to the silk wrap still held by Calisto.

"I got it for you."

"Got it?"

"I mean I bought it. I paid for it." Calisto felt stupid and awkward again, and to hide his confusion, he threw the shawl around Mimi's shoulders. She looked at him, smiled, and carelessly gathered her thick hair into a ponytail. Calisto, spellbound, stared, entranced by the strands of hair escaping from under the thin silk of the shawl; by her clear, brilliant eyes; the full lips that he wanted to kiss. And realised that he had never before felt as calm and content as he did now.

He was in love, as no one had ever been in love before. Or so he thought, because that's what everyone who's fallen head-over-heels in love always thinks. This feeling dissipated his arrogance: he no longer wanted to boast of his nobility, about houses, yachts and groves, or to play the hero. His ambition was simply to love, to be near her.

Calisto invited Mirella to lunch and she accepted. They went into the first restaurant they saw. It was nothing like the ones Calisto normally frequented. There was a time-faded menu on the counter at the entrance; a small terrace, covered with a dirty, grey awning; and it was packed with people. But Calisto was oblivious to all that and more – the shabby furnishings, the flies crawling on the tables, and the stale air, heavy with tobacco smoke and the smell of hot cooking oil. Under other circumstances, he would never have stepped into such a place, but now his thoughts of Mirella set aside all other considerations.

As he and Mirella scanned the room for an empty table, Calisto suddenly saw Giacomo coming out of the kitchen.

They were both surprised. Giacomo was dumbfounded for a moment, then cast an evil glance at the smiling Calisto and his companion. His feelings for her were just as strong as the young Conte's, but he controlled himself and embraced his "friend."

"Gia, brother! I'm so glad to see you!" said Calisto.

"How did you end up here?" Giacomo asked.

"Mirella and I decided to have lunch together. Oops, sorry Giacomo, I haven't introduced you." Calisto laid an affectionate hand on Mimi's shoulder. Giacomo felt angry.

"This is Gia," said Calisto "Mirella…." He realised he did not know her surname.

"Esposito. Mirella Esposito," Mirella chimed in, laughing.

"I'm pleased to meet you. Giacomo Pelagatti."

Giacomo lowered his eyes, and thought with annoyance that the spoiled Conte always got what he wanted. When would he, Giacomo, get a break? He held down multiple jobs. Today, he had carried crates of fish in the harbour from six in the morning. When he had finished there, he had run over to a greengrocer's shop to lug more boxes. And at night, when he was not entertaining his rich "friend," Giacomo, who was fluent in English, made translations and wrote articles for online publications. All this exhausting work was a part of Giacomo's plan to escape from the fate for which it seemed he was born. His mother wanted him to work as a waiter, like his father, but Giacomo hated the thought of being obliged to serve the rich and successful. He despised his father's work and was ashamed of his background.

"There's a free table," Calisto said, pointing, and he moved with speed to throw himself onto a chair at the still uncleared table.

"Come and sit down," he called to Mimi. She walked over to the table and sat opposite him. Giacomo looked around uneasily, slowly approached them, and also sat down.

"Now let's have lunch," Calisto said. He raised a hand to call the waiter.

A short, rather elderly man came up and, with practiced professionalism, collected all the dishes on a tray, rolled up the dirty tablecloth, and took them away. Moments later, he returned and spread a fresh, starched tablecloth on the table and placed on it fresh sauces and a salt shaker.

The waiter seemed very tired. In the crowded, airless restaurant at lunchtime on a hot day, his white shirt was an instrument of torture. It was sweat-soaked at the back and under the arms, and beads of sweat stood on the forehead of his wrinkled face. He took out a small notebook and a pen, put on a good-natured smile and asked: "Have you decided what you would like to order?"

Giacomo's face reddened, and he lowered his head and stared at the table. Calisto did not notice; his gaze was divided only between the beautiful Mirella and the waiter.

"We'll have...," Calisto began, but was interrupted by the waiter.

"Giacomo, son, these are your friends. Why didn't you say? I would have served you straight away, and with VIP service."

Calisto did now look at Giacomo: "Yes, Giacomo, why didn't you say anything?"

"Claudio Pelagatti," the waiter said, holding out his hand to Calisto.

"I'm pleased to meet you. Calisto Conte." They shook hands. "And this is my friend, Mirella Esposito." Mimi nodded her head and she too offered her hand to Giacomo's father. Giacomo grimaced contemptuously.

"Giacomo, I think, needs no introduction," Calisto finished, winking at Giacomo.

"Let me treat you to pasta," said Claudio Pelagatti. "Giacomo has already eaten in the kitchen, but that's not a problem. You can have a bite to eat with your friends, can't you, son?"

"Leave me alone!" Giacomo suddenly yelled.

People sitting at the surrounding tables turned to stare. Claudio Pelagatti went pale, looked around timidly, and began to nod his head and smile apologetically.

Giacomo jumped up from his chair so abruptly that it overturned. He ran up to his father, who stared at him with horror, and roared: "Why do you smile at them all like a fool? Why do you fawn over them, racing around like you're running a marathon? They don't care!" Giacomo glared all around, his nostrils flaring, his hands clenched into fists. "They just come here to eat and drink. They don't give a damn about you, your idiotic smile, and your sweat-soaked white shirt."

Claudio's lips trembled. Mirella looked at Giacomo with sadness. Calisto was dumbstruck. All the staff of the restaurant gathered to observe, the restaurant owner at their head. The diners whispered and shook their heads.

"Son, what are you saying?" was all the unfortunate Claudio could say.

"You can all go to Hell!" shouted Giacomo. He raced to the exit.

"Excuse me…," Claudio said, smiling despite having tears in his eyes. He chased after his son.

Calisto remained silent, looking around blankly. Mirella looked thoughtful, then frowned and jumped up to run after Claudio.

She found him leaning against a tree.

"Are you all right?" she asked softly.

"It's nothing, my dear, don't worry." He wiped the tears from his face with his shirt sleeve. "He sometimes gets like that. He's a good kid – very kind."

Claudio wanted to stand up for his son, whom he loved more than anyone or anything else, and for whom he worked so hard, almost never taking a day off. He had been saving money for Giacomo and putting it into an account for him ever since the boy was born. It was all for his son that he constantly smiled at customers, worked his fingers to the bone, and wore that hateful white shirt even in forty-degree heat.

"Giacomo is angry that I have been a waiter all my life. But I can't do anything else."

Mirella barely held back her tears.

Returning to the restaurant with Claudio, she looked for Calisto. He was standing at the bar, talking with a large man, the owner of the restaurant. They both looked at Giacomo's father. The large man nodded his head, took several Euro notes from Calisto's hands, put them in his pocket, and embraced Calisto.

Calisto walked up to Mirella and Claudio. Looking at Mirella, he smiled and winked.

Turning to Claudio, Mirella said: "Don't be upset. Giacomo knows everything you do for him. He loves you. Give it time; things will cool off."

Claudio looked at her with renewed hope, and gave her a tired smile.

Calisto promised Mirella that he would find Giacomo and do everything possible to reconcile father and son. Finding Giacomo did not take long: he was in a bar on the waterfront. After a long conversation with Mimi, he agreed to apologise to his father. Calisto felt like a hero, and Mirella felt proud of her gifts of persuasion. The three of them then decided, especially as it was a Friday evening, to celebrate in a trendy club. After all, as St Augustine said, custom is second nature.[23]

But a new drama was about to break out.

On the other side of town, Féde had decided to take desperate measures. She would make herself irresistible and go to the nightclub that Calisto and his friends frequented. She used curlers to make her hair appear fuller; lined her eyes to make them appear larger; and put on red lipstick to make her lips seem lusher. The short dress she chose emphasised the rounded contours of her body.

....

[23]   This idea was expressed by the theologian and founder of medieval philosophy, Saint Augustine (354–430) in his work *Contra Julianum* (*Against Julian*).

"What are you doing here?" Calisto asked in annoyance as Féde approached the table where he was sitting with a group of other young people.

"I wrote to you, and I phoned you," she began. "You didn't answer, so I came." She wanted to hug him, but Calisto flinched and recoiled from her.

"You'd better leave," he replied coldly. "I'm busy tonight."

"Leave? I've only just arrived!"

"But I didn't call you," Calisto snapped. Then, after a moment's thought, he said, with apparent affection: "Féde, baby, I'll phone you tomorrow."

He put his arm around Féde's waist and led her to the exit. A female voice called out: "Calisto, where are you going?"

Féde saw a tall, beautiful girl, with a shock of gorgeous thick hair. The girl approached Calisto's table. Féde now noticed that next to Calisto's chair there was an empty seat, with a glass of wine and a black handbag on the table in front of it.

Féde glared at Calisto. He lowered his eyes. Féde, usually so gentle and kind, hit him in the face with all her might, screamed, and ran from the club.

She ran all the way back to the Chalet Martina, tearing at her hair with its unnatural curls and weeping bitterly. Outside the restaurant, her stomach churned and she fell to her knees. Barely able to control her nausea, she got up and entered the restaurant. Looking for her father, she went into the kitchen, smelled garlic and felt sick again. "It's nerves," she thought. Then she saw Adriano.

"Daddy! Dad!" Féde exclaimed. She threw her arms around his neck and began to sob.

"What's the matter, my olive?" Adriano asked, hugging her. "Who's hurt you?"

"Daddy, Daddy. What should I do? How can I go on living?"

"My dear, just tell me. You only…."

"Yes, I'll tell you everything. But only you."

Leaving out the most intimate details, Féde told Adriano about her first bitter love; about how Calisto had been avoiding her; about the meeting at the club. As a loving father, Adriano's heart was breaking because of the pain his daughter was suffering. As a man, he could provide answers to Féde's questions, but as a father he wholly shared Féde's anguish.

"Daddy, what kind of love makes you want to stop living?" Féde asked in despair.

"This is not love, my darling, but sin," answered Adriano. "I'll tell you a story. Listen carefully."

Féde nodded.

"I was twelve years old when something terrible happened in our town. I've never come across anything like it since, nor a more dreadful human tragedy."

"We had a cheerful and dreamy young neighbour called Nera. She met a happy-go-lucky guy called Theo and fell so deeply in love with him that she told the whole world about it. To the delight of all who knew them, Nera and Theo got married. There was nothing stronger than their love. Two lovely girls were born to them. They were happy for exactly seven years and three months. Then Theo met Rose, and fell in love with her just as deeply as he had once loved Nera.

"Nera, on discovering that her Theo now loved someone else, declared: 'If Theo no longer loves me, then I will not live. And I will take the children with me.'

"And she did. She locked herself in the house with her two beautiful little girls, closed the windows, turned on the gas oven, hugged the children, and talked to them about love as gas filled the small apartment. Nera told the little angels about her love for their father, about their father's love for her, and about his new love. So all three of them died because of love.

"Theo was distraught. At the funeral, he tore his hair, threw himself on his daughters' little coffins, shed bitter tears. For four whole months, he was inconsolable. Then he married again, because he was still in love.

"Such is love."

Adriano looked into Féde's eyes. His voice trembling with emotion, he said: "Love for the earth, children, parents, life and the greatest love of all, for God, that's love, my sweetest daughter. Love! But the love you are crying for, that just comes and goes … nothing more."

Adriano fell silent. There were tears in his eyes.

Féde was also silent … her tears dried up … she felt better. But the poor girl did not know then that still she had not drained her cup of suffering, and that the last, most bitter drop, was still to come.

11. WHY?

Bitto Leone decided it was time for Ernesto to step into the ring, with Cenzo Rossi as his sparring partner.

"Cenzo," Bitto said, "Wear a helmet and gum shield. Wait, run to the coaching room and get Ernesto a spare gum shield."

"For Ernesto?" Cenzo asked. "Coach, I'm sorry, I'm just wondering: who will Ernesto be working with?"

"With you!" Bitto snapped.

Cenzo looked at the coach in bewilderment. Although bigger and taller than himself, this good-natured, always smiling guy was a completely inexperienced fighter. Cenzo was certain he knew in advance how this fight would end for Ernesto.

"Hurry up! How long do I have to wait?" His train of thought interrupted by the coach's hoarse voice, Cenzo went off to fetch the spare gum shield.

Bitto then called out to Ernesto, who was working on the sack: "Ernesto, come over here!"

"Yes, Signor Leone."

"Take the helmet, and Cenzo will bring you a gum shield. Get dressed and get in the ring."

"What for?" Ernesto asked naively.

"You will dance again," Bitto muttered.

Ernesto stopped talking and began to put on his helmet.

"This is for you," said Cenzo, tossing the spare gum shield to Ernesto. "You, this … be careful," he added, and went to put on his gear

A few minutes later they were both standing in the ring. Bitto, leaning on the ropes, explained to Ernesto the rules of sparring. Ernesto nodded his head enthusiastically. Cenzo shifted from foot to foot, throwing his hands forward.

"Box!" shouted Bitto.

Cenzo began to move around the ring, circling Ernesto like a predator his prey, except that this predator was not hungry and did not want his prey at all.

"Cenzo, work!" came Bitto's displeased voice.

Cenzo approached Ernesto and struck him several times.

"Ernesto, defend yourself," Bitto shouted. "Block, move to the left!"

Ernesto took a step to the left and dodged another blow.

"Work, Ernesto!"

But Ernesto did no more than move around the ring, hands held to his chin, and Cenzo's blows rained down on him. Although he spared his adversary, Cenzo worked precisely, with increasing strength.

"Rest," Bitto said irritably. "Ernesto, come here. Why are you not working? You're like a punching bag, only with legs."

"I don't have time," Ernesto replied. "And I don't understand how."

"How? How I taught you! Your task is to get away from the blow and suddenly attack. Understood?"

Ernesto looked at Bitto and did not seem to understand anything.

"Very well, I will try, Signor Leone."

"Box!" the coach shouted for a second time, and the same situation repeated itself. Cenzo moved, suddenly reducing the distance between them, and struck Ernesto with blows to the body and head. Ernesto was sweating and breathing heavily. He looked miserable and confused.

Bitto frowned deeply and shouted even louder: "Ernesto, why do you need such long arms if you have them glued to your face?"

Cenzo had cornered Ernesto and was about to throw another punch when Ernesto suddenly took a step to the side, deftly ducked under Cenzo's arm, turned around and landed a left punch straight to Cenzo's head. The blow was so strong that Cenzo staggered, and collapsed to the floor of the ring. Ernesto threw himself on his knees in front of him and shouted to the whole hall: "I'm sorry! I didn't mean to do that!"

Bitto was dumbfounded, as was everyone watching. A crowd of Cenzo fans had gathered at the ring expecting to see him knock down the ever-smiling Ernesto.

Cenzo struggled to his feet, grasping the ropes.

"That jab,"[24] he said, stunned. "And, Coach, he's left-hand-ed...."

"Yes...." Bitto said, thoughtfully. "Cenzo, how are you?"

"Fine."

"Can you still train?"

"Yes, I can," Cenzo replied, though his head was spinning.

"You have to be more careful."

"Yes, Coach," Cenzo replied softly.

"Ernesto, come with me," Bitto muttered and led him to the coach's room.

Bitto Leone's office was a small room with a window overlooking the boxing gym. By the window was a table littered with papers, and next to that an old leather sofa, with a blanket and a pillow. To the left of the entrance, almost the entire wall was occupied by a large bookcase with folders; but space remained for two posters depicting boxing's greatest stars: Rocky Marciano and Muhammad Ali. In the corner of the room there was a washbasin, and next to that a table with a teapot. Unwashed dishes were scattered everywhere. A cup on the table bore the inscription: "To my dear Bitto from D."

Ernesto looked around curiously. He was especially drawn to the poster depicting Muhammad Ali.

....

[24]   A sharp blow to the head with a straight hand.

"Ali was the greatest athlete," Bitto said, going up to the poster and exactly answering Ernesto's unspoken question. "Do you know what I remember most about him?"

"What, Signor Leone?"

"His invincible faith in himself. That was his advantage over his rivals." Bitto paused. "He also worked hard on himself, notwithstanding his belief that he was born a true champion."

Ernesto peered into Ali's face, spellbound.

"And this is the invincible Marciano," Bitto went on. "He is Italian, although he was born in America. He possessed extraordinary endurance and unshakable willpower. Think about it, Ernesto, forty-nine fights in the professional ring, and not a single defeat. That wasn't luck, son, that was down to sheer hard work: daily runs of more than ten kilometers, and more than twenty-five kilometers when preparing for fights. And more than five hundred punches in a single workout. That's what it means to work."

Bitto continued to look at his idol with admiration. But a moment later he frowned, and his face assumed its usual stern expression. "Stop staring," he said, walking over to his desk. "Sit down." He motioned Ernesto to a chair. "Tell me, why did you come to my gym?"

Ernesto was about to answer, but the old man continued: "I want to understand the true reason." He looked straight at Ernesto. "I see no thirst for victory in you. What do you expect of me?"

"Signor Leone," Ernesto began timidly, "I want to be strong."

"You are already strong, Ernesto. Nature has endowed you with extraordinary abilities. Today, I was finally convinced of that."

"Yes, I understand."

"So why do you need to be strong?"

"I'll tell you, just promise that no one will know about it."

"Son, I know how to keep other people's secrets. I keep them all here," he pointed to his head, "and here." He put his hand to his chest. "They will leave with me."

"I believe you," Ernesto said softly. And he went on to tell Bitto about everything that had been so much on his mind lately: the murder of his father, and his own irresistible desire for revenge.

Bitto heard him out, his expression inscrutable but serious. After Ernesto finished, he said: "Listen, I've never trained criminals within the walls of this gym. Especially murderers. I've never done it, and I'm not doing it now. If any of my students ever went down the wrong path, I don't know about it, and I don't want to know. Guys come to me, and I help them to become good athletes, real men. Believe me, son, you won't solve a single thing by force. And shedding someone's blood is a crime for which you will have to answer. That is a dark business."

Ernesto stared silently at the coach for several minutes, then jumped up from his chair and began to walk around the room nervously. "I don't want to shed blood. I wish no harm on anyone. I just want…."

He stopped and fell silent; his eyes wandered aimlessly around the room. "Please understand, Signor Leone," he said in a weak, sad voice, "I just want justice." Then he cried like a child.

At the sight of the big boy crying, old Bitto's face contorted in pain. His hands were shaking. To stop the treacherous trembling that had tormented him for the past three months, he clenched his fingers tightly into a fist.

Then Bitto said in a hoarse voice: "Ernesto, there is no justice on earth, but you are still too young to understand that. Calm down."

With an effort, Bitto got to his feet, walked over to a decanter of water, and tried to fill a glass, but the water splashed onto the floor. He tried again, succeeded, and handed the filled glass to Ernesto.

Ernesto took the glass, raised it to his lips, and drank the water greedily in one draught.

"Well, that's good," said the coach.

"Signor Leone, why is there no justice? After all, there are laws. Grandma Ceci said that we need to be kind and live according to the laws that the Lord taught us. Why then is there no justice?"

"Why? How can I tell you, son? Many people don't live according to the laws that your Grandma Ceci spoke about." Bitto thought, then continued: "Ernesto, as a man who has lived longer than you and seen a lot, I tell you, stop thinking about what can't be changed. Don't torture yourself. Live, rejoice! And as your coach, I will say, you are endowed with extraordinary strength that needs to be developed. And your height and long arms are a very important advantage for boxing. You are tough, resilient, and extremely hard-working. Trust me, an old man: with hard work, you will succeed in boxing. Don't deprive yourself of the opportunity to change your life. Consider a career as a professional boxer, and I will train you."

"I will think about it, Signor Leone," said Ernesto. "Thank you. No one except Ceci, the Marino family and, of course, Signor Grasso, has ever spoken to me like you."

Bitto patted Ernesto on the shoulder. "That's enough talk for today. Go … and think carefully about what I've told you. Only you – not I, not the Marino family, God bless them, not my friend Rino – none of us can influence your life. Go. Until tomorrow…."

"Yes, I'll see you tomorrow, Signor Leone," Ernesto replied, and headed for the door.

"One more thing, Ernesto: just call me 'Coach.'"

"All right, Signor … Coach!" Ernesto exclaimed, and smiled broadly.

Bitto laughed, and waved his hand.

In the locker room, Ernesto met Cenzo Rossi: "Cenzo, I want to apologise to you," he said.

"For what?" Cenzo chuckled. "You really hit hard. You will train hard and become a champion." As he said that, he thought to himself: "Oh, you!" Becoming a champion was his own dream. Since childhood, he had thought only of boxing and world fame. He was not endowed with outstanding abilities. The success that he had so far achieved was the result entirely of his hard work.

"Cenzo," Ernesto said, "I hit you by accident."

This innocent phrase caused a storm of emotions inside Cenzo; emotions that had been growing since the contest, but had not so far been able to burst out.

"Are you saying it was an accident?" he cried. "Yes, the fact of the matter, you fool, is that you haven't endured as many painful training sessions in this stuffy gym as I have. You haven't suffered a single day of the fatigue I feel. You haven't done any of that, you just 'accidentally' hit me, and I stretched out in the ring like a bag. You understand?" He was purple with anger. "No. It's as clear as day: I won't be a champion." He sat down on the bench, clasping his head in his hands.

Ernesto rehearsed in his head phrases that he might now say. Not knowing which one to use, he remained silent.

Cenzo calmed down and looked at Ernesto, who was hunched over and staring at him stupidly. Ernesto's long legs extended from short boxer shorts, and a stained tee-shirt hung over his broad chest. Cenzo suddenly laughed. He laughed and laughed, and Ernesto laughed with him. Casually observing them, one would have thought that these two were close friends who understood each other without using words.

Cenzo's nervous laughter stopped as suddenly as it had begun. He went to his locker and took out a wide black tee-shirt with "Everlast" printed on it.

"Here," he said, and threw the shirt into Ernesto's hands. "It brings good luck. A present for you. Just wash it."

Ernesto looked at the sweat-soaked shirt. It was a treasure such as he had never before held in his hands. Such was his delight, his mouth fell open.

"Thank you," he murmured. "I love your gift so much. I will take great care of it."

"You're weird," Cenzo said, laughing, and he started to change his clothes. Ernesto also turned to his locker.

On the way home, Ernesto telephoned Rino Grasso's number. Rino answered sleepily: "Ernesto, what are you doing?"

"Signor Grasso, I'm sorry to disturb you. I wanted to know…."

"So find out."

"I wanted to ask about my case."

"Ah … Ernesto, I'm working on it. I have one person…. He's promised to tell me when he discovers something."

"When?"

"Dude, don't be so hasty. In this case, haste will not help. And, most importantly, so many years have passed." Rino heard Ernesto breathing heavily into his phone. "Cheer up! We will find them. Or, at least, we will find out what happened to them."

"Thank you, Signor Grasso."

"Thank me later. Just remember that when Rino Grasso makes a promise, no hurricane, epidemic, or whatever, will prevent him from keeping his word. Do you understand?"

"I understand."

"How are your workouts? I keep meaning to stop by to watch you, but I just don't have time. Work, you know, home, children…."

"Okay, Signor Grasso. The coach praised me." Ernesto wondered, should he tell him about today's success and about the conversation with the coach? He decided to report his success, but keep silent about the conversation. "I sparred with Cenzo today," he blurted out.

"Wait, do I hear you right?" Ernesto heard the sound of Rino falling from his chair. "You sparred with Cenzo Rossi today?"

"Yes, Signor Grasso."

"And won?"

"Yes."

"Amazing!"

"Actually, it happened by accident."

"By accident? They tied him to the ropes, and you accidentally hit him with a club?"

"No, of course not. I just jabbed him and he went down."

"Maria! Are you hearing this?" Rino yelled at the top of his lungs. "Ernesto says he accidentally landed a jab on Cenzo Rossi and he went down!"

"Oh, I can't….!" said Maria, as if she understood the meaning of the word "jab" and knew who Cenzo Rossi was.

"I told you, Ernesto! You're a nugget of gold. I knew it!" Rino laughed. "I took him to Bitto Leone. I was the first to see talent in him."

Rino seemed to have forgotten that Ernesto was on the other end of the line. "Ernesto, are you still there? Are you asleep?"

"I'm listening, Signor Grasso."

Ernesto's news had made Rino happy for the night. "Don't worry about your business," he said. "Wait until we hear something."

"I will wait, Signor Grasso."

"Yes, wait." Rino, forgetting to turn off his phone, continued with loud expressions of self-congratulation and joy.

Meanwhile, Bitto Leone's gym had emptied. The coach turned off the lights and went to his office. He looked at his congealed, cold rice porridge and stale salad, turned away from them and took a piece of long-cooled pizza from its box. He brewed tea. The pizza was tasteless, and the tea was not sweet, not even with five teaspoons of sugar. The diseased organism that was Bitto's body no longer obeyed him. The trembling in his hands increased by the day; he could no longer taste food or drink; even whisky might as well have been water burning his throat; it brought no taste with it. The previous week, after a payment was refused because he could no longer sign his name in the way that he had for more than half a century, he had finally gone to a doctor. The diagnosis did not surprise him; he already knew he had Parkinson's disease. Now he could only buy time: there was no one to look after him, and only one person needed him, someone very dear to him. Thinking about his situation tired him. He tried to hide his illness, and did all he could to keep his condition stable.

He tossed aside the unappetising pizza and collapsed into a chair. He reached for a silver-framed photograph. The picture was of a young woman. Her gaze was somehow strange, almost insane. The camera had captured a moment when she tried to cover her pretty face with a small, fragile hand. Bitto stared at the already familiar features, as if seeing them for the first time. He did so for a long time, Then he returned the picture to its place and picked up the telephone. When it was answered, he asked: "How is she today? Calm? ... I understand. I'll be there as usual."

Setting aside the telephone, he turned to music. The deep, hoarse voice of the unsurpassed Fausto Leali filled the whole boxing hall:

> ...e capì di aver vissuto troppo in fretta, adesso che
> stava stretto nell'imbuto dei perché
> perché, perché, perché...[25]

It was a song that he had heard hundreds of times before. He covered his eyes with his hands and sat until sleep overcame him.

....

[25] "...and realised he had lived too fast, and suddenly found himself in a whirlpool of why, why, why, why...." (Italian).

12. TWO-FACED PATRON

The next day, Ernesto told Bitto Leone of his desire to become a professional boxer, not for revenge, but for his future, adding that Ceci would have supported his decision. The coach was delighted.

From that day onwards, Bitto took Ernesto seriously. Tens of kilometres of runs; hundreds of push-ups; exercises for the muscles of the arms, legs and abdomen; thousands of hits on the bag…. In physique, Ernesto became a different man: it was as if a talented sculptor had re-shaped his body, giving him a new, perfect form.

The beach season was coming to an end, and there was less work in the Chalet Martina. Ernesto was happy to perform any tasks Martina gave him, such as carrying incoming vegetables, fruit, fish and meat from the carpark to the kitchen. All the while, he proceeded step by step towards his goal, sparing neither time nor effort.

Bitto arranged for Ernesto to fight Big Tony, an experienced boxer and renowned knockout fighter.[26] When the day arrived, Ernesto took a day off from the Chalet Martina. He began his day with a run. Dog, Ernesto's faithful companion, seemed to understand the importance of the day. She ran faster than usual, barked louder, and energetically scattered the lazy gulls.

"What do you think, Dog," Ernesto asked her, "can I win today?"

....

[26] A boxer who has a knockout punch, often winning by knockout.

Dog barked loudly, put her front paws on his shoulders, and licked his face.

"I know you believe in me," Ernesto laughed, clasping her muzzle in his hands and gently stroking her.

Gazing at the sea, he thought of the evening's bout. He didn't want to hurt anyone. He recalled how his sparring partners in the Bitto Leone gym, including Cenzo Rossi, all fell, one by one. Every time, he felt guilt, and suffered emotional distress.

Bitto scolded him for showing emotion, but Ernesto still apologised – in the locker room, unbeknown to the coach. Now, with the fight with Big Tony looming, Ernesto worried about the power of his own left hand, forgetting about Tony's strong uppercut.[27]

Ernesto thought about Ceci and why he was so sure that his grandmother would approve of these cruel, unjustified fights.

Dog licked his hand and whined. She panted, her tongue hanging out.

"I understand," said Ernesto. "We'll run home; catch up!"

They ran to Ernesto's cabin on the beach, Dog barking loudly, scattering the gulls once again. Coming abreast of the Chalet Martina, they plunged into the cool sea water. Ernesto laughed. The sea calmed him, taking away his anxiety.

At a quarter past seven in the evening, Ernesto arrived at Bitto Leone's boxing club for what was to be his first real fight. He looked around: at the parked cars, and at the entrance to the building, and he froze, unable to take another step.

"Ernesto," called Bitto Leone, who was looking out. "Where have you been? Don't you see what time it is?"

....

[27] A classic upward punch; used in close combat.

"Yes, Coach," Ernesto replied timidly. "The clock behind you shows eighteen minutes past seven."

"So hurry up," Bitto roared. "Or have you changed your mind?"

"I'm coming, Coach." Ernesto followed the angry Bitto indoors.

An hour later, in new gloves, red shorts and a white coat, Ernesto entered the ring. Bitto Leone walked beside him. He rubbed his shaking hands, his face serious. Before entering the hall, he had stopped Ernesto and said: "Ernesto, son, this is your first fight. Do you remember everything I told you in the locker room?"

"I remember, Coach."

"That's good. Let's go." Bitto patted the boy on the shoulder. His heart was restless.

Entering the hall, Ernesto examined the audience with childlike curiosity. The front three rows were occupied by men talking loudly and smoking. The air was saturated with the suffocating smell of their smoke. No one seemed to be paying attention to Ernesto, the black rookie boxer in a white coat.

Big Tony was already in the ring. He was talking animatedly to a short, sturdy man wearing a tracksuit and sporting a massive gold watch on his wrist. This man was saying something, waving his arms. Big Tony, who seemed to be chewing, nodded his head and laughed.

As Ernesto climbed into the ring, Tony gave him a contemptuous look.

Surprising everyone, Ernesto jumped up to Tony, smiled broadly and joyfully greeted him: "Hi! It's me, Ernesto!"

There was laughter in the hall. "What an idiot," some were heard to say. "That nerd is training with Leone?"

Bitto's face coloured a little, but remained motionless. Grimacing, Big Tony looked inquiringly at the man in the tracksuit and massive gold watch. Bitto pushed Ernesto aside and shook hands with the tracksuit and gold watch man.

Then the referee moved to the centre of the ring to announce the contestants. Heavyweight Verzilu Tony; weighing ninety-seven kilograms; one meter and eighty-nine centimetres tall; twenty-five fights behind him; fifteen victories won by knockout. And heavyweight Baby Ernesto; weighing ninety-four kilograms; one meter and ninety-two centimetres tall; appearing in the professional ring for the first time.

The audience applauded Big Tony and shouted his name. Ernesto looked around in confusion and smiled stupidly.

Then the referee called both boxers to him, reminded them of the rules of the fight, and with a movement of his hands invited them to greet each other. Flaring his nostrils, his broken, crooked nose giving his face a menacing look, Big Tony glared at Ernesto. Ernesto smiled kindly.

The gong sounded: the fight was on. Big Tony rushed to the attack and struck Ernesto with a series of accurate blows to the body. Ernesto dropped his hands in surprise. Tony, taking advantage of his opponent's weak defence, struck him with the strongest of uppercuts, from which Ernesto swayed. Another powerful blow from Tony and Ernesto was on the floor.

Ernesto looked at the referee as if through a fog. Shielding Tony with his fat body, the ref was leaning over and counting: "One! Two!.."

"Get up, Ernesto!" commanded Bitto. "Get up now!"

The audience cheered, chanting Tony's name.

Ernesto scrambled to his feet as the referee reached the count of five. The referee fixed his small eyes on Ernesto's face, assessing whether he should continue the fight, then gave the command to carry on.

Again, Big Tony went on the attack with a series of crushing blows. But this time Ernesto held his hands high, lowered his chin, and dodged, as Bitto had taught him.

"Move!" Bitto shouted. "Don't let him back you into a corner!"

The gong sounded, ending the first round. Ernesto sank onto the stool in his corner. Bitto climbed into the ring: an obvious effort. He treated a cut to Ernesto's eyebrow, gave him water to drink and some advice, and for himself tried to calm the trembling in his hands and the doubts in his soul.

The gong opened the second round. Yet again, Big Tony went straight on the attack, striking hard. Ernesto circled around the ring, trying to maintain his defence.

At the end of round two, Ernesto again sat in his corner, Bitto tending his wounds. The audience loudly chanted Tony's name.

After the sixth round, when Ernesto collapsed onto the stool in his corner and looked into the hall, for a moment one spectator caught his attention. His face seemed familiar, his glaring eyes two sparkling, sinister lights. It was Alberto Conte.

A few days after their chance meeting at the traffic light, Alberto had sought out Ernesto. When he discovered that Ernesto had a fight coming up, he made sure of going to see it. Alberto had assessed Big Tony, looking hard at his face and big strong hands. He rejoiced at the thought of Baby Ernesto's defeat. He hoped that Tony's crushing blows would destroy the boy; the boy who had suddenly reminded him of a terrible sin.

Round seven. Big Tony had not expected this inexperienced black guy to last so long. He pounced on Ernesto, inflicting fierce blows, blows that would have knocked many boxers to the floor, never to get up again. But this boy, apparently made of iron, continued to circle around the ring.

To his own surprise, some of Tony's shots missed their mark. He was getting tired – and annoyed. He wanted to finish this fight, and soon. The audience, too, was becoming impatient for Ernesto to be knocked out. They yelled at Tony to hurry up and finish the guy.

Ernesto too, was tired, but he was not ready to give up. He drew up schemes of attack in his head, as if he were facing a school exam, not a dangerous opponent in a boxing ring. He began to close the distance between Big Tony and himself, and deliver single blows, putting all his strength into them. With seconds remaining before the end of the seventh round, Big Tony rushed furiously at Ernesto, wanting to end the fight there and then. But he made a mistake. Ernesto deftly dodged to the right. Tony's own momentum sent him flying onto the ropes; he touched them, quickly turned and, stumbling on his opponent's strongest left jab, collapsed in the ring, much to his own amazement. The referee began the count. Tony could not get up and was knocked out.

The spectators held their breath, staring at the ring. Then a dull murmur was heard, followed a moment later by joyful exclamations. They chanted Ernesto's name. Ernesto stood motionless, his hands down, smiling in bewilderment. Bitto rushed to hug his pupil.

Alberto Conte had of course followed the battle closely. When Ernesto dealt the decisive blow, he jumped to his feet as if scalded. His eyes reflected sheer horror. It was as if he himself had been defeated by Ernesto.

The elder Conte decided to get closer to the one he was most afraid of. He hoped to meet Ernesto at the exit after the fight. But Ernesto came out with his coach, Bitto Leone. So Alberto got into his car and waited until Bitto was gone. Then he drove up to Ernesto. Ernesto was very surprised to see the black Mercedes and its driver, the one who had so unsettled him recently. Getting out of his car, Alberto began a dangerous and cunning game: "Congratulations, Ernesto. Impressive debut."

"Thank you."

"I like unpredictable situations," Alberto began. Ernesto wondered what this strange man wanted from him. "Entertainment evokes animal instincts in a person, raises feelings hidden in the soul. You, Ernesto, have great power, and not just in your beautifully-shaped body. Your power is deep inside."

Alberto paused. Ernesto looked at him questioningly.

"Ah, I see I have confused you," Alberto said, forcing a laugh. "I was waiting for you. I wanted to invite you to dinner. Let's talk and celebrate your first victory. What do you think?"

"I don't know," Ernesto answered. "I don't know you."

Alberto laughed again.

"So this is where you get to know me. Believe me, you have nothing to lose." Alberto affected the sincerest friendliness. "Let's just talk. Please, respect a kind old man, especially one who so much admires your talent."

"OK," replied Ernesto timidly. It would have embarrassed him to refuse, and Ceci had taught him to be polite with his elders.

"Well, that's great," said Alberto happily, rubbing his hands. "Let's go to a place where they cook excellent steaks. Mmm.... Somewhere I'm sure you won't have been before."

Ernesto nodded, and moved to take the front passenger seat in the black Mercedes. He had never before sat in such a luxurious automobile, never before touched such soft leather. It had its own aroma – very fragrant – contrasting with his own, stale smell.

The seat was so far forward Ernesto's knees pressed against the dashboard – very uncomfortable. Alberto saw this but did nothing.

Alberto felt his power over this huge, physically strong guy. He talked enthusiastically about cars, restaurants and sport.

Ernesto's stomach rumbled loudly, insistently demanding food. He was embarrassed. And his head spun. He began to regret agreeing to spend his evening with this man.

"Here we are," Alberto announced cheerfully, driving up to a small, beautiful building located on a knoll. The parking area was spacious, with a fountain, flower beds, and fragrant blooms in clay pots.

Ernesto followed Alberto into the restaurant. Alberto's face shone with a self-satisfied smile. A polite waiter led them to a separate, private room, seating them on soft velvet chairs beside a large table. Alberto ordered. Within minutes, canapés, bruschetta, meatloaf, salads, two huge beef steaks with potatoes, and a bottle of excellent wine were set before them.

Sitting there in his tee-shirt and sweatpants, Ernesto was embarrassed. He fidgeted on his chair, clutching the tablecloth, looking around uneasily. Every minute increased his anxiety. Alberto maintained an appearance of calm indifference – nevertheless following his guest's every movement with eyes that were not kind.

"Let's get started. Don't be embarrassed, Baby Ernesto," Alberto said. Was there a hint of mockery in his voice? "Help yourself. This is all for you."

Ernesto overcame his timidity and began to eat. Alberto only watched him; he didn't eat at all.

When Ernesto had satisfied his hunger, Conte picked up a glass and said: "I propose a toast to the winner. For you, Ernesto. Tonight, your star lit up."

"Thanks," Ernesto replied. "But I don't drink."

"And neither do I," laughed Alberto, "but tonight is special, and a glass of good wine can only make it better."

"No, I will not."

"Yes, boy, you still have everything ahead of you. Life is full of all kinds of entertainment and pleasures. I love pleasure. And you?"

"I don't know," Ernesto answered uncertainly. "I love spending time with my dog; I love the sea. I like to play with a little girl called Frani; to talk with the coach. He is strict, but kind."

"Is that all your pleasure, Baby Ernesto? Amazing!" Alberto laughed. "I'm not talking about these 'pleasures' of yours, but about real, adult pleasures. Understand?"

"No, I don't understand, Signor…." Ernesto realised that he still did not know the name of this man.

"Call me Signor Vero,[28] or just Vero," said Alberto. "And I will tell you about real life. Do you have a girlfriend?"

"I don't have time. I train and work a lot. I have a goal."

"Yes, Ernesto, life is short…." Alberto narrowed his eyes. "But that's not where I'm coming from. I want to tell you about pleasure and, when it comes down to it, I am talking about the brevity of life. You need to enjoy every hour, every minute, but everything has its price. For some reason, I remember one incident. It was many years ago. Two friends worked for my father. Closer than brothers, they were hardly ever apart. But then their friendship fell apart. Whether a woman came between them, or money, I don't know, but one evening one friend killed the other."

A short silence. Then Alberto looked Ernesto in the eyes and continued, almost in a whisper: "He beat his friend in a dark, deserted spot, and left him to bleed to death. And so his only friend died, alone on the cold ground. And the murderer hid somewhere in a remote place and hoped that he would escape punishment. It seemed that there were no witnesses to the crime. And who could have suspected him, a close friend, almost a brother? However, punishment overtook the killer when he least expected it. On the ninth day after the wretched killing, a great storm came with heavy rain. A wall of water, driven by the wind, fell on the sinner. He stepped unseeing into the road and a fish truck smashed into him…. Just like that."

....

[28] The Italian word for "real" or "true."

"That was as it should be," Ernesto said. "Whoever breaks the law knows about the punishment, knows what will happen next."

"Yes," whispered Alberto, "but the one who flies into the abyss is no longer afraid of his fate. He only wants tranquilization – and fast."

With that, Alberto raised his glass and drank greedily.

He then spent some moments silently staring at Ernesto.

"Do you know, Ernesto, what is your mission?"

"I don't know. I don't think about that."

"You don't? Consider the power you have been given. I saw you today; you are hardy, strong…."

Flushing, Alberto looked at Ernesto with anger in his eyes. Then, recovering himself, he said: "I just want to help you, Ernesto. I'm rich. I help talented people, and I will help you."

"But I don't need it! I have Signor and Signora Marino – and a coach. I have everything."

"That may be so, but to make a good career in big boxing, you need connections and money, which, I am quite sure, your benefactors do not have. And I, Ernesto, stretch out my hand to you and offer my patronage, and, mind you, I ask nothing of you in return."

"Thank you, Signor Vero, but I don't need anything."

Ernesto was about to get up, when Alberto said quietly: "I knew your mother."

"My mother?"

"Yes, your mother."

"What was she like?" Ernesto was eager to know.

"Skinny…. I didn't know her well. We met by chance, but I will remember our meeting for the rest of my life." Alberto's handsome features twisted into a terrible grimace.

Ernesto lowered his eyes, then said in a trembling voice: "My father and mother were killed."

Alberto turned pale: "How? That cannot be! Killed? … Both?"

"Yes, both."

Alberto opened his mouth to say something, but nothing came out. He looked at Ernesto with fear, emptied his glass of wine in a single draught … and finally asked in an insinuating tone: "And what do you know about it?"

"Not much, yet, but I'll find out soon."

"Of course, you must. How are you going to find out?"

"Ceci told me that sooner or later I would discover the truth in the most unexpected way."

"And who is Ceci?"

"My grandmother. She died."

"Ahh … now I understand," Alberto said with clear relief.

Deciding that it was time to end the evening, Alberto stood, saying to Ernesto: "We should go, I think."

"Yes, I want to go home."

Alberto drove Ernesto to the Chalet Martina without speaking further. Finally, when the time came to part, he said, "We will continue our conversation. Meanwhile, rest!"

"Goodbye, Signor Vero."

At the Chalet Martina, Ernesto encountered Adriano.

"Where have you been for so long? Rino called. He told me about your victory and that you disappeared somewhere after the fight. And why is your phone off?"

Ernesto looked at the dark screen of his phone. "So it is."

"What's wrong with you, my friend?" Adriano patted Ernesto on the shoulder.

"With me? Everything is fine, I'm just tired. Do you know Signor Vero?"

"Signor Vero?" Adriano was surprised.

"I had dinner with him after the fight."

"Well! Martina and I were waiting for you here, and you had dinner with some Signor Vero. What does this mean? What did you get hit on the head with?"

"No…. I got hit, of course, but not much. It just happened."

"And what did this gentleman want from you? Is he a manager?"

"No, he's not a manager. He's rich. He said he wanted to help me."

Adriano thought how strange that was, and then said: "You rest now, Ernesto. We'll deal with your Signor tomorrow."

"Yes. Until tomorrow."

Ernesto went off to his cabin. Adriano looked after him thinking: "How very strange…. I must tell Martina about this."

13. AND THE THIRD ONE

Frani's seventh birthday was celebrated at the Chalet Martina. The weather was as bright and sunny as the birthday girl herself. A large tent was set up, and decorated with bouquets of scarlet flowers, inflatable unicorns and golden stars. The air was filled with the scent of vanilla and cocoa. Happy children's laughter rang from all corners of the Chalet Martina.

Frani looked like a fairy taken straight from the pages of a children's book. She wore an airy white dress studded with scarlet roses; her hair was tied with a bow, which was itself adorned with a shiny stone. Her spontaneity, inborn grace and charming smile were all very touching.

"Today, Ernesto, you will be with me all evening," Frani said importantly, taking his hand.

Ernesto replied kindly: "I will fulfil all your desires." The birthday girl jumped up and down and clapped her hands with joy. All the girls who came to say Happy Birthday to her looked with genuine admiration at the huge, smiling Ernesto.

She raised her curly head and said with pride: "Ernesto is a boxer."

Led by Frani, Ernesto played hide and seek with the children. The children ran around the room delightedly.

Equally happy, Adriano ran to and from the kitchen. Sometimes he stopped and looked at little Frani playing with the other children, and his eyes became moist.

Martina too was in festive mood. She chatted with all the guests, joked and laughed. Joy shone in her eyes.

Only Féde was quieter, more modest than usual. She helped her parents, running between the guests with a tray in her hands, but she was downcast, thoughtful, silent. If she smiled, it was only for a moment, and with such sadness in her beautiful olive eyes that some of the guests asked Martina what was the matter. But Martina only sighed, shrugged her shoulders and said: "You know how it is with the young; eternal sadness for no reason."

Martina did, however, know full well what caused Féde's suffering, but was unable to help her.

Frani received many birthday gifts: lots of her favourite unicorns; handbags; hairpins in the form of roses, peonies, lilies, and even violets; children's perfume; smart notepads and pens; and from her parents a gold brooch.

Rino Grasso came with his wife Maria and daughter Marisa, who Ernesto had saved from drowning. "Here, Frani, is our gift," Rino said importantly, presenting Frani with a large box wrapped in pink paper. Frani straightaway opened the present and gasped in delight as she pulled out a doll's pram fit for a princess.

Her response made Rino equally happy. "Amazing!" he said, running his plump hand over the birthday girl's curly locks. "And for you, son," he said, turning to Ernesto, "I also have a surprise, but more on that later."

Rino then turned to the buffet table, drawn by the aromas of Adriano's culinary masterpieces. "Rino is very hungry, and no Grasso does business on an empty stomach."

So Ernesto had to wait, tormented by curiosity.

Adriano continued to bring out hot snacks and kept muttering that there was not enough food. Martina laughed and said that for the number of dishes he had prepared there were not enough guests.

Actors arrived: a prince with a small pointed beard, and a princess, with curly pink hair. The show began: the children jumped, danced, guessed riddles and laughed infectiously.

Féde sat alone at the farthest table, watching the general merriment and thinking sadly about her own situation. The joyful voices, laughter, and even the music echoed in her heart with dull pain. She struggled with this feeling and, so as not to burst into tears, set mind games for herself. Working through the alphabet, she recalled the names of artists and writers. When the turn of composers arrived, she decided that it was better to move on to capital cities. But no matter how hard she tried to restrain herself, to distract herself from sad thoughts, she again plunged into darkness. It was as if another Féde, unfamiliar to her, had settled inside her and was constantly crying and whining as she, her double, recalled the details of her unhappy love, repeating that her despair was natural, inevitable – and that it was pointless to fight it.

Ernesto had noticed the change in Féde. He saw her suffering, and although he did not know its cause, he wanted to help. He was devoted to the Marino family; they had accepted him as their own, and he considered it his duty to take care of all of them. He took a large plate, collected some snacks from the buffet, added three types of pizza, and made his way to Féde's table.

"This is for you," he said, placing the dish in front of her.

Féde looked at him with sad eyes, smiled weakly, and said: "Thanks, Ernesto, but I'm not hungry."

Ernesto was silent, unable to think of anything to say.

"Why is it only virgins can tame unicorns?" Féde suddenly asked.

"Hmmm…. Perhaps because the unicorn is a symbol of purity."

"Yes, maybe…." Féde looked thoughtfully into the distance. "So, purity is characteristic only of virgins?"

"I…." Ernesto blushed. "I don't know. I'm not well versed in such matters."

Féde looked at him with contempt, and said in a caustic tone: "Well, that's not surprising, Ernesto. You have grown big, but your brain is no larger than a pea."

She looked defiantly at Ernesto, hoping that he would finally leave her alone. But Ernesto smiled and replied kindly: "Ceci used to say, 'when people feel bad, they offend those who are nearby. It's their way of protecting themselves.'"

He went up to Féde and hugged her tightly. The girl wept in the strong, friendly embrace of a big man with a good heart.

She murmured:

> The saintly hermit, midway through his prayers
> stopped suddenly, and raised his eyes to witness
> the unbelievable: for there before him stood
> the legendary creature, startling white, that
> had approached, soundlessly, pleading with his eyes.[29]

"Ernesto! Ernesto!" came the voice of Rino Grasso.

Ernesto stood in indecision and looked at Féde. She wiped away her tears and said: "Go. Everything is fine."

Ernesto hurried to Rino, who was looking rather pleased with himself.

"Now, son, I'm ready to tell you about your surprise," he drawled with a wink.

"Please, tell me. Is it about my parents?"

"Yes. Didn't I tell you that nothing is impossible for Rino Grasso?"

"They talked?"

"Don't I always keep my word?"

"Signor Grasso, please tell me quickly. What did you learn?"

....

[29] "The Unicorn" by Rainer Maria Rilke (1875–1926).

"Everything," Rino exclaimed triumphantly.

"AND?" Ernesto asked.

"And tomorrow morning you and I are going to the Ascoli Piceno prison."

"You have found them, Signor Grasso?"

"Yes. Rino Grasso always finds everyone."

"I can't believe it!" exclaimed Ernesto. "So soon…. Tomorrow, I will see them. Tomorrow, I will look into their eyes."

"Not quite." Rino spoke cautiously. "Tomorrow, Ernesto, you will look into the eyes of only one of them."

"Why only one?"

"Calm down, son, don't boil over. Otherwise, the lid will fly off the teapot." Rino pointed to Ernesto's forehead. "The fact is," he continued, "one of them died in prison; or rather, he was killed."

"Killed! Who…?"

"How would I know? It happens there. Maybe they didn't share something, or someone. He was on a walk and was stabbed in the back with a knife. He died like a dog. For what? At the prison they don't really understand it. But it doesn't matter. What we can say is that one has already been written off, and the second is still sitting there. They gave him some extra years for getting into a dust-up. I didn't ask for details."

"And the third one?" Ernesto asked. "Is he dead too?"

"The third one?" Rino hesitated, took a deep breath, then continued in an unsteady voice: "Why should there be a third one all of a sudden?"

"Signor Grasso, it was you who told me there were three of them."

"I may have said that, but I could have been wrong. It was many years ago. Does it make a difference?"

"I remember exactly, Signor Grasso, you said there were three of them."

"Don't upset me," Rino said, offended. "I tried, I found out for you. I unearthed these people. I came running to you thinking you would be happy. I thought we would go tomorrow to look at the bastard who killed your father. You could say all you wanted to say, maybe spit in his face once or twice … but not beat him! And, by the way, Ernesto, it wasn't easy for me to arrange this visit for you. I had to make a few things up: that you are a journalist, a writer, that you're writing about this case from twenty years ago, and so on. And you, aren't you happy?"

"Thank you, Signor Grasso. Of course I am!"

"That's better." Rino was delighted. "So, are we going tomorrow?"

"Yes, definitely!"

"Fine. I will come for you at ten in the morning. Now, let's see what else old Adriano has to offer."

The next day, riding in Rino Grasso's car, Ernesto thought about the upcoming meeting. Would it change anything? What should he do next? Would his pain subside? And who was "the third one" who had robbed him of his father and mother? The unanswered questions tormented him, and he could not change what lay ahead.

The sky that morning was wonderful: boundless blue, strewn with fluffy clouds that gathered in a variety of shapes. Ernesto loved to watch the endlessly changing, amazing things that happen in the sky, and was always fascinated by the boundless height of the heavens. It gave him a feeling of deep awe and – important today – looking at the sky calmed him.

As ever, Rino kept up a torrent of words throughout the whole journey, accompanying his words with emotional gestures. He spoke of Ernesto's recent fight with Big Tony, then abruptly switched to his personal problems, connected either with Maria, the children, or a neighbour. Ernesto listened and thought how funny this fat man Rino was.

They arrived at the Ascoli Piceno prison. Seen from the car park, the prison was a red brick building behind a high fence with thick bars. Ernesto shuddered.

Getting out of the car, Rino stood and smoked, looking towards the prison. After some minutes, a burly man in uniform approached the fence. Rino met his eyes, gave him a slight nod, threw away his cigarette, opened the car door and said: "All as agreed. Now, Ernesto, you will go through those gates," he pointed to the prison entrance, "and you will be smart. Remember, you are a journalist, a scribbler. Take this notepad."

Rino reached to the back seat and picked up a small notebook with a patterned cover, taken from his elder daughter's desk that morning.

"Don't forget your pen. And put on a serious face – like this." Rino demonstrated a serious face. "Okay. Let's go."

After that, Ernesto felt as if he was sleepwalking. He was met at the gate by the uniformed man, at whom Rino winked. Without speaking, the man led him to the entrance of the building, where he was ordered to leave his mobile phone. His notebook was examined. He was allowed to keep that, but his pen was put with his phone and he was given a lead pencil instead.

Ernesto was then taken to a small hall with tables and chairs. Sullen-faced men dressed unmistakeably as convicts were each paired with a woman dressed in a way that said just as clearly that she was from the outside. The women spoke quickly, showing photographs and children's drawings.

Ernesto was taken to a vacant table and told to sit. He was scared; his mouth was dry. He tried to remember the conversation he'd been thinking about all night, but he couldn't. Coherent thoughts seemed to have taken fright and fled. Waiting for the arrival of the prisoner who was being punished for the death of his father, Ernesto felt great anxiety.

Finally, a man dressed like all the rest appeared at the edge of the room. He was looking around fearfully. Seeing Ernesto, his eyes showed horror. He seemed to want to turn back, but a broad-shouldered prison guard led him to the table where Ernesto was sitting.

"Oliver Stratty," the guard said, seating the terrified prisoner on the other side of Ernesto's table.

"You're not a writer," Oliver Stratty said in a trembling voice. "You look so much like him," he whispered. "Oh yeah. I understand."

"Hello, Oliver Sutty," said Ernesto coldly. Now that his father's killer was sitting in front of him, anger drove all fear from his soul, leaving firm confidence in its place.

"Stratty," the prisoner answered quietly.

"What?" Ernesto was confused.

"You said Sutty. My name is Stratty," the man repeated, nodding his head.

Ernesto carefully examined the convict: thin, grey hair; an emaciated and yellowed face, deeply wrinkled; eyes of indefinite colour, empty, with an extinct look. His hands shook; his nails were bitten to wounds that festered in places.

"Hello, Oliver Stratty," said Ernesto. "I came to…."

"Don't go on!" Oliver interrupted him, glaring into his face. "I know why you came."

"Okay, why?"

"You came to torment me."

"What?" Ernesto shouted – so loudly that all eyes turned in their direction.

"Quiet," said Oliver, wheezing. "I know you are his son."

"So you remember my father?" Ernesto was excited by that thought.

Oliver kept silent. His inflamed eyes darted randomly over Ernesto's face.

"Do you remember how he was killed?" Ernesto asked.

"Yes, I remember that night all too well. There isn't a single day when I don't think about it." Oliver lowered his eyes as if to study the surface of the table.

"Are you sorry?" Ernesto asked grimly. The pain he felt showed in his face.

"Oh yeah, I'm sorry," the prisoner began hotly. He licked his lips, which were chapped to the point of blood. "I have been suffering for so many years. I was young then … like you are now."

Oliver now seemed to look right through Ernesto to somewhere in the distance – the distant past.

Ernesto clenched his fists, barely containing his anger.

"I didn't think it would end like that," Oliver continued. "I just wanted to have some fun."

"Why are you telling me this?" Ernesto began to boil.

"I just wanted to have dinner, so I went with them," Oliver continued. "But something happened that can't be changed."

"How did he die?"

"I didn't see your father die, he died in hospital, but I saw his agony. I realised it was very serious."

Ernesto's eyes filled with tears, and Oliver stopped.

"Go on," said Ernesto.

"There was a girl. She was pregnant."

"Yes, that was my mother."

Oliver sighed. "It's hard for me to say this, but it all started because of her."

"Are you out of your mind, you bastard?" Ernesto spoke too loudly: a guard walked towards their table.

Oliver cringed. Ernesto assured the guard that everything was under control.

The guard turned away. "Speak!" Ernesto sternly commanded Oliver.

Oliver licked his damaged lips and began again: "I was just trying to say … that if the pregnant girl hadn't been there, then A…."

Oliver looked around in all directions, then whispered: "He wouldn't have touched your father."

"Who is 'he'? The other one that was with you?" Ernesto demanded, glaring.

"With us? …Yes." Oliver responded.

"What is his name?

"Name?"

"Yes, what is his name, or what was his name? Is he still alive?"

"He's dead, the other guy is," said Oliver rapidly. "His first name was Doni, and his last name was Tancello. Doni Tancello, that's what his name was."

"But just a few moments ago you started his name with an 'A.'"

"Did I? Well, maybe I did."

"Okay, go on. What can you say about my mom?"

"Your mother was pregnant. I already said that. She lived with your father in a cabin on the plantation. And he found them there. And when he saw that your mother was pregnant, he became so furious. And he kept shouting: 'Is this from him? You and a black man decided to spoil Italian blood with this.' He called her a lot of bad words, but it doesn't matter now. Then he grabbed your mother by the arm, wanted to…."

"Speak, Oliver, speak!"

"Yes, I'm talking, I'm talking. I wanted to join in insulting her. I didn't understand exactly, but your father rushed at him like an angry beast, and there was a fight."

"Go on."

"I still don't understand how it happened." Tears showed in Oliver's eyes. "I didn't take part; I was just there."

"If you didn't take part, how is it that you've been sentenced to more than twenty years?"

"I'm telling you the truth: I never hit your father once. It was them."

"So there were three of you?"

"Yes, but I'm not telling you anything about the third one." Oliver again looked around the room.

"Why is that?"

Oliver leaned towards Ernesto and whispered: "Because he's a terrible man, and I'm afraid of him."

"But you are in prison. What are you afraid of?"

"Hey boy, you don't know him," said Oliver, still whispering. "He's rich and powerful. He can do anything."

"I don't understand. You say you didn't join in beating my father…. So, if there were three of you, why are you in prison? The second one died. What about the third? What about him?"

"The third one came out of the water dry." An evil fire lit up in Oliver's eyes.

"Are you saying he went unpunished?"

"That's exactly what I'm saying. His name was completely removed from the records of the crime." Oliver now began to nibble at the already inflamed skin around his nails. "I've been here for more than twenty years. Back then, my sister was very ill with a tumour in her head the size of a walnut. We needed money, big money. Well, the family of this third person got wind of my own family's situation and came first to my mother, then to me. Immediately after their visit, my mother ran to me. She was crying. She went on her knees in front of me, asking for my sister. She said: 'Have pity on her. I know you'll get through everything. Agree to their terms. Do it for your sister: do it for me. Please! I beg you!' She sobbed in front of me, stroked and kissed me as if she would never see me again.

"And the next day they came to me: 'Take all the blame on yourself. Say that you and your friend, Doni Tancello, did the beating. Keep quiet about the third one – he was not there! Do that and we will transfer two hundred thousand to your mother's account.'

"Can you imagine? So much money! Neither I nor my poor mother had ever known such people. The lawyers promised that I would be given no more than ten years. They said I would get out still young … and with money. But they gave me twenty years. They said 'aggravating circumstances' – injury to the pregnant woman, done by a group; and they added another crime – motivation by racism. The judge was an ardent fighter for the rights and freedom of people of different races, something like that. So I got twenty years. But my sister didn't survive. She died just one year later, and the money has long since been spent."

Ernesto sat in silence, struggling to understand the meaning of what he had heard.

"The visit is over," the guard suddenly shouted.

"Wait," Ernesto exclaimed. "One more minute!"

"Oliver Stratty, please say, what is the name of the one you are doing time for – the third one?"

"I can't," Oliver said. "I cannot!"

"Please! Please! I'll make him answer for everything."

"Oh no," shouted Oliver. "You can't do that. It's not in your power." He got up from the table and walked towards the guard.

Ernesto also stood. He watched in anguish as the prisoner retreated. Tears choked him. But suddenly, in front of the door leading to the cells, Oliver Stratty stopped and shouted to the whole hall: "Alberto! His name is Alberto!" Then he laughed loudly and disappeared behind the door. His insane laughter echoed around the hall for what seemed a long time.

Ernesto got out of the prison and back to Rino Grasso as fast as he could.

"So, how did it go?" Rino was eager to hear.

"I don't know."

"What? Didn't you meet him? Didn't you see him?"

"Yes, we met," Ernesto replied. "But he is the least to blame. There were three of them."

Rino rolled his eyes. "So there were three," he said thoughtfully.

"And the third one's name is Alberto," Ernesto added sternly.

"Alberto," repeated Rino, clearly afraid. "And what is his last name?"

"I don't know his last name; I only know that his name is Alberto and that he is rich."

Rino sighed. After a pause, he declared: "Of course, it will be easy to find someone called Alberto."

Another pause. "Okay, let's go. There's nothing more to do here. Get in the car."

Ernesto started towards Rino's car, but before getting into the car, he turned and looked once more at the prison. Could he *still* hear the ominous laughter of the desperate prisoner?

Oliver Stratty died that same night. He hanged himself in his cell.

14. BITTO'S SAD LOVE

Bitto Leone's health worsened by the day. His thunderous voice died away, seeming to retreat deep inside him. His face assumed an indefinite expression; a mask under which he hid himself. The stern coach became a frail old man.

One Sunday, just as Ernesto returned to his cabin from his morning run, his phone rang.

"Ernesto!" It was Bitto.

"Coach, good morning!"

"I need your help."

"Help?" Ernesto was surprised. "Certainly. Yes. What can I do for you?"

"Come to me; as soon as possible."

"Is something wrong?"

"No!" Bitto seemed irritated by the suggestion. "I just need your help."

"Should I ask Signora Marino for time off?"

"All right, Ernesto, just hurry, or we might be too late."

"Are we going somewhere?"

"Never mind that," Bitto growled angrily. "Come on, get moving!"

"Yes, Coach, I'll be with you very soon," Ernesto said meekly.

"Ernesto," croaked Bitto.

"Yes?"

"Can you drive a car?"

"A car?"

"Yes, a car. A thing with four wheels, a steering wheel…."

"I learnt, but since I got my license I've driven only three times, and that was with an instructor."

"Never mind. I'll be waiting for you," said Bitto.

Precisely twenty-three minutes later, Ernesto ran into Bitto Leone's gym. Bitto was sitting on a bench near the ring. Ernesto was surprised by the coach's appearance. He was wearing wide-cut jeans, the kind that had been in vogue twenty years previously, and a light brown fine woollen jacket over a white tee-shirt. His pointed leather shoes, once bright red, were worn in places. His hair was combed, his face clean-shaven, but with a fresh razor cut near his right ear spoiling the effect.

"Signor Coach, you are so smart today!"

"Am I a girl to look smart? Cut the talk; we're late. Let's go!"

Ernesto moved to help Bitto get up from the bench, but Bitto pushed him away.

They went outside to the garage.

"Here is my beauty," Bitto said softly. He opened a canvas cover, beneath which a red Alfa Romeo was hidden. He ran his hand gently over its contours, and tried to smile.

Ernesto gasped, taken aback by the beauty of the car, which was the same age as himself.

"Get behind the wheel," Bitto said. He opened the driver's door.

Ernesto climbed into the seat. He checked the controls…. Most of them seemed familiar.

Bitto got into the passenger seat. "Right, let's go," he said impatiently.

Ernesto turned the key and the old Alfa's engine burst into life.

"Where are we going?" Ernesto asked.

"To Ancona."

Apart from Bitto's instructions, they did not speak on the journey. "Turn right! …In one hundred metres, turn left…."

Two hours later, they reached the Ancona hospital complex. The unpractised Ernesto found parking the vehicle the hardest part of the journey. Bitto was indignant, and grumbled as he got out of the car. Ernesto stayed behind the wheel.

"What? Do you need a special invitation?"

"I thought I'd be waiting for you in the car," Ernesto replied.

"You thought! Get out, now!"

Ernesto got out of the car and followed Bitto to a small, bright building called Casa Sabrina. They entered a pleasant reception area. Bitto motioned Ernesto to one of several soft, white sofas and told him to wait, himself continuing to the front desk. The young woman at the counter smiled at him and made a brief telephone call. A man in a white coat soon appeared to take him further.

Ernesto flipped through some booklets that had been arranged fan-like on a table beside the sofa. The booklets were illustrated with photos of smiling people. All the people seemed infinitely happy. An elderly woman in a wheelchair, a man supporting himself with a crutch, and a girl in a hospital bed were all happy about something. A picture of a family particularly drew Ernesto's attention. He looked at it for a long time: dad, mom and two lovely children, holding hands and looking into the distance with joyful smiles.

Ernesto remembered his own childhood. There were evenings when, as a little boy, he had lain in bed and dreamed that he would fall asleep, and the gentle voice of his mother would wake him. Her gentle hand would caress his head and face. He would get out of bed and run to the kitchen, where his father would be sitting at the table, reading a newspaper. The three of them would have breakfast. Ernesto would tell them of a dream that had frightened him in the night. Mom would kiss him and his father would hug him. Then they would say, "It's time for school," and Ernesto would run to get dressed. At school, friends would be waiting for him.

At lunch-time, they would eat sandwiches their moms had made. At the end of the school day, Dad would come for Ernesto and they would go hand in hand to the beach, where they would play and run into the sea with bare feet. They would be so happy together. Returning home, they would end their day with a family dinner, after which Mom would read Ernesto a fairy tale in which love and goodness overcame evil. Then she would kiss him and say that he was the best boy in the world, and that she and Dad would always love him and would always be there.

"Ernesto!" Bitto's voice commanded a return to reality.

Bitto was pushing an elderly woman in a wheelchair. She was wearing a blue cambric dress and a white sweater. Her thick grey hair was combed smooth. She was staring at the floor.

Ernesto stepped closer. "Good afternoon, Signora," he said loudly. Continuing to stare at the floor, she didn't seem to hear him.

Sighing, Bitto said: "Daniela Leone is my wife."

"Very nice to meet you, Signora Leone. My name is Ernesto Bruno. Your husband trains me." He had intended to say more, but stopped short.

"She hears, Ernesto, but she won't answer you. We are going for a walk." Bitto pushed the wheelchair towards the exit; Ernesto followed.

Outside, the weather was warm but windy. The sun mostly hid behind grey clouds, but sometimes bright rays of warmth peeked out. The trio made their way to an arcade where carved benches stood beneath dense greenery. Bitto stopped by a distant, empty bench.

"Here we are, Dana," said Bitto, parking the wheelchair beside the bench. "This will make you feel good." He arranged a blanket to cover her legs.

Ernesto stood by, not knowing what to do. He couldn't take his eyes off the face of the woman. She must have been very beautiful in her youth, he thought. Her features were beautiful even now: a smooth nose, a well-shaped lip. Only her refusal to interact betrayed her illness.

"Don't stand over her like that," Bitto growled. "Sit down!"

Ernesto obediently sat down on the bench and tried not to look at Signora Leone.

Sitting beside him, Bitto was silent and looked into the distance.

After some minutes, Bitto said: "Dana wasn't always like this. She was the most beautiful girl in school. I liked her from the very first day she joined my class. I was afraid to look at her. I was shy, lost for words. She was always cheerful, and attracted the attention of all the boys. She took part in every school excursion and concert, danced well, and sang beautifully. Her voice was mesmerising. I admired her, feared her, and adored her. I wanted nothing more than that Daniela would pay at least some attention to me.

"I was not good at my lessons, and didn't take part in all the extra activities. I hid in the back row so I could see her without being noticed. Cursing my own timidity and weakness, I watched and dreamed. I secretly followed her home. I knew her schedule by heart and all the places she went. I was her secret admirer and bodyguard.

"So the years passed, and still I didn't dare approach her, to tell her how I felt; until one particular moment that changed my whole life.

"Daniela was at a rehearsal. I was waiting for her in the school yard when three high school students approached me, one of whom was not indifferent to Daniela. He knew that I followed her everywhere. Now he was going to assert his seniority and intimidate me. The guys started bullying me, laughing at me. Unable to stand it, I hit one of them on the nose. Remember, Ernesto, I wasn't boxing then.

"All three then turned on me, raining blows on me from all sides. I lay face down on the ground. And then Daniela appeared, and ran to help me up. Covered in blood, I wanted to escape from her, disappear and never again be seen by her. But she would not let me go. She insisted on taking me to the school nurse, and afterwards walked home with me. After that, we were always together, and I started boxing."

Bitto fell silent. Not knowing what to say at such a moment, Ernesto decided that it was best to say nothing.

Signora Leone sighed loudly. Getting up from the bench, Bitto leaned over and kissed her gently on the forehead. Still, she stared at the floor.

"It's nothing, Dana dear. I'm near. Don't worry." Bitto stroked her motionless hands.

He continued his story: "When we finished school, Dana went to college. I didn't. She studied and worked, I trained. We got married. At first, we rented a small apartment. Dana believed in me. I won fight after fight. She was always there. Sometimes, I was so bludgeoned that for several days afterwards I couldn't get out of bed. She took care of me. I became a professional – made money. We moved to America. It was hard there. It was especially hard for her: she didn't know the language. When I disappeared off to the gym, she had to wait for me all alone in our apartment.

"We were unable to have a child. Daniela suffered greatly over that. At first, she kept everything to herself. Then the tantrums began, and the first attack."

Bitto covered his face with his hands for some moments. Then, scarcely audibly, he continued: "I began to get involved with other women. I was rarely at home. She suffered alone, while I was out having fun. How much I have paid for that. I didn't see her illness. Every day, I lost a little more of the one I loved – not noticing.

"One day, I received a call from St Anne's hospital. They said Dana was with them, in a serious condition. I rushed there. She was drugged, sleeping peacefully. All night, I sat beside her. I asked for forgiveness; I promised that I would always be there; and hoped that what happened that night would never again happen to my Dana. But it happened again. Her condition worsened by the day."

Dana groaned. Bitto bent over to look into her eyes, as if looking for her former self, but she made no further response. The old Dana was deeply hidden – buried – in the woman they had come to visit.

"When she came to," Bitto continued, "she asked me to take her home to Italy. And that's what I did. We got back home. With the money I had left, I bought my own gym and started coaching. Dana felt better in Italy, but not for long. One evening, I came home from work and she was not there. I searched all over the city, not finding her. The next day, the police called and said that they had her. She had grabbed a baby from a woman walking along the promenade. When the police caught up with Dana, she screamed that she would not give up the baby, because they would kill her. My beloved wife has been living here ever since. I visit every week. For more than ten years, my Dana has not acknowledged me – but I'm with her."

Ernesto looked with horror at his mentor, the man who had seemed to him an indestructible wall, now revealed as a wretchedly unfortunate husband.

"Well, Ernesto," Bitto said quietly. "I didn't bring you here and tell you this story to make you feel sorry for me. I wanted to ask you…."

"Of course, Coach. I'm ready to do anything for you."

"Look, Ernesto," Bitto pointed to the grass, "I'm like that dry leaf. The wind of fate is throwing me in all directions, and I can no longer resist. Once I was healthy, full of strength, and believed that I would remain so forever. But now my body will not obey me. Do you see what's wrong with me?" He showed Ernesto his shaking hands. "I have forgotten the taste of food, lost my voice, can't sleep at night. I can't even drink a glass of water without spilling it on myself. And it can't be stopped. I have Parkinson's disease."

"Parkinson's? So this is...."

"Yes, Ernesto," Bitto interrupted. "The disease is incurable, and over time it will get worse."

Ernesto looked at him sadly.

"I want to ask you," Bitto continued, "when I get worse ... only then ... bring me here – to her."

"Yes, Coach, I'll bring you."

"And one more thing." Bitto took some papers from the inside pocket of his jacket and handed them to Ernesto. "This is a power of attorney from me in your name, to manage my accounts and ... the right to the gym."

"Aw, come on. What are you saying? Why?" Ernesto stood up, the better to turn and face Bitto.

"Calm down, Ernesto. Sit down." Bitto waved Ernesto back to his seat. "I'll explain to you later what to do with these papers. You see, Dana and I have no one: no children, no relatives, and I have become attached to you, as to a son. I want you to take care of us." Bitto looked at Ernesto, who took his hand.

"Yes, Coach. I'll do everything."

"That's good," said Bitto. His gaze slid off into the distance.

They sat in silence for a while. Everything had been said. Intermittent sharp gusts of wind rustled the trees; more dry leaves fell to the ground.

15. YOU WILL BE MINE

Love is a great feeling that can empower a person, fill the heart with joy, and at the same time poison with doubt, bitterness and pain. Do we know what this feeling will do to us? The lucky ones are those who find a quiet haven in the arms of a loved one and remain forever in complete serenity. Deeply unhappy are those who have made their way through violent winds and sharp rocks, but never found their love, their harbour. No, it has perished in the vast expanses of a cruel, cold world. No more screams or moans are heard, the bitter tears of disappointment are not seen behind the wall of selfishness, cynicism and vulgarity.

Calisto Conte longed for Mirella. He had broken the hearts of gullible girls many times, but he could not master the one he loved. Despite her youth, Mirella was a wise young woman. She was aware of the power of her beauty, which she had inherited along with the blood of her vicious father. But she distrusted men; that she had absorbed in the womb. Mirella revelled in her power over the young Conte. She felt great sympathy for him, almost love, but her calculating mind commanded that she should play with his feelings.. Her goal was to become the young Signora Conte. And, following Patricia's instructions, she understood that her main, perhaps her only, asset was her virginity. She could not, and did not want, to sacrifice that to lust, or even love.

Oh, how skilfully Mirella played her game. She teased Calisto: she displayed her charms, covering them with the thin fabric of a light dress; gave him alluring eyes full of sweet promises; allowed him to enjoy the heady aroma of her delicious hair and even hot kisses.

At first, Calisto was amused by this game. He admired Mirella's mind, said that she was the most worthy of all the girls he knew. But as the game went on, the languor became painful; became an unbearable torture. He was easily irritated; he would return home gloomy, silent, and dissatisfied. His handsome face carried a smile less and less often. Patricia noticed the change in her son. She asked him what was the matter, but he dissembled, telling her of some troubles at the university. She didn't want to be overprotective, so thought it would be best for him to solve his problems himself, and did not persist.

Alberto, on the other hand, had lately been too busy with his own anxieties, so had not noticed the change in his beloved boy. Sensing from his father's nervousness and irritability that something was going on, Calisto tried to avoid him. He heard Alberto's strange cries at night, noticed the insane fury that sparkled in his eyes, but preferred not to know the cause. He knew of Alberto's secret life, but did not condemn him for that, and did not think about what it meant for his mother.

The only person with whom Calisto willingly shared his thoughts and experiences was Giacomo Pelagatti. It seemed to Calisto that Giacomo, despite his oddities, loved him with true friendship, or at least respected him as his closest comrade. Foolish Calisto! You'd do better to trust the first passer-by you happen to meet. Asking for advice from someone who himself loved Mirella made no sense.

Calisto asked Giacomo to help him influence Mirella in his favour. His plan was that, as if by chance, Giacomo should go to the coffee shop on the university campus where Mirella had breakfast each morning and start a conversation with her. It would be necessary for Giacomo to go each day until Calisto's goal was achieved.

Calisto allocated a budget for this "covert operation," enough money for a hearty lunch and even a glorious dinner, as well as breakfast. A rich young man in love had no reason to skimp on the details when his fate was at stake.

Rejoicing at the unexpected opportunity to get closer to Mirella, whom he loved no less passionately than Calisto, Giacomo gladly accepted the money and the conditions of the "operation" with pretended indifference, as if rendering a friendly service. In truth, he too was experiencing an agonizing, irresistible desire to possess Mirella, and hoped to win this game. He believed that he was the more worthy to be near Mirella, and was confident of victory. He began to despise Calisto as a minion of fate.

Giacomo arrived early at the coffee shop that Calisto had said Mirella favoured. He settled down to work on an article for a travel blog. After some time, the door opened and Mirella walked in. Looking up, he feigned the most sincere surprise.

"Giacomo," Mirella exclaimed happily, walking over to his table. "What a surprise, and how nice to see you. Why are you here?"

"Mimi! I didn't expect to see you here. I came here to drink coffee and to finish an article."

"But why here, on our campus?"

"Mmm…." Giacomo hesitated for some moments, then said unsteadily: "I came to see Professor Totti."

Mirella looked at him attentively.

"Professor Totti? That's a new name for me. Which department is he from?"

"From the Department of Linguistics," Giacomo answered quickly, at the same time realising that he was entangling himself in a lie. "He works here part-time, as a Consulting Professor. He comes from Milan. I'm taking lessons from him."

"Interesting," Mirella said thoughtfully. "This is the first time I've heard any of this."

"Yes, it's a new program to exchange experience between teachers. Not official yet, you understand," Giacomo said with a significant wink. "How are you doing?" He was keen to change the subject.

"Wonderful," Mirella replied, with a good-natured smile.

Giacomo took a close look at Mirella: a blue hoodie, tight jeans that emphasized her slender legs, and white sneakers. She stood close to him and the sweet smell of her perfume made him dizzy. Confronted with the beauty of this extraordinary girl, he felt utterly powerless.

"I'd be glad if you would keep me company," he said, pulling out a chair to reinforce his invitation.

"Won't I bother you?" she asked, looking at his open laptop on the table.

"Oh, I can finish that later." Giacomo quickly closed the computer. "Right now, let me treat you to breakfast."

"I'll be happy to have breakfast with you, but I can pay for myself," Mirella said, waving to the waitress.

Many other young men would have accepted it if a modern girl wanted to pay for herself, but not Giacomo. He felt Mirella's refusal as a personal insult. He pressed his lips tightly together, his eyes clouded over, spots rose on his face. He remembered the day he felt shame and disgrace in the restaurant where his father worked as a waiter. Clearly, Mirella perceived him as the son of a pathetic waiter, a mere shadow of the incomparable Calisto Conte.

As this storm of emotions boiled deep inside Giacomo, Mirella, with a carefree smile, gave her usual morning order to the young waitress.

Then she turned to Giacomo and said enthusiastically: "It's good that you are here. It can be lonely being here alone, especially on days when the weather is cloudy and windy. I don't like wind and damp."

Spellbound, Giacomo stared at her as she gazed out of the window.

"It's as if nature is sad about something," Mirella continued thoughtfully. "It makes me sad too. When I was little, I thought that when it was grey and rainy outside, somewhere in the world someone's soul had passed into eternity. The soul is good and bright, and nature is sad for her passing. What do you think?" She turned to look at Giacomo.

He quickly looked away from her face. "I don't think nature cares about us. It's just a process. I don't look for hidden meaning where there is none."

"Maybe you are right, but I still feel sad. I like to think that when I'm gone, it will rain."

"Well, it will, for sure." Giacomo laughed. "If suddenly you were gone," he continued more seriously, "then I myself would cause the most severe downpour that can be."

Mirella looked into his excited face; his jokes were good.

Giacomo went each morning to the coffee house where Mirella had breakfast. He looked forward to their meetings. He tried not to think about Calisto, but Mirella herself often made him a topic of their conversation. For Giacomo, that was the moment when the magic of their meetings dissipated. He had to give stupid advice to Mirella, read their correspondence, and even help choose gifts for his rival. More than ever, that reinforced his feeling of insignificance. But Mirella did not notice, and believed in the sincerity of Giacomo's friendship with Calisto.

One day, she asked, "If a man swears his love to a woman, not wanting to marry her, then what are his confessions worth? I don't believe in love without commitment."

"Don't you think," argued Giacomo, "that your views are like old prejudices? I would say medieval."

"Why?" Mirella objected. "If a girl does not want to give herself to a man before marriage, why immediately speak of the Middle Ages?"

"Because no one lives like that anymore. People meet, feel sympathy, try out if they are suitable for each other, even live together, and then get married."

"Try out! How very significant that you, a man, should use those words. 'Trying out' is mostly done by men. How many such 'trials' will a girl have before finally becoming a wife?"

"Mimi, I wasn't talking about that at all." Giacomo laughed.

"No?"

"No, I wasn't even thinking about you," Giacomo objected. "I was just making a general observation."

"So let Calisto try someone, but not me. I have my terms," Mirella said, folding her hands across her chest and pouting her plump lips.

She's playing, thought Giacomo. He said aloud: "Maybe we should change the subject."

Giacomo became more and more attached to Mirella, whilst Calisto became more and more annoyed. He called Giacomo every day and demanded a detailed account of that day's conversation with Mirella. He even asked Giacomo to record each new conversation on his phone. Indignant, Giacomo said that he would not do such a humiliating thing. Calisto hung up, called back a few minutes later, apologised, and asked Giacomo to continue the "covert operation." He was still hoping for a positive result.

Giacomo, thinking of Mirella's views on marriage, suddenly decided on a desperate step. The next morning, he went to meet Mirella wearing a smart shirt and jacket, and carrying a huge bouquet of white roses. In his jacket pocket was a small box, and inside the box was the ring that his father had given to his mother on the day she accepted his proposal of marriage.

When Giacomo arrived at the coffee shop, Mirella was sitting at their usual table and the waitress had already brought her coffee. Giacomo straight away went down on one knee in front of her and said: "Mirella Esposito, I have loved you since the day I first saw you. I don't want to 'try' you. I know that you are the best girl in the world. I want to live with you all my life. Mimi, dear, I ask you to marry me."

The waitress clapped her hands. Mirella dropped the spoon with which she was stirring her coffee. A vague smile fixed itself on her face; an expression of her utter bewilderment. A string of the most unexpected thoughts flashed through her mind, but none of them were that she should agree to marry him.

"Giacomo, my dear Giacomo," she blurted out, standing to lift the unfortunate man from his knee. "Giacomo, my friend…."

Giacomo, as if struck by lightning, froze in place. In his unfortunate heart, something seemed to break, explode, and disappear. He understood everything. But he wanted to hear her refusal. He needed to.

Gathering all the strength of his will, he repeated with desperate determination: "Do you agree to be my wife?" He stared sternly into Mirella's eyes.

"I … I can't," she murmured.

"Thank you," Giacomo said softly, placing the bouquet of flowers in front of her. She looked at him, not knowing what to do.

He grinned at something, silently turned around, and with a confident step made for the door.

Mirella recovered herself just enough to call after him: "What about Calisto?"

Giacomo paused, turned to look back at her, and sneered: "Don't worry about Calisto! He will never find out!"

With that, he kicked the door open and was gone.

On the street, he telephoned Calisto, and when Calisto answered said angrily: "She won't be yours!"

"Why not?"

"Because for that you will have to bring her to your house and make her Signora Conte!"

16. LIVE, FÉDE!

A luminous haze looms out of the thick darkness. It comes closer; now very close, the light becomes blinding. Féde covers her face with her hands. She hears the clatter of hooves and a loud neighing. She opens her eyes and sees the dazzling radiance and extraordinary beauty of a snow-white unicorn. Spellbound, she reaches out to touch him, but he rears up and neighs, shaking his silvery mane. Féde shrinks back, fearing the unicorn's powerful hooves will crush her. But the mythical beast turns around, raises a sparkling cloud of magical dust, and retreats back to the darkness. Féde runs after him, stretching her arms towards the magic light, but the unicorn easily outpaces her.

She awoke, her heart thumping. Listening to the beat, like the drumming of hooves, she tried to remember the indistinct images of a dream that was already gone forever.

Every night, the fantasies of her dreams took her to a world where she was different, where the love that dwelt within her was still carefree and strong, not poisoned by betrayal and disappointment. By day, she hid her feelings in a back corner of the far room of her consciousness, keeping that room securely locked. But although feelings can be hidden, locked away, any love that still lives radiates warmth and light. As soon as she closed her eyes each night, the most unquenchable part of her soul took the key and pushed open that cherished door. In the deep quiet of each night, she could again enjoy her lost happiness.

When morning came, cold reality insisted that those beautiful visions, where love still bloomed, were no more than dreams; just dreams.

Féde, move on from what is past. Set aside the lingering glimmer of that old love. The hope you hold on to is as unreal as your dreams. Live! Rejoice! Your world has changed. Joy and contentment await you.

But the only future Féde could foresee was painful, lonely, scary. What to do? How to live on? The questions were unanswerable, it seemed. Even so, a flicker of hope persisted: What if, when he finds out, he wants to be with her? Perhaps it's not too late. Perhaps all three might yet be happy together.

"Hello!" Féde heard Calisto's voice on her telephone.

"Hello, Calisto," Féde said, timidly.

"Hi, Féde."

"We need to talk."

"What about?"

"Not on the phone. Can we meet today?"

"Today?" Calisto drawled. "Maybe another day?"

"No, today! Can't I count on at least one meeting?"

"Okay, don't boil over, I'll come."

"No. I'll come myself. Tell me where."

"Porto?"

"No, too crowded. Our conversation will be serious."

"What, are you going to kill me?"

"I'll think about it," Féde answered with a laugh. "No, seriously, let's talk in private."

"I'm intrigued! Come to the car park at the port at seven."

Féde walked through the city towards the father of her unborn child. Trembling with excitement and fear, she recalled his cold, cruel silence in recent months. What if he refuses her? Doesn't even want to listen. What if he doesn't believe her? Such thoughts made her heart shrink.

Calisto was waiting for her as arranged. On seeing Féde, he got out of his car, taking his time and giving her an indifferent look.

"Hello, honey," he said, with a forced smile.

"Hi," Féde replied. She offered her lips to him, but he turned his cheek. She shuddered, embarrassed and confused.

"So, what's this all about?" Calisto asked with obvious mockery, looking around.

"I wanted to talk to you," Féde said softly, her voice trembling.

"Okay, speak."

"I…," Féde hesitated. "How are you?"

"I'm fine," Calisto replied, reluctantly. The conversation had hardly begun, but already it was tiring him.

"I want you to know that I don't resent…." she began. "I'm sure you had your own reasons…. I forgive you everything." Féde tried to hide her excitement. She wanted to smile, but she could not. Her voice trembled.

Calisto looked at her pale face. She had dark circles under her eyes, swollen eyelids, parched lips. His mind conjured up an image of Mimi: so beautiful, by contrast.

"It's good that you forgive me for everything," he said cheerfully. "If that's all, then, I'll go."

"No, that's not all," Féde said softly. Her eyes filled with tears.

"Why are you crying?" He knew that tears would be followed by accusations, reproaches and sobs.

"I'm expecting a baby!"

"What?"

"I'm pregnant."

Calisto's self-confidence suddenly deserted him. "Are you sure?"

"Yes!" Féde said, happily.

Calisto tried to remember exactly when they had their last date, but he could not. Then another thought struck him:

"Congratulations!" he said, laughing nervously. "Who is the father?"

Féde reacted as if she had been slapped on the face. "The father is you!" she almost screamed.

"Hang on a minute, Féde. Take it easy. Remember who else you've been with."

It was a knife, plunged right into Féde's heart. Just a few months ago, this man had been the most tender person in the world. Now he had made himself disgusting to her; everything about him sickened her.

"Only with you," she replied coldly. "I have only been with you, and it's your baby, Calisto Conte." Her eyes sparkled with a fire which he had never before seen in sweet, quiet, timid Féde.

"Ah, forget it! It doesn't concern you anymore!" she said. She examined Calisto defiantly. She wanted to remember him just as he was at this moment: with that stupid, frightened look on his face; his crumpled tee-shirt; stains on the toes of his red suede moccasins. She would no longer deceive herself about him; not dream; not cry about someone who – in truth – had never existed.

"Goodbye," she whispered. She turned and began to walk quickly away.

"Féde!"

She stopped. Foolish hope flickered for one last time.

"If you need anything," Calisto said, "a reliable doctor ... or money for ... well, you know ... tell me, I will give it to you."

Féde was gone. She wanted to run, hide, disappear. After she rounded the corner of the house, where Calisto could not see her, she leaned against the wall, covered her face with her hands, and sobbed convulsively.

A passing woman stopped to ask her what was the matter. Did she need help? For Féde, the questions seemed to come from a swirling fog. She tried to smile, said thank you, no help was needed, and wandered on.

She had no plan on where to go or what to do. All her thoughts were hopelessly jumbled. She trembled: her legs were so weak she could not walk straight.

She staggered so close to the road that her hair was blown by the draught of passing cars. The drivers honked loudly, but the noise they made scarcely penetrated the heavy thoughts racing through her mind. It was going to be impossible to look her parents in the eye; impossible to tell them the truth; impossible to continue to live.

With that, a new and unexpected thought dawned. It was so simple and clear. Why hadn't she thought of that before? One movement … and the end of her suffering. One moment … no more decisions … freedom!

Did Féde consider her parents? Yes; this would be the only way to cleanse the shame from their family.

Did she think of the pain and suffering she would inflict on her loved ones? No, she did not think about that; her own pain and suffering at this moment was stronger.

Did she think about punishment from above? No, she didn't think about that either. Can there be worse torment than she was experiencing now?

She made up her mind. Now she had only to overcome her fear of the last step.

But now something else: it seemed to her that, among the headlights of the passing cars, she could see ahead, near the road, the silhouette of a snow-white unicorn. He shook his silvery mane, looked at her, and disappeared. Féde smiled sadly. "See you soon," she thought, took a deep breath, closed her eyes and stepped forward.…

A strong kick to the side knocked her to the pavement.

When she opened her eyes, cars were still passing on their way, as before.… "Féde, Féde.…" came the voice of Ernesto.

He helped her up. One thing was certain: she had not expected to see him.

"Ernesto, what are you doing here?"

"I was walking home from training. I saw you standing near the road – too near. I waved my hand, but you didn't see. I came over. Your eyes were closed, your foot was already off the pavement. If I had not come then, in a moment you would have been lying on the road under the wheels. Are you unwell? What is it?"

"Whatever is wrong with me is none of your business," Féde snapped.

"I'm human too," Ernesto countered.

Féde was surprised. She had not expected Ernesto to persist in that way.

"If it's gratitude you want, don't bother to wait," she said. "Nobody asked you to interfere."

She turned and walked away from him.

Ernesto turned in the same direction and walked beside her.

"Are you going to follow me now?" Féde was indignant.

"No, I'm taking you to the Chalet Martina. That's where I'm going."

"Well try this," Féde shouted, and ran towards the sea.

Ernesto ran after her. Whatever was wrong with her, he knew it would be dangerous to leave her.

Féde ran along the beach past restaurants, loud shouts, children's laughter…. All these echoes of other people's lives increased her anguish.

Ernesto continued after her. "Féde, wait," he shouted.

"Leave me alone!" Féde shouted back, but stopped.

"What happened to you?" Ernesto pleaded, with the greatest sympathy and concern.

"What happened to me?" Féde replied venomously. "Here's what you want to know. I'm pregnant by a scoundrel who doesn't want me or my baby. I don't want the baby either. And I don't want to live any more."

She stepped closer to the astonished Ernesto. "Now you can understand what's wrong with me," she finished. She made as if to run again, but immediately stopped, and sank down on the sand. She then sat motionless, as if frozen, head down.

Ernesto did not dare to approach her. He stood not far from Féde, watching her and thinking about what he had heard. Ernesto felt awkward, sad, and vexed. All these feelings mixed in his soul. He watched and waited perplexed, looking from the sand to the sea, and back to Féde.

Minutes passed. Féde raised her head and stood up. She walked calmly to the sea, scooped up some water with her hands and splashed it on her face. Then she turned to Ernesto and said quietly: "Come, please."

Ernesto immediately did as she asked. Féde smiled and sat down on the sand. Ernesto sat down beside her.

"I'm sorry I was rude to you," she began. "Today was a most awful day … the worst day."

"I understand."

"Really?"

"I understand that whoever it was has hurt you terribly," said Ernesto. He thought it best to then keep silent.

Féde looked at the water as it splashed her feet. After she had turned over Ernesto's words in her mind for a while, she said: "Yes, he hurt me terribly."

"And you are expecting his child."

"Yes."

"And you don't want to … live. Is that why you stepped out on the road there, at the crossroads?"

"Yes," Féde answered quietly.

"But that's wrong!" Ernesto exclaimed. "You shouldn't have done that, Féde. Life is given to us to live! Sometimes we have to fight to move forward, while we are still awake, while we are still breathing, while we live. And you too must do that."

"But what if it's hard, too hard? Too hard to breathe? Unbearable? What then?" cried Féde. Her eyes flashed, again wet with tears.

"Live! Still live, no matter what."

"For what?"

"For the sake of life itself. After all, it is a gift from above," he said quietly, and looked at the sky. "We cannot, we must not give it up."

Féde looked at Ernesto: such a strange fellow to have spoken the truth. Everyone has such a person in their soul; you just need to look inside yourself, hear the voice that speaks the truth. And if you listen to that voice, you will find happiness, peace of mind: everything will become clear and understandable, light and easy. You will raise your eyes to the sky: sunbeams will break through the clouds. Here is one, and another, and another: a multitude of rays will illuminate the tops of the mountains, the valleys, the forests, the sea, and the faces of humanity with their brilliance. Your heart will fill with joy; you will understand that you are not alone in this world: that there is an invisible, strong hand that will lead you, will not let you fall, will take care of you. You just need to believe, to trust – and there will be no more fear, no more suffering.

Féde dipped her feet in the water, frightening away a shoal of tiny silver fish. The wind gently ruffled her hair. Overhead, a seagull cried. Féde wiped away her tears and smiled. This extraordinary world had returned to her: she could still see, hear, and feel it. Her fear was gone; she no longer despaired. She was ready to confront all difficulties, with faith and a renewed love of life.

"Ernesto, can I ask you one thing?"

"Yes, sure."

"Keep what you saw today as something that remains only between us."

"Yes, I understand that."

"Thank you. And one thing more…." She took Ernesto's hand: "I'm sorry for the unkind, stupid things I said to you."

Ernesto smiled at her, and she smiled back as he said he understood that too, and that forgiving and forgetting all of that would be no problem.

"And thank you," she continued, taking his hand and squeezing it, "for saving me from death."

They embraced.

"I want my child," Féde said with new confidence. "Do you think, Ernesto, I will be a good mother?"

"Most certainly, you will be the best mother."

"And you are the most unusual godfather." Féde laughed and ruffled his hair.

Ernesto kept Féde's secret. But everything was revealed when, a few weeks later, Féde lost the child. She woke in the middle of the night in excruciating pain. Martina and Adriano took their daughter to the hospital, where everything possible was done, but the child could not be saved.

A great sadness settled on the Marino family. So friendly and happy a few days ago; now a deep abyss had settled between them. Avoiding one another, each hid in their own corner, struggling with pain and despair.

Féde lay in bed, staring out of the window. She refused to eat, and avoided talking to anyone. She blamed herself for the loss of her child.

Martina wandered along the seashore, reproaching herself for excessive severity, harshness and inattention to her eldest daughter. That had not protected her, had not saved her.

Adriano started drinking. With the company only of a bottle, he sat for many hours, unable to believe that his affectionate, beloved daughter had fallen into so much suffering. It was so wrong. Surely he could have prevented all this, helped his daughter, warned her; but he had not.

Ernesto felt himself tossed into the chasm between Féde, Martina and Adriano. He puzzled over how to return them to their former unity, peace and happiness. He lost weight, and even missed workouts. But he did not lose hope.

Late one evening, with all visitors to the Chalet Martina gone, the courtyard was empty but for Adriano sitting alone at a table. He poured whisky into a glass, drank it down in one draught, poured another, and knocked that back too. Ernesto walked up and took the bottle from the table.

"That doesn't help, Ernesto," Adriano said, reaching for the bottle. Ernesto did not yield. Instead, he emptied on the floor what was left in the bottle.

Adriano snorted, got up from his chair, and swayed unsteadily over the short distance to the bar. He began turning over empty bottles, opening cupboard doors, pulling out drawers.

"Martina, the snake, has hidden everything from me. As if I … Eh!.. Nobody here understands me," grumbled Adriano. "Of course, I'm just the cook here. 'Adriano, come here! Adriano, come on! Adriano….'"

Adriano stopped to examine Ernesto's face as if through a thick mist. "You came to find me, Ernesto," he said, laughing drunkenly. "I'm … I'll … find something to drink and join you. Now…."

Adriano opened the cupboard beneath the sink and climbed into it with his whole bulky body. "Here she is. Hee, hee!"

Groaning and swearing, Adriano extracted himself from the cupboard, holding a bottle of rum in one hand, whilst using the other to hold on to the edge of the sink to pull himself out. Lurching and swaying, he returned to the table.

"Now I will tell you a sad story, Ernesto," Adriano said, pouring himself a full glass of rum. Ernesto wanted to stop him, but Adriano pushed his hand away and said in a slurred voice: "No! I need it. You understand?"

He took a long drink, wiped his mouth with his jacket sleeve, and looked intently into Ernesto's eyes.

"And now, my boy, Adriano will tell you something about his life. I confess to you that I myself was a scoundrel. Yes, a scoundrel. Listen carefully."

He drank more rum. "When Martina told me that she was expecting a child from me, I got scared and ran away from her. Yes, I did. And no matter how good a father I become to my children, I will never forgive myself for that. I ran away, like a coward, to Milan, to work as a chef in a restaurant. But Martina decided that she would keep the child. This is what my Martina is all about. She didn't call, she didn't write … she did nothing to remind me of herself and our child."

Another drink. "Disgraced, abandoned, she carried our child. And one dark and windy night, I woke up and saw Martina, all in white. Everything … everything glowing white. This light made a chill run right through my body. I stretched out my hand to her. She shook her head and left. Suddenly, that hurt so much.

"The next morning, I ran to her. I left everything: Milan, the restaurant, my precious patronage, all the women who loved me. I threw it all away … and ran to my darling Martina. All the way, I thought of what I would say. I decided I would crawl on my knees in front of her until she forgave me, a traitor. But I didn't have to grovel at her feet for long. When I came to her, she looked at me as if her whole soul had turned inside out, and she said: 'Think carefully, Adriano. If you return, then you are mine forever!'

"Without hesitation, I kissed her hands and said: 'Martina, my Martina, my soul, I am ready to do everything for you. I will love you. I will love our child. I will be the best father. You make me so happy.'

"I hugged her, and kissed her stomach. I wanted our child to know that the shepherd had returned to the fold."

Adriano looked at Ernesto as if looking through him. There were tears in his drunken eyes. He smiled, but suddenly the smile vanished and he said through his teeth: "But I suffered my well-deserved punishment for betrayal and cowardice. Our son died. He died in my arms. We buried our angel, and part of me was buried that day … most of me."

"On my knees," he continued, "day and night, I begged God for forgiveness. I prayed that He would forgive me my sin, so that Martina would not be punished, and would not remain childless. I will bear punishment all my life, I prayed, if only my Martina can be blessed with a baby. And the Merciful Lord heard me. He gave us Federica, my poor Féde! Now she suffers, for *my* sin.

"You see, Ernesto? I have now experienced all the bitterness of what I myself did twenty years ago. So don't you tell me not to drink! I can't bear this pain.… I don't want to remember.… I don't want to feel anything, … so I drink."

He poured himself yet another full glass of rum. Ernesto snatched it from his hands and threw it to the floor. The glass shattered. Having stared at the fragments for some moments, Adriano burst into a wild, desperate laugh.

And then the door opened and Martina appeared. She walked up to the table, snatched the bottle and sent it after the glass. She took Adriano firmly by the hand and said: "Stop torturing yourself! It won't help. You atoned for your guilt. We lost one child twenty years ago. We must not now lose another!"

Tears streamed down Martina's cheeks. "Let's go, Adriano – home! She needs us. Our daughter needs us." She hugged her husband. As the couple united in their love and pain, fear and despair retreated.

So Adriano and Martina went home to their children; determined never to part again; resolved to endure this test – and, whatever might lie ahead for them – together.

17. THE REAL SIGNOR CONTE

Alberto and Patricia Conte were going to a charity dinner marking the opening of a hospital department for patients with leukaemia. Alberto had donated a significant amount of money to the cause.

He loved such events, not for a high, noble goal such as saving lives, but for the moment of glory for himself. Doctors, officials and journalists praised him for his mercy, humanity and generosity. In truth, he did possess the small degree of self-awareness necessary to be secretly amused by the paradox that such a vicious person as he was could be hailed as a benefactor of mankind, someone who helped people, and gave them hope. Whenever he went on a stage to be thanked and applauded, he felt a surge of pride. He kissed small children, hugged women, and shook hands with men who had found a new life without pain and torment. His dark soul rejoiced.

He put on a tuxedo made for him by famous designers. Usually, he looked long in the mirror, admiring himself, but not tonight. Tonight, he looked in the mirror only involuntarily – seeing a pale, aged face with inflamed eyes; a face in which arrogance and complacency had been replaced by fear and suffering.

He waited for Patricia in his office. He sat at the table and for the hundredth time leafed through the same small collection of books, looking at the pictures of brutal executions. He peered into the faces of people condemned to a terrible death. His mouth dried up from the fear that settled in his soul and made him think about retribution, about torments which he might yet have to endure.

For many years, he had lived with confidence in his impunity. But meeting the son of Omar, whom he had killed, made him think, and he realised that there was something – some kind of force – that did not depend on him, that was not subject to his mind. That thought tormented him dreadfully. Nightmares and terrible visions haunted him: ugly faces lay in wait for him, hid in dark corners, between trees in the twilight; their bleached eyes effervescing with hellish brilliance. Ominous laughter seemed bent on driving him crazy.

His fear surprised and ashamed him, but he could not overcome it.

"Are you coming, Alberto?" Patricia asked, standing in the office doorway.

He raised his eyes and stared at her. She was still beautiful. A long dress of grey silk emphasized the slenderness of her figure and the whiteness of her skin. Her thick, dark hair was tied up high and adorned with a golden tiara fashioned as a branch of delicate leaves studded with diamonds.

"Yes, yes," said Alberto, "I'm coming."

"You'll miss your favourite part of the evening if we're late," Patricia teased him.

"I've been looking at the Iron Maiden.[30] The unfortunate people who were hit by her spikes must have been praying for a quick death. How amazing it is that someone should want their death to come as soon as possible."

"Yes, of course, it whets the appetite." Patricia's tone was harder now, getting beyond teasing. "You stay with your tortures; I can go alone."

....

[30] An iron cabinet, the inside of which is lined with long, sharp spikes.

ANASTASIIA MARSIZ

Alberto gave her an angry look. It seemed she knew about the tortures in his soul and had taken the opportunity to stick in another spike. She hates me, he thought.

"I'm coming too. You must wait. You're not going anywhere without me, Patricia Conte. Get out and close the door!"

Patricia left, not at all displeased that she had succeeded in irritating Alberto.

Very soon, the door opened again.

"I told you … get away!" yelled Alberto, expecting to see his wife. But it was Calisto who stood in the doorway.

Calisto's eyes betrayed the sudden fright he felt, but he stuck to his intended approach and, with a tentative smile, said in a low voice: "Dad, it's me … I wanted to talk to you."

"Ah, Calisto," Alberto replied, much calmer now. "Your mother and I are just about to leave for the city. We can talk later."

Alberto looked carefully at his son. "I assume that our conversation will be about a matter of importance?"

"Yes, Dad. How is it that you know everything – and understand everything?" Again, he accompanied his words with a smile.

Alberto stood up and hugged his son, and again his distracted mind turned things upside down: how awful it would be not to hear the voice, not to see the face, and not to smell the hair of the person dearest to his heart. He was again seized by fear, vague, undefined, but nonetheless very real. A nervous trembling ran through his body, a cold sweat broke out on his forehead. For once, though, something was different: the fear was not for himself.

"Son, we'll talk it all through. Wait for me at home." Alberto kissed Calisto's forehead.

"Okay, Dad."

"Everything's good then," the elder Conte said, making for the door. But then he stopped, turned to his son and said, very seriously: "Calisto, take care of yourself."

"Dad, I will, of course!" Yet again, Calisto smiled for his father.

Alberto nodded and left the office.

The Contes were half an hour late for the dinner. All the other guests were already seated at their tables, music was playing, barely heard above the hum of chatter and laughter. The waiters fussed around, carrying food and drink to the tables. The organisers checked their watches. Why was it that important guests were always late? When Alberto and Patricia appeared at the entrance, several men in tuxedos rushed to greet them, shook Alberto's hand warmly, complimented Signora Conte on her dress and good looks, and led the couple to a table where officials, bankers and judges were already assembled, together with their magnificently adorned ladies.

Patricia greeted the men, exchanged friendly kisses with the women, responded graciously to compliments and courtesies, and took her place at the table. Alberto, meanwhile, was hurried to the stage.

As he climbed the half-dozen steps to the stage, Alberto noticed a particular person in the hall – a tall, dark, young man, dressed as a waiter. The man grinned and disappeared behind a pillar. Alberto's face instantly turned pale, his hands trembled, and his mouth dried up.

"Signor Conte, please step forward." The chief organiser of the evening urged him to take a position centre-stage.

"Yes," said Alberto, bewildered, "Let's get started." He moved to sit on the chair that had been reserved for him. From his place he searched the hall for the man he was sure he had seen, but who had now disappeared.

"Good evening, ladies and gentlemen," a man in a tight tuxedo began. Stammering and wiping sweat from his forehead, he went on to thank the owner of the hotel for providing the room, and the chef for his gourmet dishes. Then he pronounced, with excessive feeling, the names of all the benefactors who, with their good deeds and generous donations, had enabled the realisation of this wonderful project. The benefactors, to an explosion of enthusiastic applause, rose from their seats and smiled broadly, nodding their heads.

A picture show followed, so that all could see the splendid new wards, laboratory and operating theatre.

Even from where she sat, Patricia had been able to see the sharp change in Alberto's demeanour. She followed his gaze, but could not see anything unusual. Looking at him intently, she tried to attract his attention.

A strange – but perhaps not so unusual – feature of the Conte marriage was that whenever they were seen in public, Alberto and Patricia Conte presented themselves as caring and loving spouses. When they walked together, they held hands, gently looking into each other's eyes. With every step, Alberto admired his beautiful wife, and Patricia responded with repeated looks of deep affection. Everyone could see that the Contes were deeply in love, and an example for all of an ideal partnership. However, as in a well-known fairy tale, the magic disappeared as soon as they left an event, even if the clock was not at that moment striking midnight.

"And now I am glad to introduce you to a person who has made a particularly valuable contribution to our common cause. Thanks especially to him, our dreams have become a reality. Let us welcome our esteemed Signor Alberto Conte!"

This announcement was greeted with generous applause.

Just at that moment, though, Alberto saw the tall, dark waiter look out from behind a column. He did not clap, as everyone else did, but shot a venomous glare straight into Alberto's face. Alberto was struck with such fear that he became breathless. Dizziness followed; his sweat soaked his shirt. Worst of all, he could not take his eyes off the face that pinioned him with its clear knowledge of the evil within him.

"Signor Conte." The organiser held out a microphone. Alberto took it with a trembling hand. There was silence in the hall as everyone prepared to listen, smile and clap. Everyone, that is, except Patricia, who could see the gravity of her husband's situation, even though she could not see the cause.

Alberto looked around the hall, looked at Patricia, and again at the dark waiter by the column. Many of the assembled guests exchanged glances, some murmured. Someone even grinned.

Trying to conceal his growing alarm, the organiser looked questioningly at Alberto. "Signor Conte…?"

"I…," Alberto began, in a hoarse, strangled voice. "I'm glad … I mean…."

Alberto fell silent. He looked again at the waiter with the terrifying glare. The hall was waiting. Patricia had a strange, wry smile on her face.

"Cursed freak!" Alberto suddenly yelled. He dropped the microphone and rushed headlong down the steps from the stage and across the hall to where the tall dark waiter was standing. To Patricia's horror, and the surprise of all present, he grabbed the waiter by the throat.

"So you followed me here, you Jamaican rat! You want to destroy me, but you won't!" Alberto laughed demonically, and in front of all the esteemed guests, twisted the throat of the unfortunate, frightened waiter, who, apart from his dark skin, had very little resemblance to Alberto's mother's Jamaican lover.

Patricia rushed to her husband and, seizing his sleeve, shouted: "Alberto, let him go! You will strangle him!"

Alberto turned to her and hissed: "That's what I want to do – kill him! Crush him, like a bug!"

"Come to your senses, Alberto," Patricia pleaded.

Her strength to endure this vile person, to remain silent, to hide her hatred for him, was just about gone. Only her shame in front of all the people who were witnessing this madness was stronger than her hatred of Alberto.

Mustering all her strength, she threw her whole body against Alberto, but he pushed her back with such force she fell to the floor.

Finally, the hotel security guards, who had been expecting a quiet evening, came running. They surrounded Alberto, Patricia and the waiter on all sides. Alberto, breathing heavily, looked at all those standing in front of him with a venomous look, as if he were a hunted animal about to attempt a desperate last dash for freedom.

He seemed to abandon any such plan, though, when a tall man in a dark suit arrived to join the circle. With an impassive but firm expression, he addressed Alberto in a restrained low voice: "Signor Conte, I am Paolo Grossi, the manager of this hotel. Out of respect for your family, we will not contact the police."

Paolo Grossi bowed respectfully to Patricia, who said nothing, but nodded her head in gratitude. The security guards helped her up from the floor.

"You won't go to the police?" Alberto laughed. "Just look who I caught!" He waved a hand to indicate the waiter. "He was following me. Come on, admit it, Gian-Bob."

Alberto again grabbed the unfortunate waiter, this time by the collar, and began to shake him.

"Sir, my name is not Gian-Bob," the waiter insisted, "and I am not following you. I don't know you at all. I'm seeing you for the first time."

"You lie!" shouted Alberto. "You are Gian-Bob, and you've been following me for weeks."

The security guards moved as if to restrain Alberto, but the hotel manager stopped them. He stood close to Alberto, lifted his hand away from the waiter, and said in the softest voice: "Signor Conte, this man is not lying. His name is Kamal Zaki. It seems you mistook him for another person. If our employee insulted you or your family, we will look into the matter, and he will answer according to the law. You can safely leave this matter in our hands."

Paolo Grossi motioned to the guards, and they grabbed the waiter by the arms.

"Why not Gian-Bob?" Alberto asked quietly, looking around in confusion. He peered into the face of the man being held by the security guards, and instead of the insolent, mocking face of Gian-Bob, he saw the pale, frightened face of Kamal Zaki. Rather than whitish, laughing eyes, the waiter had dark brown, sad eyes. Finally, Alberto realised that his fear had cruelly tricked him.

The unfortunate, innocent waiter was taken away. "But it is not my fault. Believe me, please. This is the first time ever that I have seen this gentleman…."

The Conte couple, taking advantage of the moment, quietly slipped out of the hall and hurried to their car. For the five minutes it took to reach the main road, they drove in silence. Then Patricia said softly: "Alberto, you need to see a doctor."

"I wonder, my dear, which doctor are you sending me to?"

"To the one, Alberto, who will straighten your brain."

"But my brain is fine."

"You showed it tonight."

"Things didn't go the way I expected, but nothing much happened."

"Wake up!" cried Patricia. "You poison and destroy everything you touch. That waiter will lose his job. Why didn't you say that you imagined it all? Why didn't you stop them? Why? I'm scared, Alberto. I feel that something bad is about to happen … something terrible."

"Did you forget to take your pills today, honey?" Alberto asked sarcastically.

"What?" Patricia croaked hoarsely. "How dare you laugh at me? When all is said and done, it was you who brought me to this state!" She began to pummel him with her fists.

He struggled to keep hold of the steering wheel and almost drove into the oncoming traffic. Pulling to the side of the road, he stopped the car, grabbed Patricia by the shoulders and shook her.

"Listen, you stupid woman. Mind your own business! Don't you dare tell me how to live. Understood?"

For a few seconds, Patricia stared blankly at her husband, her eyes full of horror. Then she shuddered all over and, breathing heavily, said: "Repent! Repent before it is too late…."

Alberto laughed in her face and lowered his hand.

"Repent, Alberto! If you don't repent, you won't be saved."

Alberto stopped laughing, frowned, and said: "'Whoever believes … will be saved.'[31] But I do not believe … and I do not ask for mercy. You know, dear, that repentance was not part of my plan."

He turned away from Patricia and looked out of the window. There were clouds in the sky, but a scattering of stars shone through a clear patch. One star was much brighter than the others. But a large cloud moved in and even the brightest star first turned pale and then disappeared altogether.

"You understand, Patricia," said Alberto in a different, sad voice. "My soul is like the sky. Only one star shines for me. I'm afraid of that one star, the light of my life, going out. If that were to happen, everything will plunge into darkness, disappear. Then I myself…."

He turned to Patricia and looked at her with such despair in his eyes that she shuddered. "That's what I'm afraid of, Patricia. But I don't want to repent, and it's already too late. I have no forgiveness." He trailed off, but then his eyes lit up again: "I don't need it. I don't need this repentance of yours. Don't you dare speak to me about it ever again!"

······································
[31] The Gospel According to St Mark, 16:16.

At their home, Calisto was waiting for them. Just as in childhood, he was standing looking out of the window of a large room, through which the lights of arriving cars would shine. He pondered the upcoming conversation with his father, and smiled. He had firmly decided to marry Mimi. She would belong to him, and he to her – happiness! The thought made him feel so good. And it had been so easy: all that had been needed was to decide.

His parents arrived. Calisto rushed to the door.

Patricia entered first. Her face was pale, her hair dishevelled. The diamond-studded golden tiara with delicate leaves was not on her head but in her hands.

"Hi, Mom. Did you have fun?"

"We certainly did," said Patricia with angry sarcasm. Walking past Calisto, she declared: "I'm going to bed."

Alberto followed Patricia in. "What's the matter with her?" Calisto asked.

"You don't know your mother?" Alberto replied wearily. "Why are you standing here?"

"I was waiting for you. Have you forgotten?"

"Ah, yes…. You wanted to talk to me about something."

"Something important."

"Is it about money?"

"Not exactly, although money will be needed."

"I'm tired, son," Alberto said, taking off his jacket.

"Dad, I want…." Calisto began, but hesitated.

"Go on," Alberto said impatiently; his body wanted to sleep.

"I want to get married."

"What?" Alberto's cry could have been heard throughout the house.

"Get married," Calisto repeated softly.

"And who is the lucky girl?"

"Dad, you will understand when you see her. You will like her."

"Where is she from? Who are her parents? Do I know them?"

"No, you don't know them. Her parents … adoptive parents… They…. Her father is a builder, and her mother…."

"That's enough for me. I'm not interested in knowing who the adoptive mother of this beautiful foundling is."

"She's not a foundling. Her parents are dead and a rich lady takes care of her."

"And who is the Signora?"

"Signora Ricci."

"I don't know any Signora Ricci."

"Dad, that doesn't matter."

"Where is she from?"

"From Cupra."

"Cupra Marittima?" Alberto's voice declared horror, even fright.

"Yes, from Cupra Marittima. Does that matter?"

"It matters … that you will not marry this girl."

All Calisto's resolve evaporated. He was utterly bewildered. Never before had his father spoken to him in such a tone.

"But, Dad, I love her."

"Ah. You love her," hissed Alberto, his eyes flashing with anger.

"Yes, I love her."

"Have you not heard, my dear boy, that love has to be paid for, fought for, and sometimes even died for? Do you stand ready to walk out of here, just as you are – without a name, without money, without an inheritance – to walk out of here and go to her, your love? Just as you are. Are you ready? Answer me."

"Dad, what are you talking about?"

"I'm talking about the fact, son, that if you love her so much and marry her, you will give up the Conte name and face the consequences. I will deprive you of everything. I will curse you. My father married me to your mother, and I will marry you, when I want, and to whom I want."

Calisto stood silent, bowing his head dejectedly. His apparent submission pleased Alberto, who smiled, put his hand on his son's shoulder, and said: "Think it over, son. And remember that in this house everything will be just the way I decide. I hope you understand that."

"Yes, I understand."

"Well, that's good. I'm going to bed. And tomorrow...." Alberto looked intently at his son, "see that you don't even think about your stupid idea. Goodnight. And don't forget that you are a Conte."

"I won't, Dad. Good night."

For Calisto, that night was long and sleepless. He was tormented by the desire to possess Mimi, but could not go against the will of his father: not out of respect for him, but out of fear of shame and poverty. He could not live like that: he did not know how, and had no wish to find out. Without Mimi, he would be sad, but he could live. How was it that he had suddenly decided that this was love? Why get married?

By morning, Calisto well understood the absurdity of his decision to marry, and was grateful to his father for dissuading him. So his first and only love passed – but the pain of wounded pride was another matter: that continued.

18. BY ALL THE RULES
OF REVENGE

Mirella sat in the coffee shop. The sun's rays reached through the window and gently touched her face. She closed her eyes and smiled, feeling that this day would be special. She was awaiting Calisto's proposal. He had called her the night before and excitedly told her that everything would be decided soon. Anticipating the sweetness of victory, her dreams raced ahead. She envisioned herself as Calisto's wife, and now she was just waiting for the wedding ceremony. Her head would be decorated with a beautiful diadem, a well-deserved reward for her wisdom and patience.

As she looked out from the window on this warm, autumn day, everything pleased her: wicker pots with bushes of crimson heather beneath the windows of the coffee shop; butterflies fluttering in the flowerbeds; an oleander spreading its magnificent branches; even a grey cat, basking in the sun. And the students hurrying past seemed to sense that today was a special day for her, and smiled.

Then Mirella spotted a familiar figure: a young man with a cheerful, confident step, head held high. It was Giacomo, and he too was smiling. She hoped that he was in a hurry to consult with his mysterious teacher and would pass the coffee shop without so much as looking in. But no, he was walking straight towards her. He opened the door and stood on the threshold.

The waitress, the one who had witnessed his unfortunate confession, gasped as he entered, and almost dropped a tray of cups. He winked at her and grinned, as if to say: "Look, there is nothing left in me of the former fool in love."

He made his way to Mirella's table. She sat motionless. A sunbeam highlighted her face; her glossy hair fell over her shoulders in thick curls. She was beautiful. Giacomo sighed heavily, and was immediately angry with himself for his involuntary reaction.

"Hello, Mimi." He spoke with mock gaiety and, without waiting for an invitation, sat down opposite her. Mirella gave him a look of surprise.

"Good morning, Giacomo," she replied. She tried to be calm and friendly, but her voice trembled slightly. "I didn't expect to see you here."

"No, of course you didn't expect me," said Giacomo, placing emphasis on the "me." He laughed. "You were looking out for your handsome Conte prince."

"Why are you speaking to me in that tone?"

"Oh! My tone does not suit the court. Am I not like you, my dear Signora Conte?"

"Giacomo, do stop this stupid performance. I understand that you are angry with me, but I never meant to offend you. I just loved Calisto, that's all. You and I can still be friends."

"Friends? No, Mimi, we're not friends any more. How naive you are. Someone whose love you have rejected can't be your friend."

"I'm not guilty of anything before you, Giacomo. I thought you were my friend, but you…."

"Well, tell me, what am I?"

Making no reply, Mirella returned her gaze to the window.

"Then I'll tell you," Giacomo began. "If you think that I am here because of you, because you are dear to me, you are mistaken. I came because he asked me to."

Mirella turned quickly back to face him: her face brightened; her eyes lit up with delight.

Giacomo had been waiting for this: all part of his game of revenge. Now he could continue.

"Conte commands," he said, "the servant Pelagatti executes." He gave her a look of pure hatred.

Mirella responded with a look of bold defiance. She now felt confident of winning this battle.

"Just imagine, Mimi," Giacomo continued, "that this time, playing the role of messenger gives Pelagatti great pleasure."

"Giacomo, do hurry and get to the point."

"Mimi, you must be patient. I have a parable for you." Giacomo looked mysterious. "I wrote it especially for you."

"If that is so, then do please tell me," she said.

Giacomo smiled contemptuously, and began: "There lived in a certain kingdom a poor orphan. She earned her bread with hard work, wherever she had to. Nature had not endowed her with outstanding beauty, or a sharp mind, or any special talent. But in her dreams, the poor orphan saw herself as a beauty, a smart girl, and certainly a rich woman.

"Once, when the girl went to the well for water, an angel appeared to her in the form of an old tramp. He asked her for water. The orphan gladly gave him a drink. The angel tramp asked the girl who she was and where she came from. She told him of her miserable life. She was thin, like a skeleton, and ugly. Her dress was old and patched, her shoes torn. The angel took pity on her and decided to bestow a gift on her. 'I want to thank you for your kindness,' he told her. 'And you may choose – wondrous beauty that will conquer the heart of everyone who looks at you; or wisdom to live happily and comfortably, so that everyone you meet on your way, whether it be a husband, a wife, or a small child, will love you and thank you for your good deeds.'

"The moment the angel uttered the last word, the orphan blurted out: 'I want marvellous beauty – for everyone who sees me to love me.'

"'Since you decided so,' said the angel, 'let there be beauty!'

"Instantly, the girl was transformed. Her face became extraordinarily beautiful; her figure slender, but not a picture of hunger, as before; lustrous, golden-tinted chestnut hair fell in thick strands on her shoulders; and her clothes transformed into silk and brocade, decorated with precious stones secured with golden thread, like the daughter of a king.

"And she met a young man on the road. A kind, strong, brave man, but he was of low birth; he was a poor man. This young man fell passionately in love with the orphan with a beautiful face and royal robes. He loved her as one can love only once in a lifetime. And he threw himself at her feet. He asked for her hand in marriage; swore to love her for as long as she lived. He promised to conquer all the kingdoms of the earth and lay them at her beautiful feet – if only she would become his wife.

"But the orphan in royal clothes thought no, he was just a poor man, and she refused him. She would wait for a prince.

"Then she met another young man, a real prince. He saw the girl with dazzling beauty, in magnificent clothes, and he fell in love. He decided to marry her. But his father, the king, having learnt that she was not of royal blood, but a poor orphan, forbade his son to marry her. Furthermore, he said that if the prince went against his will, the will of the king, he would drive him out of the royal palace and deprive him of his inheritance.

"The prince thought about this, sighed for a day or two, and refused the beautiful orphan in royal robes.

"Afterwards, she did not wait for her prince, but remained alone, wandering around the world. She found no true friends, no love, no happiness, or even the wealth which her callous, greedy heart so longed for. The royal clothes wore into holes; her beauty faded completely."

Giacomo paused and looked fixedly at Mirella. She returned a cold look. Doubts had risen in her mind, and her recent certainty of victory was yielding to unease.

"Did you like my story?" Giacomo asked.

"It is instructive," she replied dryly. "One thing I don't understand: what are you getting at?"

"My beautiful orphan, Calisto Conte asked me to tell you that, due to some circumstances that are stronger than his love for you, he cannot keep his promise." Giacomo grinned maliciously.

"You are lying!" Mirella shouted, choking with anger.

Giacomo laughed out loud, and then, sighing, said: "No, my dear, I am not lying, your handsome prince has abandoned you."

Mirella's eyes filled with tears. Only those who get close to a strongly desired goal but finally lose it can understand what she felt at that moment.

"Why so upset?" Giacomo asked. "There are many princes in the world. One of them may yet take you to his palace. Meanwhile, you can rejoice that you are not carrying a little Conte under your heart."

"What?"

"Yes, there was one stupid girl who believed the honeyed words of the beautiful Calisto, but … it came about that she and her child were left without the name Conte. By comparison, your position is very bearable."

"Giacomo, why are you telling me this? Who was this girl? What child? What are you saying?"

"You know, Mimi, I'm getting bored," Giacomo said, getting up from his chair. "I have told you all I came to say."

Giacomo was about to leave, but Mirella grabbed his arm and said firmly: "Tell your friend, Calisto Conte, that I will be at the autumn fair in Cupra tonight. Perhaps he will come."

Giacomo jerked his arm away, grimaced, and replied: "I will definitely pass that on."

That same evening, Calisto and his comrades – the gloomy Giacomo and the cheerful Orsino – wandered the streets of Cupra. Calisto stared intently at the face of every passing young woman, looking for the girl he could not let go, the girl he passionately desired, no matter what.

Music played loudly. The lights of the attractions sparkled and shimmered with all the colours of the rainbow. The smell of candyfloss and popcorn filled the air. Many cheerful groups gathered, men and women talking animatedly, exchanging jokes and laughter. Children rushed around like colourful flocks of little birds, shouting merrily.

Finally, Calisto saw her. Thin yellow dress, high breasts, slender legs … her delicate face, lustrous hair. He froze in place, smiling stupidly.

The rest of the scene continued as it was: passing men, women; chatter, laughter; sweet smells; colour; children running … but Calisto stood motionless, never taking his eyes off Mirella. Surrounded by friends, sipping a cocktail from a tall glass, she frequently burst into ringing laughter.

Giacomo too had seen her. His heart sank, aching with pain. He felt awkward, confused and helpless. His desire for revenge could not be reconciled with his still-persisting love and longing.

Mirella had seen Calisto; their eyes met and she smiled. Then she kissed the guy who was closest to her – on the lips. Furious, Calisto turned and walked away. Giacomo followed his friend, but first grinned and waved to Mirella. On catching up with Calisto, he put his arm around his shoulders and said cheerfully: "What are you, brother, completely soft?"

This did nothing to lessen Calisto's anger. "I'm not soft," he growled. "Let's go for a drink."

"That sounds like a good idea," said Giacomo. "Where's Orsino?"

"He was here a minute ago," Calisto answered, looking around. "There he is." He pointed. "Do you see him?" Orsino was not far behind, but was half hidden by a large candyfloss.

"Orsino, which poor child did you snatch that from?" Calisto shouted. He and Giacomo both burst into laughter.

"I didn't snatch it, I bought it." Orsino put a large piece of the sweet confection into his mouth, as if to affirm his ownership of it.

Calisto and Giacomo continued to laugh, covering, but not altogether forgetting, their gloomier thoughts: the one suffering from hopeless love, the other pondering an insidious plan.

"Come with us to the bar," Giacomo said to Orsino. "We can get a hot drink."

"I thought we were going to the concert," said Orsino, his lips half stuck together by the candyfloss that he continued to eat.

Barely audibly, Giacomo said: "You will still have a concert today."

The three of them entered the nearest bar and seated themselves at an empty table.

"A bottle of rum and something to eat," Calisto called out to the bartender, who nodded to confirm he had heard.

The scene remained cheerful enough as they worked their way through the food and drink the bartender brought to them. Then, as they made significant inroads into a second bottle of rum, Giacomo turned to Calisto and said: "You, brother, are suffering for this girl. Is she really worth it?"

"Don't call Mimi a girl." Calisto slammed a fist on the table. The fist and a slight slurring of his words testified to the quantity of rum he had already consumed.

Orsino looked with bleary eyes from Giacomo to Calisto and back again.

"I call Mimi that," Giacomo said. "Do you know why? Because she acts like a street girl. That's why."

"I don't agree with you. She is kind and sweet, and I am not worthy of her. That's what I can tell you," Calisto said. He clasped his head in his hands, leaned his elbows on the table, and froze, seeming to get stuck for some moments. Then he re-filled his glass with rum, drank it, and looked steadily at Giacomo.

In turn, Giacomo poured himself another glassful and, all the while returning Calisto's stare, drank it straight down. Then he wiped his mouth with the sleeve of his jacket and said: "You listen to what I, your devoted friend, have to tell you. Mimi is an experienced, prudent person. She began to 'befriend' you – he poked Calisto in the chest – for what she saw as her own advantage, to become a member of the Conte family. The way to achieve that, as she thought, was through a young and stupid son. And so, a cunning plan was born in her pretty head."

"Plan?" Calisto asked, vaguely amused, it seemed. "And what was her plan?"

"To make you fall in love with the idea of love: driving you to madness by keeping you at a certain distance, hiding behind false modesty and pretended convictions, and then setting her condition – that she had to become Signora Conte. And you have to give little Mimi her due – her plan worked; you were ready to marry her."

Giacomo looked inquiringly at Calisto and grinned. Then he lowered his eyes: "But our cunning Mimi didn't foresee one thing, the necessity of your father's consent to this ridiculous marriage."

Giacomo poured yet more rum and drank it. Calisto and Orsino did the same.

"So, what next?" Giacomo continued. "Our beautiful Mimi invites you to an autumn fair. She dresses up…. Why? What for? That was to arouse desire in you. No, sorry, not desire, love. And today I saw – and Orsino did too – that when she saw you, she immediately threw herself on the neck of the guy who happened to be nearest. What was she thinking? Only about touching the string in your heart that she will play until … it breaks."

"Are you saying," Calisto asked, "that it was all a game, right from the beginning … our first meeting … in a restaurant on the beach?"

"Yes. That is exactly what it was," Giacomo said. "And one more thing," Giacomo lied without thinking, "I made inquiries on campus about your sweetheart."

"Why didn't you tell me this before?" Calisto asked.

"Did I need to, when you had already turned her down? Besides, it would have hurt you to know…."

"To know what?"

"Mimi only played hard-to-get with you." Giacomo lied again.

"What?" Calisto, jumped up from his chair.

"Sit down; don't shout," Giacomo said quietly. "Please, sit down."

Calisto resumed his place at the table and looked incredulously at Giacomo. Orsino looked at both of them in surprise, vaguely shook his head, and poured more rum.

"Is it true that she was only difficult with me?" Calisto asked.

"That is what I was told by the most reliable sources. Your Mimi has a very loving heart … and, judging by the rumours, is very experienced."

"That just can't be true," Calisto thought, dumbfounded. He gulped more rum. He could not speak. Giacomo had succeeded in doing all the damage he intended. Mimi's clean, bright image was all but gone, covered with patches of some kind of sticky, greasy dirt. As never before, he regretted, with pain in his heart, that he was a Conte. He wanted to hide from everyone who knew his father and mother; start a new life. He suddenly felt so alone, so small, so insignificant. And what if not only Mimi, but everyone around, even his friends, smiled at him, praised him, declared their love for him only because he was a Conte, Conte Junior. He shuddered: anger seized him – anger directed at all the false friends, and especially the pretend lover. He had believed her – had thought she was sincere. He had fallen in love, opened up, bared his soul … and suffered. He thought he had offended her, betrayed her love – her love! – but now he realised how ridiculous and pitiful he had been. How stupid!

"She must answer for it." Giacomo's hollow voice interrupted Calisto's private soliloquy.

"What?"

"Mimi must answer for everything." Giacomo had divined Calisto's thoughts and he skilfully continued in his own vile role.

"How?" Calisto asked.

"We must give her what she loves so much," Giacomo hissed angrily. "What I heard of again and again, as she played a double and dangerous game with Calisto Conte."

"Do I understand? Are you suggesting…?"

"Exactly that. Together."

Calisto looked at him in horror.

"Trust me, she will remember it forever," Giacomo persisted. "She loves these games. That's something else I was told."

A flame of resentment ignited in Calisto, one which he no longer had the power to extinguish. An uncontrollable desire set his head spinning, his ears roaring, and his hands trembling.

"I will arrange everything." Giacomo spoke quickly so as not to miss the moment.

"Mm … huh…?" Calisto mumbled.

"You stay here…. I'll come straight back." Giacomo sprang from his chair and ran out of the bar.

Making his way through the crowd, Giacomo looked for Mirella. Up on a stage, a band was playing – loudly. Many people were dancing. Giacomo searched for the yellow dress that he had seen his victim wearing earlier. Finally, he saw it. He found a path through the dancers, quietly approached Mirella, and whispered in her ear: "He's changed his mind."

Mirella turned to face him. Their eyes met: hers enthusiastic and pure, his full of cold hatred.

ANASTASIIA MARSIZ

"He'll be waiting for you at half past eleven on the beach, near the abandoned boats."

"Why there?" Mirella was surprised.

"Because it's romantic."

Mirella looked into his eyes, but then a dancer accidentally pushed Giacomo from behind and, losing his balance, he fell onto her. He jumped to his feet and laughed strangely.

"So what should I tell him … that you won't come?"

"No." Mirella answered hurriedly and, biting her lip, said: "I will."

"Good," Giacomo said. "Then I'll go." He was about to leave, but Mirella grabbed his arm; her touch seemed to burn him.

"Thanks," she said timidly, and smiled.

Giacomo jerked his hand away, turned and walked away with quick steps. A bitter doubt began to creep into his soul: what had he done? He, like the last coward, ran from the one he loved … whom he wanted to punish, destroy … dishonour. A shiver ran through his body. He looked back at Mirella: her face beamed with joy. Of course, he knew that she was not thinking about him – the miserable, impoverished Pelagatti, but about Calisto Conte. The fire of anger, hatred, contempt for himself, for her and for the whole world, again seized him. She was choking him, taking complete possession of his heart and mind. Anger overcame love.

19. FIRE OF RETRIBUTION

Ernesto was woken by a piercing female scream. Dog lifted her muzzle, pricked up her ears, growled, then rushed to the door and set up a loud barking. Ernesto got out of bed, hurriedly put on sweatpants and a sweatshirt, opened the door and stepped outside. A cold wind blew in from the sea.

The woman's cry was repeated. Barking menacingly, Dog bounded towards the abandoned boats at the very end of the beach; Ernesto ran after her. The screaming continued; then a heart-rending cry of distress was followed by a dull groan.

Ernesto realised that interfering with whatever was going on could mean mortal danger for himself, but he just had to keep going. As he approached the old boats, he saw some movement in the darkness. Dog stopped and growled menacingly. Moving closer, Ernesto discerned three men: one was holding the hands of a girl who was lying on an old boat, the other two stood over her.

"What are you doing?!!" Ernesto shouted.

"Go away!" came a hoarse, male voice.

Dog barked loudly.

"I won't leave until I know who's screaming!"

One man separated himself from the group and walked up close to Ernesto. His face seemed familiar. "Get out of here," he hissed menacingly.

Ernesto knew that wasn't what he had to do. He brushed the man aside with his shoulder and strode purposely forward to stand next to the girl lying on the boat. The big man who was holding her made as if to punch him, but Ernesto easily dodged his fist and responded with one on the chin. The big man staggered and fell backwards over an old boat. Another man rushed at Ernesto with his fists. With the agility of a boxer, Ernesto dodged to the side and the attacker flew past him, lost his balance and fell to the sand. Then the third guy rushed towards Ernesto with a knife. Dog seized the assailant's arm in a death grip; he screamed in pain. Growling, Dog held on tight and kept squeezing until the knife fell to the ground. One of the other criminals quickly recovered the knife and thrust it into the side of the animal. She yelped and unclenched her jaws. With a howl of his own, Ernesto rushed towards her.

Suddenly, a police car siren was heard, not far away.

"Let's run!" one of the villains shouted.

The big man grabbed the uninjured arm of the guy Dog had stopped and pulled him along. A couple of minutes more and they were no longer visible.

Ernesto now turned to the girl. She had hidden behind the boat during the fight.

"How are you?" he asked quickly.

"I will live," she answered, sobbing.

"That's good," said Ernesto.

He returned to Dog. She was wheezing. In the darkness it was impossible to see the wound. He picked her up as tenderly as he could and carried her to the sea. It was just a little lighter there. He lay Dog on the sand and knelt beside her. Her breathing became erratic, and she began to tremble all over.

He felt for the wound and pressed it with both hands. She lifted her head to look into his face and seemed to say with her eyes: "Don't. Leave it. I'm going to die anyway."

"Am I hurting you?" Ernesto asked in a trembling voice. "Okay, I won't do that. Forgive me." He held her close and caressed her. "Don't leave me," he whispered. "Don't die!"

A convulsion ran through Dog's body. She looked into Ernesto's eyes for one last time, and then was gone.

All was quiet: no wheezing, no breathing.

Unbearable pain gripped Ernesto's heart. Now it was his turn to gasp for air. A dear friend, loyal, courageous, was gone forever. She had given her life for him – for the person who played games with her, took her jogging beside the sea, let her swim in the cool water. They had shared their lives, and they had shared love.

"I'm sorry…." A choked female voice interrupted his reverie.

There stood the girl he and Dog had saved from the three men. Pale and dishevelled, with streaks of mascara on her cheeks, and her dress torn, she was a sorry sight.

"May I sit with you?" she asked.

"Of course: please do."

She sank to the sand with a groan.

"I'm really sorry about your dog. She saved you," the girl said.

Ernesto couldn't answer: tears streamed down his cheeks.

After some minutes, he said: "Her name is Dog."

"That's a good name."

"She came to me by herself," Ernesto continued. "One evening, she just came … and she stayed with me."

"I never had a dog," the girl said. She carefully ran her fingers over Dog. "You must have loved her very much."

"Yes." He paused. "I lost everyone I loved, or could have loved. My mother died when I was born, and my father was killed even before that. My Grandma Ceci also died."

"I didn't know my parents either," the girl said sadly. "My mother died when I was still a baby, and I never saw my father. He may still be alive; I don't know."

After a pause, the girl continued: "I am so grateful to you for what you…." Choked by the recollection, she broke off.

"You don't have to thank me. It was Dog who saved you."

"Thank you, Dog. Thank you so much!"

"I'm really sorry about what happened to you," Ernesto said. "It shouldn't be like that."

"No," the girl replied. "It shouldn't … and I don't know how I can go on living." She burst into tears, covering her face with her hands.

"Well, don't cry," Ernesto said, trying to calm her. Then he hesitated, not knowing what to say next.

He tried: "My name is Ernesto Bruno. And you?"

"Mirella Esposito."

"Mirella Esposito, don't cry. As time passes, so will your pain. Time changes everything, erases everything … and even the things that you can't forget don't hurt as much …." He fell silent, gazing sadly at the sea.

"How can time erase what I can't forget?"

"Given time, you will find that you think about this night much less, and something else, something good, will happen in your life, and…."

"How can I survive until the day I forget?"

"Just live and do what you have to do."

Saying no more, Ernesto stroked Dog and looked at the water.

"What do you think, Ernesto Bruno," she suddenly said, "is someone looking down on us?" She raised her tearful eyes to the sky.

"Of course! He's watching. And nothing can be hidden from His sight." Ernesto followed her gaze up to the sky.

"I want to believe it," Mirella said wistfully.

"You don't believe?"

"I believe that evil must be punished."

"Grandma Ceci said that evil would find its pit and fall into it without fail."

"So let them all fall into their deep hole and rot there. Then I'll forget. Only then!"

Ernesto also wanted the evil to finally stumble, fall into the deepest, darkest hole, and stay there forever. He thought about Dog, his mother, his father.... He was filled with indignation against those who had deprived him of all that was dear to him. With all his heart, he also wanted justice....

Calisto, Giacomo and Orsino ran to Calisto's car. Giacomo groaned at the pain in his arm. His thoughts were confused, but one stark reality was clear: he had fulfilled his desire for revenge, but it was surely inevitable that he would suffer retribution for his crime.

With shaking hands, Calisto unlocked the car. He and Orsino helped Giacomo into the front passenger seat. Before taking his place in the driver's seat, Calisto looked all around and listened. The sound of a car engine was receding into the distance. That was all.

In the car, Calisto felt safe: everything was left behind. But his heart was thumping, his mouth tasted vile, a cold sweat had broken out on his forehead, his palms were wet, and he felt dizzy. Maybe it wasn't just nerves; he had drunk a lot of alcohol.

Something vile and disgusting was growing in his soul. It seemed to have tentacles that pinched and pulled. "What will your father say when he finds out? Will he find out? Of course: he always knows about everything. What will he say? How will your mother look at you?" He could picture her: cold eyes, a judgmental look, contempt.... She would never forgive him for this. She would not understand. "What is there to understand, Calisto? You crossed the line. You betrayed love. You committed a crime, a sin."

And Mirella, if he ever saw her again. Yes, he would meet her, and she would look at him with those beautiful eyes, but not as before, not at all as before. Calisto shuddered; he gripped the steering wheel tightly.

ANASTASIIA MARSIZ

Orsino was anxiously looking out of the window, fearing police pursuit. "No one seems to be following," he said out loud. Then he added: "That's good."

"They will find us anyway," Calisto said. His pale face twisted into a strange smile. He accelerated the car; barely got around some sharp bends; braked and accelerated again.

"Calisto, why are you driving like that?" asked Giacomo in a weak, hoarse voice.

"Like what? Everything is fine." Calisto laughed manically.

"Calisto, take it easy!" shouted Giacomo.

"Who's driving: you or me?" Calisto demanded to know, taking his inflamed red eyes off the road to glare at Giacomo.

"Look out!" shouted Giacomo, pressing himself into the seat.

There was a screech of brakes as, at the very last moment, Calisto pulled hard on the steering wheel and the car barely missed hitting a concrete fence.

"Are you completely out of your mind?" shouted Giacomo.

Orsino, shaking with fear in the back seat, yelled: "You're going to kill us, driving like that. Stop! I want to get out!"

Calisto laughed. He didn't even think of stopping. He was so sick, so disgusted at heart.

"Stop the car now!" Giacomo demanded.

Grinning, Calisto shot a glance at Giacomo and asked: "Did you know, Giacomo, that my father loves poetry? Thanks to him, I have been reading the works of Petrarch since childhood."

In Ripatransone, Calisto turned onto the old road. This road was winding and dangerous, especially at night.

Calisto's face flushed; his eyes sparkled. Giacomo fell silent; he realised that he could not stop Calisto.

"Did you hear what I said about Petrarch, brother?" shouted Calisto hysterically.

"Yes," the terrified Giacomo managed to say.

"I have learnt many of his beautiful sonnets by heart. Girls love them. Poetry moves them. That's why I learnt poetry. Orsino, do you hear?"

Calisto looked in the rear-view mirror for Orsino. Orsino, terrified to death, beads of sweat running down his red face, was firmly gripping the door handle with one hand, and holding the seat belt tightly with the other. He grimaced, closed his eyes, and seemed to be praying.

"Orsino, are you asleep?" Calisto asked.

"No, I'm not sleeping."

"So, my friends, I have remembered Petrarch's sonnet thirty-two," Calisto said, pressing the car yet harder along the winding road.

> O earth, whose clay-cold mantle shrouds that face,
> And veils those eyes that late so brightly shone,
> Whence all that gave delight on earth was known,
> How much I envy thee that harsh embrace!
> O heaven, that in thy airy courts confined
> That purest spirit, when from earth she fled,
> And sought the mansions of the righteous dead…[32]

As Calisto reached "the mansions of the righteous dead," he turned the steering wheel sharply to the left. Giacomo and Orsino screamed as only people looking their own needless and terrible death right in the face can scream. Giacomo threw himself on the steering wheel, but to no avail – the car veered beyond its balancing point on the edge of the road and rolled down the cliff. On reaching the bottom, the car burst into bright flames. Still inside were the three comrades –

----

[32] Petrarch wrote in Italian. This translation into English is by Alexander Fraser Tytler, Lord Woodhouselee (1747–1813).

three notorious scoundrels, three children – for whom their inconsolable parents would shed copious tears.

At the same time, and not so very far from where Calisto, Giacomo and Orsino met their end, something jolted Alberto awake. He ran to Calisto's bedroom. The bed was empty; untouched; still awaiting its sleeper. Clutching his head in an attempt to extinguish the inferno that roared within it, Alberto rushed to the window, flung it open and, with dry, whitened lips, whispered into the night: "Calisto…. Son…."

20. YOU WERE A FRIEND
TO ALL OF US

Nothing else changes a person's life – soul, heart and mind – so much as deep grief. Everything that previously worried or pleased loses its meaning in the face of death, especially when death strikes suddenly.

How to find consolation? Where to find peace? How to hold on and not be drawn deeper and deeper into the whirlpool of bitter loss?

Some get angry, despising those who dare to be happy. Others, feeling all the bitterness of loss, lose themselves, becoming their own shadow. They yearn for a world where there is neither pain nor sadness; a world filled only with serene memories, grief never having crossed the threshold; a world that does not, and could never, exist. They hide like a snail in its shell.

Yet others respond to the pain of loss by opening their hearts, offering their hands to their fellow beings, especially those who also suffer. The one who seeks salvation in real love, selfless and great, can and will be healed. But the road to healing is narrow, and can be steep, and it takes a diligent seeker to find it.

Ernesto was sitting on his bed with his phone in his hands. Next to him lay the body of Dog, wrapped in a blanket.

A gentle knock; the door opened, and there was Féde.

"Hello, Ernesto," she said softly.

"Féde! Hello! You have come!" He stood up to welcome her.

"Ernesto, how could this happen?" She ran her hand over the blanket under which Dog was lying.

"I can't believe it myself." Ernesto smiled sadly.

"Oh dear. Everything at once. My child, now Dog." Her eyes filled with tears. She sat down and made an effort to control herself.

"Ernesto, don't despair. All the rest of life is still ahead. My tears for my child have somehow cleansed my soul. Everything superfluous, everything empty, everything that prevented me from living, has disappeared; evaporated. I feel reborn. New thoughts, new feelings. It is as if a long night has ended, and in the fresh daylight I see the wonderful beauty of this world, hear the birds singing, feel the wind blow … as I never did before."

Féde looked at her friend for a long time, then took his hand and said: "Ernesto, thank you for the fact that I'm alive."

He smiled softly.

"Everyone is waiting for you out on the street," she continued. "Mom has arranged everything." Féde looked sadly at the bed.

Ernesto knelt down beside the bed and wept like a child. Féde hugged him and whispered: "Come on, Ernesto, it's time to go."

He nodded, carefully picked up Dog and obediently headed for the door.

The old Adriano minibus stood outside the Chalet Martina. The entire Marino family had gathered beside it.

"Ernesto! Ernesto!" Frani's thin voice called his name. The little girl ran to him. "Dog, my Dog," she exclaimed, and wept.

Adriano picked up Frani and hugged her. He whispered in his daughter's ear, stroked her hair and kissed her cheeks. The girl buried her face in his shoulder and wept plaintively.

Adriano had lost weight and it had not improved his appearance. He looked several years older, even haggard, but his chin was neatly shaved, his hair combed smooth, and his clothes were neat.

Martina smiled affectionately at Ernesto, clasped his body against hers and kissed him on the forehead. Adriano, with Frani in his arms, followed suit, followed by Andrea, Féde and Antonio. The Marino family had connected, rallied and proved that they were indeed a family.

When everyone was seated on the bus, Rino Grasso and Bitto Leone appeared around the corner. Fat Rino walked quickly, almost running, pulling Bitto along by the wrist. Bitto was shaking all over: moving his ailing body at Grasso's pace was difficult.

"Wait!" Rino shouted, running up to the bus, out of breath. "We are coming too!"

Ernesto hastened to greet them. Rino hugged him tightly and spoke passionately: "My friend! How awful! How did it happen?"

Ernesto didn't offer an answer, just a sad smile.

Bitto tried to squeeze his pupil's hand with his own weak hand. His face was motionless; he was unable to express his feelings, but there were tears in his eyes.

Ernesto hugged Bitto, said "Thank you" in his ear, and helped him onto the bus.

The winding road they followed took them through a picturesque landscape, but everyone regarded it gloomily and sat in silence, immersed in sad thoughts. A huge, bluish cloud filled the sky, threatening a downpour.

After fidgeting in his seat for ten minutes, Rino Grasso broke the silence by repeating his earlier, unanswered question: "How did it happen?"

Martina gave him a look of disapproval.

"I don't know," Ernesto answered. "It was just chance. Dog led me to the place."

"Rino, don't torture Ernesto with questions," Martina said sternly. Rino fell silent and returned to staring out of the window.

Ernesto contemplated the blanket beneath which Dog lay. Sitting next to him, Bitto Leone tried to offer consolation. He shook his hand with his own shaking hand. Frani sobbed from time to time, holding tightly in her small hand a rubber sausage – Dog's favourite toy. The Marino boys looked out of the window in silence. Martina sighed softly, from time-to-time glancing anxiously at her husband.

Adriano drove up to the gates of a park that provides space for owners to bury their beloved pets.

"Now…," said Martina, looking around, "They are waiting for us."

Everyone got off the bus.

A tall, thin, uniformed man stepped up to meet them, and a park worker with a face of professional compassion spoke briefly to Martina before motioning for everyone to follow him. He led them along a narrow path that meandered between neat banks. The banks were densely populated with small stone slabs with images of dogs and cats – beloved pets, dear friends who had gone from the lives of their owners for ever, but left a deep impression in their hearts.

They came to a shallow pit, next to which lay a stone slab with the image of Dog with a rubber sausage in her teeth and the inscription: "You were a friend to all of us."

The farewell to Dog was solemn and mostly silent. Dear animal, faithful, devoted friend, you are no more. Another tragic death. Another victim of human malice, cruelty, vile intrigue and meanness.

Still that big cloud covered the sky; becoming more menacing by the minute. An angry wind got up, blowing leaves, raising dust, ruffling the mourners' hair, even picking up and carrying withered dead flowers. The Cypress trees rustled gloomily. Raindrops began to splash. There was a strong clap of thunder, and then the cold rain poured down.

Adriano picked up Frani and ran with her to shelter beneath a nearby gazebo. Taking Féde's hand, Martina hurried after Adriano. The boys followed their mother, covering their heads with their jackets. Ernesto, however, continued to stand, his eyes fixed on the photograph of Dog. The rain that flowed down his face mingled with tears.

"Ernesto, let's go!" Rino shouted, tugging on his sleeve. But Ernesto didn't move and didn't answer.

Frowning, Rino took Bitto by the arm and led him to the gazebo.

Ernesto looked again at the photograph of Dog, pressed his cheek against the wet stone and whispered: "Good-bye my friend. I will always remember you."

It was damp and cold in the gazebo. Leaning his head against a wet jamb, Ernesto looked out of the rain-splashed windows and listened to the sound of the water flowing off the roof. Cold, black sadness gripped his heart, but even stronger were his thoughts on injustice. It tormented and choked him that he had never found his father's killer, the one whose name he repeated every day. This Alberto killed his father; deprived his mother; destroyed the dam that held back the turbulent streams of life, the fast, muddy waters that carried Ernesto into an unfamiliar world, full of grief, suffering, misunderstanding and cruelty. Now he felt solid ground beneath his feet; now he had confidence in himself, in his strength; now he was ready to face his enemy – he just needed to find this Alberto, make him finally answer for his crime.

Sighing heavily, he looked around at all the Marinos, at Rino Grasso and Bitto Leone – good people all of them, who had gathered on this rainy day to share his difficult moment, to encourage and console him. Someone had directed each of them to a strange, useless orphan – in whom each of them had seen a great man, and fallen in love with him for his kind

ANASTASIIA MARSIZ

heart and pure soul. He wiped away a tear with his fist, then said, smiling: "It's so good to have you all by my side."

Adriano spoke up: "Ernesto, I'm telling Martina that we need to find an apartment for you. It's already getting cold, and it's damp on the beach, and anyway…." He faltered, blushed a little, then paused and added: "You don't have to live there."

"Yes, Ernesto," Frani exclaimed. "I don't want you to live on the beach either." She pouted her lips. "You're not the chair keeper any more … and you are my best friend."

Smiling, Ernesto lifted Frani from the floor and kissed her on the cheek. She laughed loudly, and her laughter made everyone smile.

"Ernesto doesn't need an apartment," Bitto Leone said in a trembling voice.

"Why not?" Martina was outraged. "He must have an apartment!"

"He's leaving," the coach said quietly, lowering his eyes.

"How? Where to?" Féde exclaimed in fright. All eyes turned to Ernesto.

"Yes, I need to leave," he answered in a guilty voice.

"Where are you going?" Martina asked sternly.

"To Milan," Ernesto said quietly.

Bitto came to the aid of his pupil: "He will train there with a good coach: a friend of mine. He will make a champion of Ernesto."

"Then I want to go to Milan too," Frani announced, jumping up and down.

"Bitto," said Rino Grasso suddenly, as if coming to his senses, "you are the best coach. Why would Ernesto go to Milan, to some unknown coach? Why did you invent this tale?"

"No, I'm not a good coach now," said Bitto sadly, raising his shaking hands as evidence. "I can't so much as drink a glass of water without spilling it. I'm done. And the guy needs to move on; he has a great future."

Rino was silent. Everyone looked at each other anxiously.

"And when did you decide?" Martina asked.

"The coach told me two weeks ago," Ernesto replied. "But I didn't tell you because...." He glanced at Féde. "Well, I didn't want to upset you."

"So you would have waited until the day you left and said: 'Thank you for everything. *Ciao!*'" Rino was offended by the mere thought.

"Please forgive me," Ernesto said. "I'm very, very grateful to you all, for everything. You, all of you, are my family."

Tears welled up in Martina's eyes, Adriano gently took her hand.

"I never thought," Ernesto went on, "that anyone other than Ceci would ever care for me. Thank you, Signora Marino for helping my grandmother, and for taking me in to Chalet Martina." He walked up to Martina and kissed her hand. "Thank you, Signor Marino, for feeding me, talking to me. I remember every word of yours." Ernesto firmly shook Adriano's hand. Adriano's eyes became wet.

"Thank you, Signor Grasso, for your help, for bringing me to the coach." Ernesto stepped towards Rino, who smiled and hugged him.

"Coach," Ernesto turned to Bitto and looked at him affectionately. Bitto waved his hand and tried to smile. "You helped me understand who I am. You believed in me, in my strength." With the agility of a boxer, but gently, he sprang to the coach's side and held him tightly. Bitto affectionately patted him on the shoulder.

"Thank you, dear Frani, for teaching me how to play. That was something completely new for me."

Ernesto tried to bow, as little Frani had taught him, but Frani threw herself on his neck and said: "Don't leave, Ernesto."

"Don't worry, Frani, I'll be back, very soon."

"Don't forget me," Frani said softly, through tears.

"Dear Frani, I won't ever forget you. How could I possibly forget you?"

Adriano's old bus was returning to Cupra. The rain had stopped, but the sky was still overcast. Everyone was silent, all thinking their own thoughts. Life goes on, and no experiences and worries can change the future course of history – where everything will change, everything will pass.

"Signor Grasso?" Ernesto said softly to Rino.

"Yes, Ernesto." Rino answered reluctantly; he had been sinking into a doze.

"Can you please give me the address of the farm where my father was killed. I know you have it."

"Why do you want it?" Rino was alarmed.

"I want to go there before I leave … just to see. Please, Signor Grasso."

"Only to look?" Rino was incredulous.

"Yes, only to look."

"All right, Ernesto. I'll tell you the address. But there must be no nonsense. You understand me?"

"Yes, Signor Grasso," Ernesto replied happily. "No nonsense."

"Can I go with you?"

"No, please don't," Ernesto replied hastily. "I'll go alone."

"Okay," Rino said, and sank into thought.

When Ernesto approached his cabin on the beach, he saw Mirella sitting on the sand, near the door.

"Ernesto!" she exclaimed, jumping to her feet.

"Mirella! I didn't expect to find you here."

"I was waiting for you," she said softly, looking around anxiously. "I need to talk to someone. I tried calling Patricia, but she doesn't answer. I didn't know where to go. And I really need to talk to someone. I'm sorry." Her eyes darted around; her lips were dry; she trembled all over.

"It's all right. I'm here now. Take a seat." He pushed an old chair towards her, but it was wet from the rain. "Oh, that's no good," he said. "Let's go indoors."

Ernesto opened the door of his cabin to let them both in. Silence: nothing, no one there. Just as Mirella expected, but for Ernesto very hard. Dog's bowl was on the floor, her toys were scattered around.

Mirella could see what a sad scene this was. She bit her lip and said in a choked voice: "Forgive me, Ernesto. You won't want to talk now." She looked over the poor dwelling of her hero and shivered.

"It's true, I'm very sad. I buried Dog today."

"I'm so sorry," Mirella said, lightly touching Ernesto's arm.

He smiled weakly. "How can I help you?"

"I wanted to say, I went to the police today." Her voice shook. "I went to report them."

Ernesto looked at her sadly.

"So…. Yes…. They told me that they're all dead!" The words came out very fast. "All three of them! Gone! Just like that!"

Something akin to insane delight flickered in her eyes.

"How did they die?" Ernesto asked.

"At night … they crashed their car…." Mirella seemed to be looking at something far distant, through the wall. "Their car fell off a cliff. It caught fire. And they all died. All of them."

Mirella looked at Ernesto with horror. Her eyes flashed; her lips trembled.

Taken aback, Ernesto shuddered. Then he was struck by the thought that the power of justice had prevailed. No, it didn't make him happy, but the news of the death of the three scoundrels was not unexpected: on the contrary, it seemed natural.

He gave Mirella a blanket to help her get warm, and turned to boiling a kettle.

After some moments, Mirella said "Ernesto. Maybe this is the will of Providence."

Ernesto paused in the middle of the room and looked back at her. The same thought had flashed through his head.

21. LAST GOODBYE

It was twenty years since Alberto Conte had taken his son in his arms for the first time. For a long time he peered into the baby's face, and inhaled the wonderful aroma of purity and innocence inherent only in the very, very young. He kissed the newborn's tiny feet, and tears of tenderness filled his eyes. A new feeling of love was born in him – sincere, immeasurable and real. And in Conte's dark soul a light flared, warming his heart and reviving hope for simple, quiet happiness.

Alberto did not miss a single day of Calisto's life. If it had been possible, he would not have missed a single minute. He was there when his son said his first word, took his first step, and for the first time wrote his name. When the young Calisto was ill, Alberto spent days and nights at his bedside; talked to him, read books to him, played chess with him. Alberto cherished Calisto, protected him … and spoiled him.

Much was in Alberto's power – but not everything. In the mortuary, he gazed at the body of his only son. Pain dug claws into his heart. Despair slid into his soul like a snake, paralyzing and exhausting him. Confronted by death, he was powerless.

Covering his son's face with trembling fingers, Alberto whispered through dry, chapped lips: "Forgive me, son. I'm sorry, so sorry!" He burst into sobs. His legs gave way, and he would have fallen if the mortuary attendant had not rushed to seat him on a chair. He stared blankly at the attendant, then again at Calisto's lifeless body. Finally, he jumped up, screamed, backed away, and rushed from the building, clutching his head in his hands.

Returning home, Alberto froze as he entered the house. It was quiet, gloomy, cold. Here his son had lived for all of his brief life. It was from here that he had left, such a short time ago, never to return.

Beside himself with pain, Alberto flew into his office, and in a frenzy began to tear up papers, manuscripts, books – everything he had collected over the past thirty years. Then he took all the torn paper he could hold in his two arms out of the office and straight to the fireplace. There he used some of the paper to start a fire, feeding it with more and more as it burned. The flames licked around each fresh offering of paper, then overwhelmed and devoured it, reducing it to ash.

Then Alberto turned to the cabinet where the family photograph albums were kept. He found a picture of two-year-old Calisto. The little fellow was holding a green plush frog in his hands, smiling with delight. Alberto bit his lip, clenched his fists until they hurt, kissed the photograph and returned it to its shelf. Then he took an album and tore out all the photos in which he himself appeared, throwing each one into the fire as he did so. With tears in his eyes, he watched as the bright flames, sometimes turning green or blue, destroyed the mementos of a happy past.

At that moment, Patricia came into the room. "What are you doing?" she shrieked, rushing to the fireplace. She tried to pull from the fire a picture of Calisto, aged five, sitting on his father's lap, but Alberto roughly pushed her away.

"Get out! Get away from me!" he roared.

Patricia was filled with horror and disgust. Alberto had never seemed so despicable and paltry to her, with face distorted by convulsions, tousled hair, red eyes, and dry lips twisted and trembling.

"Get out! Get away!" Alberto repeated, and he pushed Patricia with such force that she fell to the floor. She moaned plaintively, but Alberto ignored her and continued to throw photographs into the fire.

With difficulty, Patricia rose from the floor and staggered back to her husband. She stood behind him and placed her hands on his shoulders. She felt unbearably sorry for him, this hated man who, overnight it seemed, had lost weight, become haggard, and gained a decade or two in age.

"Go away! Don't touch me!"

"Calm down, Alberto," said Patricia, massaging his shoulders.

Alberto paused, then turned to his wife, looked into her eyes and said: "Oh, Patricia!" He turned to kneel in front of her. Clutching her hand, he whispered: "What have I done? It was me. I killed him!"

"No," Patricia said, "it was an accident."

"Not so. I killed him. I killed him," he kept saying as if delirious. "And you, Patricia, I have ruined you." He hugged her knees. "Forgive me. Forgive me, Patricia. I'm sorry." He sobbed like a child. Patricia wept, and stroked his hair.

Three very different families became equal in the face of death. The following day, they all had to say goodbye to their almost-grown children – sons who would never again hug father or mother, never have children of their own, never again see sunlight, but would lie in the dark, damp earth ... leaving behind memory, pain, suffering, insatiable longing.

Gina Norte learnt of her son's death early in the morning, just as she was about to go to work. She sold fruit and vegetables in a small shop near her home. She had raised Orsino alone. His father, Sani Norte, had run away with a girl from Munich, leaving Gina alone with the three-year-old Orsino. From the absconding father, Orsino had received only an old tape recorder, and Gina, huge debts and a short letter:

> Gina dear, I loved you, as you know. But everything passes, everything changes ... and I have found my happiness. After all, one of us should be happy.

Raising Orsino alone was difficult for Gina. She worked from early morning until late at night, often leaving little Orsino at home alone, shedding tears. As she ran to work each day, she prayed to God that on her return her son would still be there, alive and unharmed. There was little time she could spend with the child, so Orsino grew up mostly on his own; first in front of a TV, then at the computer she gave him as a birthday present.

When she was able to be at home, Gina sewed, to earn extra money. As he grew older, Orsino helped, making patterns, and even sewing when she was exhausted. He loved his mother, but did not know how to show his feelings. He was a quiet, taciturn and withdrawn child.

Following the tragic death of her only son, Gina despaired and spent much of her time in bed. She soon died, alone in her small apartment.

The unfortunate waiter, Claudio Pelagatti, had always worked selflessly for the happiness of his son Giacomo. Grief-stricken, he spent all his savings on the young man's funeral. He bought the most expensive burial suit; chose a huge bouquet of flowers; and paid for the most prominent place in the cemetery that he could afford. He believed that Giacomo had loved him, although he had never been told that, or received a word of gratitude from him.

Claudio endured his grief in the same way as he lived – quietly, alone with himself. He was accustomed to obeying and bowing. Now, resigned to his fate, he lowered his head even further. He sat trembling at Giacomo's desk, sorting through the notebooks. He ran his fingers over the computer keyboard, so recently touched by Giacomo. Weeping silently over all his child's small belongings, he arranged them neatly on the table, inhaled their scent. Such hopeless, endless grief fell upon him that he no longer hoped for dawn, but only eternal impenetrable night and cold melancholy.

Meanwhile, his wife sobbed and lamented, mourning her only son. At the funeral service, Claudio modestly sat next to his wife, holding her hand, wiping tears from her cheeks. He listened to every word uttered by the priest, wanting to remember all the prayers, to be strengthened in faith, to remain steadfast.

Claudio maintained his silence at the cemetery as he watched his son's coffin being carried to the grave and listened to the words of consolation offered by his friends. But when the farewell ceremony was nearing its end, he suddenly cried out: "Stop!" He timidly looked around at all those present, smiled sadly, and went up to the coffin. He knelt at the graveside and sobbed like never before in his life. When everyone had dispersed, he felt unable to leave. He remained for a long time, praying for the salvation of his son's soul.

Alberto and Patricia Conte sat together at the front of the chapel. The whole of high society had gathered for the ceremony, sporting exquisite mourning clothes, with expressions of deep sympathy on their faces, offering banal phrases of insincere regret. Neither Alberto nor Patricia was perturbed by the artifice. Patricia was heavily subdued by psychoactive drugs, Alberto by dull, hopeless despair. Heedless of public decency and decorum, he sat hunched over, clasping his head in his hands, biting his lips and, with cloudy, motionless eyes, staring at the coffin in which his son lay.

"Dear God, You see our sorrow because sudden death has taken our brother Calisto from life," the priest said with passion. Alberto gave him a pained look. "Show Your infinite mercy and receive him into Your glory," continued the priest. "Through Christ our Lord, Amen."

"Amen," echoed the voices in the chapel.

On that, Alberto let out a wild groan, a desperate cry. Patricia took her husband's hand and squeezed it tightly. Burying his face in her shoulder, Alberto wept bitterly.

At the end of the mass, all those present silently made their way out.

Just beyond the outer door stood a short, stocky man in a grey suit and glasses. He was the head of the local commissariat, and was of course on the most friendly terms with Alberto. Approaching Alberto, he whispered something in his ear. Alberto looked surprised and drew him aside. Patricia silently followed them.

"Alberto, deepest condolences on your loss. How terrible it is," the commissar began. He then turned to Patricia: "Dear Signora Conte, it is hard to lose loved ones. What an irreplaceable loss. Please accept my expressions of the sincerest sorrow."

Having dispensed with the essential courtesies, he continued, "I am sorry to disturb you on such a day, but I have received some important information about your son." He hesitated a little, blushed, then said: "Sorry, please excuse me … about your tragically deceased son, Calisto."

"Speak up, Tony," Alberto said impatiently. His eyes flashed with anger, and his pale cheeks gained some colour.

The commissar threw a glance at Patricia and looked very uncomfortable.

"Don't waste time; talk," Alberto said. Turning to his wife, he said: "You can stay, Patricia."

"Yesterday a young girl came to our department and said…." The man stopped in indecision, looking again at Patricia.

Patricia had realised that something bad was on its way. Her heart sank in anticipation.

"Go on, Tony," said Alberto, sorely irritated.

"The girl said that three young men, Giacomo Pelagatti, Orsino Norte and Calisto Conte, raped her that night."

"Raped? How?" cried Patricia, staggering back. Alberto froze, staring at the commissar.

"I just wanted you to know, Alberto, in case something happens," the commissar said dryly. He shook hands with

Alberto and was about to hurry away when Alberto grabbed his sleeve.

"What is the girl's name?"

"Mirella Esposito."

"No. No, this cannot be!" Patricia cried out. She staggered, and fell senseless into her husband's arms.

Calisto was buried in the Conte family vault, next to his grandfather Sergio. Patricia was conscious, but it could hardly be said that she had recovered her senses. For her, the real world no longer existed. Her mind had closed itself to the grief and all the horror. She looked around utterly bemused. "What was happening? What was going on? Why was everyone wearing black? Why were they crying? Why was Alberto bending over a coffin? Who was in the coffin? … And with whom was her baby Calisto staying?"

On finally returning home, Patricia immediately rushed to Calisto's room. Confused as she already was, the empty room perplexed her yet more.

"Calisto? Son? Mom is home! Where are you, baby?" she called loudly.

Alberto went upstairs and stood looking at her.

"Alberto, where is Calisto?" she asked.

Alberto looked surprised and did not answer.

"Alberto, I ask you, where is my boy?"

"He is no longer with us. He's gone," Alberto finally answered, his voice shaking.

"Where is he?" Patricia screamed. "Where did you take him?" She grabbed Alberto's hand and jerked him towards herself. "Answer me, you vile soul!" she shouted into his face, pumping the arm she held. "Where have you hidden my son?"

"Patricia, he is dead," Alberto whispered weakly.

"Dead? What? …Dead?" This was impossible to believe. "No, he is not! Calisto is not dead! You lie!" she screamed, and fell to the floor.

Alberto wanted to pick her up, but as he stooped over her she hit him in the face with all her might. Panting now, she said: "You deceive me. Give me back my boy!"

Alberto looked into her face, and his eyes filled with tears. He quietly ran his hand through her hair. Patricia leaned her head on his hand, and cried.

"Don't be afraid. I am with you," Alberto said.

He lifted Patricia in his arms and carried her to the bedroom. There he laid her on the bed, sat down beside her and took her hand. He offered her a sedative, which she accepted. When she finally fell asleep, he straightened the covers, kissed her on the forehead, and returned to Calisto's room. There he lay on the bed and, hugging the pillow, cried for a long time until sleep overcame him.

When Alberto awoke, the sun was setting. Opening his eyes, he saw the bloodied face of Omar bending over him – or he thought he did. He felt Omar's chill breath on him, with its heavy smell of death. He jumped off the bed, rushed to the door, and turned around – but the ghost had already disappeared. Alberto looked at himself in the mirror and smiled a pathetic, wry smile. Then he ran downstairs, out of the house and into the garage. Jumping into his car, he raced it down the road to the olive farm. That was where he had begun his rapid and deep descent – where he had spilled the blood of an innocent man. He felt that a terrible retribution awaited him, but he was no longer running away from it – rather, he was hurrying to meet it.

Ernesto walked along an empty road. Rino Grasso had kept his word and given him the address of the olive farm where his father died. The sun was setting: the autumn wind blew cold. Ernesto shivered and plunged his hands into his jacket pockets. Nervous about his imminent visit, his heart was beating hard. He looked up at the sky; the cover of long, grey clouds was increasing. A premonition of something bad made him shudder.

As he continued down the road, a distant hillside, populated with neatly-aligned olive trees, came into view. As he got closer, he was surprised to see the car of that strange Signor Vero, whose acquaintance had so impressed him. His heart began to beat yet faster, and his breathing speeded up. Frowning, he quickened his pace, following a narrow footpath that took him into the depths of the olive grove.

Ernesto explored the avenues of trees. He was looking for the old house where the terrible drama that changed his whole life had taken place. Twilight was rapidly gathering, and with it grew a sense of anxiety. He could barely make out the darkened path, which seemed to lead only to more trees. He saw no house. He was seized with a strange turmoil.

Suddenly, he heard a familiar voice: "Ernesto!"

He stopped, peering into the darkness.

"Are you by any chance looking for me?" asked the same voice.

The man was not far away, but in the fast-fading light Ernesto could see him only in silhouette.

"I'm here! Come to me," said the voice.

Ernesto stepped forward, towards the voice. As he approached, the man turned and led the way along a different path. Very soon, they came to a small house dimly lit by a single lantern. Peering into the man's face, Ernesto was able to confirm with certainty that it was Signor Vero.

"Well, here we are, champion," Vero said, referring to Ernesto's victory in the boxing ring.

"So it's you," Ernesto said.

"Yes, Ernesto, it's me. Let me introduce myself again: Alberto Conte."

"Alberto," Ernesto repeated in amazement. His fists clenched, his face tightened, his eyes flashed, and he trembled with rage.

"Yes, I'm that Alberto," Conte said in a nervous voice, perhaps louder than he intended.

"What are you doing here?" Ernesto asked.

"I can tell you one more story," he began.

"What is this, a joke?" Ernesto hissed.

"No, I'm not in the mood for jokes," Alberto said. His eyes were cold and hard, his lips tight, his face pale. Ernesto gave him a sullen, incredulous look.

"When you were not yet in this world," Alberto began, "a young boy full of hope for a happy future met a girl. He loved her sincerely; as tenderly as perhaps only young and ardent hearts can love."

Ernesto's heart raced as Alberto walked up to the house, ran his hand over the outside wall and read, "My L. – my pier of hope." Then he turned to Ernesto and said: "I forbade painting over this inscription – in memory of your parents." He gazed into Ernesto's eyes.

"What happened to them?" Ernesto demanded, through gritted teeth.

"I wanted your mother – and that's why I killed your father," Alberto said defiantly. Then he suddenly shot both hands forward towards Ernesto and shouted: "I killed him with these hands!"

Ernesto's body was ready to fight. His temples pounded, his face was on fire, his hands clenched into fists, he felt breathless. This was the person who took his father's life, and brought his mother to her death. This was the scoundrel, the murderer who eluded punishment for his crime. Ernesto shook with rage: it seemed that he was about to attack his father's murderer.

Alberto, hands down and head bowed, stood before Ernesto in silence. He was waiting for the storm to destroy him. He longed for his release, his end.

Ernesto clenched his fingers into a fist. He was ready to deal a crushing blow for justice – a death blow for revenge. It would not be difficult to crush Alberto's skull with a single movement.

"Well?" roared Alberto. "Come on!"

With his left fist raised above his head, Ernesto rushed at Alberto, but suddenly stopped and stood motionless. Alberto stared at him in terror – his lips were trembling.

"No, you are not worthy even of that!" Ernesto spat out: and he turned and ran away without once looking back.

He ran through the trees, the thorny branches lacerating his face. Faster and faster he ran, until he stumbled on a stone, lost his balance, fell to the ground and rolled down a slope, clutching at bushes and tree roots as he rolled. When he came to a stop, he was lying in a ravine. Above him, the sky – dark now – was huge, silent, severe. Twinkling stars offered something gentler. Ernesto raised his hands, as if praying to God for forgiveness – for help. He was angry with himself, but he knew he had done the right thing. Now it was his turn to bury his face – in the damp grass – and sob like a child.

After some time, a quiet, fresh wind arose, gently caressing Ernesto before turning its attention to dancing with dry leaves and swaying the tree tops. Itself unseen, but felt and seen in its effects, it soothed and calmed him.

Alberto Conte, driven by fear, rushed home. Everywhere, he imagined he saw monstrous, ugly people. Their pale faces appeared when he stopped at dark intersections; they peered around corners; hid behind trees. On arriving home, he ran into the house, locked the door, closed the curtains, and hurried to Patricia. He wanted to hug her, close his eyes, forget himself, and fall asleep.

Out of breath, he flew to his wife's room. Patricia was sitting on the bed, swaying to left and right, and apparently looking far into the distance. She was holding a green plush frog – little Calisto's favourite toy. The old frog was faded, and white threads stuck out of his long legs. Alberto remembered how Calisto had cried when the frog was injured, asking to take it to the hospital. Alberto had said that he could cure the frog better than any doctor – and himself stitched up the damaged foot.

"Patricia," said Alberto, and threw himself on his knees before his wife.

"It's you, Alberto," she said softly, barely looking at him. "Calisto went for a walk and forgot his Nocchio. How will he manage without Nocchio? He will cry."

"Oh, Patricia, Patricia." Alberto said softly, hugging her knees and weeping. She was his last refuge, his only consolation, his only hope of salvation – and everything was shattered. She was lost in the distant past, and he…. What was left for him?

Patricia suddenly had a good idea. In her most positive tone, she said: "Alberto, look outside, in the garden, find our boy and take Nocchio to him." She held out the frog.

Alberto sighed, got up from his knees, took the frog and said quietly: "I'll go, Patricia, straight away. I will give our boy his beloved Nocchio, I promise. Now, you lie down and sleep." Once again, he put her to bed, covered her with a blanket and gently kissed her forehead. "Sleep, my Patricia. I will go."

He quietly left the room.

Moments later, downstairs, on the ground floor, the shutters banged with a thud, and something fell to the floor and shattered.

"Dévi!" Alberto called to the maid: "Is that you?"

There came no answer, other than the wind, which howled eerily in the chimney.

Alberto went down to the living room. A curtain was being buffeted by the wind; the open window behind it swung wildly back and forth; the shutter did the same, repeatedly hitting first the window, then the house wall.

On the floor was a carved photograph frame, its glass broken. Alberto bent down to pick it up, immediately cutting a finger with a shard of glass. The blood flowed fast and dripped to the floor. Putting his cut finger in his mouth, he used his other hand to take the photograph from its frame. He smiled sadly as he looked at the picture. He remembered that day on the beach. Little Calisto laughing, splashing his bare feet in the water, running away from his parents, getting caught, everyone laughing. And Patricia so beautiful, so young, so happy, her hair fluttering in the wind, a smile playing on her lips. He remembered what the sand felt like under his bare feet, the splash of water on his face, the sound of the water, the smell of the sea. It all seemed like yesterday.

"Baby Alberto." A voice familiar to him from childhood came from behind.

The photograph fell from his hand. He could not move, and was unable to utter a single word.

"Baby Alberto," the voice repeated.

This time Alberto turned around. An indistinct human form slipped through the door and into the darkness of the corridor. Frozen with horror, Alberto got up, looked out from behind the door, and froze. At the end of the corridor stood a huge Jamaican, his eyes glowing monstrously in the dark.

"Alberto," he said in a mocking tone, savouring each syllable, and then retreated through the door of the office.

Alberto's legs buckled. He grabbed the door frame. Gasping with fear, he stood and looked at the door behind which the ghost of Gian-Bob had disappeared. Perhaps it again only *seemed* to be him? Maybe….

He was dizzy and his thoughts were confused. He looked around. No one. He checked the stairs. Empty. He bit his lip, took a few steps and stopped; took a deep breath and went into the office.

Huddled in the semi-darkness was a cluster of dark figures. Seen only in silhouette, they stood bent over, so that their faces could not be seen. Alberto shrieked and backed toward the door.

"Well, Baby Alberto, finally…." The distinctive voice of the Jamaican spoke. Gian-Bob was sitting with crossed legs in an armchair in a corner of the room.

"Is that you?" Conte wheezed.

"Of course it's me. And here with me is everyone you killed."

Peering fearfully into the darkness, Alberto saw the bleak faces of all those he had humiliated, dishonoured, destroyed. Mirella's poor mother was there, and the unfortunate girls from the orphanage, and Ernesto's father.

"Do you remember them all, Alberto?" The Jamaican was mocking him.

Looking at Gian-Bob, Alberto's demeanour was transformed. Like a cornered wild animal, he was ready for a deadly fight.

"No, it was not me who killed them all. It was you, Gian-Bob. You made me as I am. You destroyed my family. There hasn't been a day when I haven't cursed you. I have longed for revenge, to crush you, to destroy you, but you always eluded me. You…."

Gian-Bob laughed loudly and clapped his hands. His eyes lit up with hellish fire.

"What a liar you are, Alberto Conte. Was it me? Or was it your obsession with revenge? You could have been a man, but you became a beast. You lived as a creature, and you will die like the last creature." Gian-Bob again burst into loud laughter.

Alberto rushed to the corner where his tormentor was sitting. He lurched forward to grab him by the throat, but his outstretched hands met nothing but emptiness, and then the back of the chair. Gian-Bob had melted away.

Alberto was shaking. He was drenched in cold sweat. His lips twisted as his eyes darted around the room. There was no one there: he was alone in a dark, empty room.

Panting, he croaked: "You won't get away this time. I know where to find you. We will meet soon, and you will answer to me for everything."

Opening a drawer beneath the table, he took out a loaded pistol, hissing angrily: "I do not repent! I will not repent! Gian-Bob, I will meet you in hell!" He put the gun to his temple and pulled the trigger.

EPILOGUE

Three years passed. Ernesto trained, had many fights. Step by step, he went for his goal and prepared for the championship. Fortune smiled on an orphan from a small town: his star rose in the sky of world boxing. Now the future champion had a long journey to make – to America, where his dreams would become reality.

He had other dreams too: he yearned for his former life, for the people who loved him as their own. So he asked his manager for permission to visit Cupra for a few days.

The Marinos knew he was coming and eagerly anticipated the arrival of their champion. At the Chalet Martina, Adriano ran around the kitchen shouting at Antonio every now and then, dropping and breaking dishes, pouring flour, and repeating that this was his last day in the kitchen.

Martina ordered colourful balloons, and she and Frani made a poster: "Welcome back, Ernesto!"

Frani devoted herself to drawing a big red heart, and Martina declared that Frani had never before sat for so long and so quietly in one place.

Féde taught all the Marinos a song, the words of which were written by Marco, her once-scorned admirer. Marco had become a frequent guest at the Chalet Martina. He spent all his free time with Féde. He helped her carry dishes to the tables, wrapped forks and knives in napkins, and even prepared cocktails, which were very much enjoyed by visitors to the Chalet Martina.

Andrea washed the floor, tables and chairs, obsessively straightened tablecloths, polished cutlery – and kept an eye on the entrance, hoping to be the first to see Ernesto.

Rino Grasso brought Bitto Leone, who now used a wheelchair, being almost unable to walk. Bitto had moved to the clinic, so as to be near his beloved Daniela. Each day, he would meet her and they would sit together under a large tree. He lived on memories of happy days in the past, and frequently thought about his beloved pupil, Ernesto.

At last, Ernesto stood outside the Chalet Martina. The summer season was in full swing, and the promenade was crowded with people who had come to walk along the shore. A merry crowd of children swept past; jostling each other, chattering and laughing. Ernesto smiled as he looked after them. As a child, he had often walked along the promenade with Grandma Ceci, sat on a bench and eaten ice cream. There was the roundabout, on which a white horse had launched him into the world of children's dreams; and the sea, the guardian of so many of his secrets, thoughts and experiences.

He sighed and entered the Chalet Martina. On seeing him, Andrea shouted joyfully: "He's arrived!"

Everyone turned to look at the long-awaited guest. He was wearing a red polo shirt that hugged his athletic figure, and carried a travel bag over his shoulder. His face shone with a blissful smile, remembered by all as characteristic of his happiest moments.

Frani made a dive for him: "Ernesto! Look, Mommy and I made a poster for you," she said, pointing her finger.

"How beautiful! Thank you, Frani."

"Welcome home, Ernesto," Martina said softly as she hugged him.

"That's lovely, thank you Signora Marino," said Ernesto, embarrassed. "I've missed you so much."

"Welcome back, Ernesto!" was heard from all sides, and everyone rushed to hug him.

Rino wheeled Bitto to Ernesto in his chair. The old coach slowly stood and, supporting himself on the arms of the wheelchair, took a step towards his pupil. Ernesto hugged him, kissed him tenderly, and whispered: "Coach!"

Tears of happiness filled Bitto's eyes. He put his hand to Ernesto's cheek.

Rino Grasso said: "Here you are, son. Well done!" He shook Ernesto's hand firmly and added: "I told you that you would be the champion!" Then he turned to everyone and asked: "Who saw talent in Ernesto?"

"You did, Rino. It's all thanks to you," Martina said, laughing merrily.

"I'm thinking," Grasso said seriously, "that maybe I'll become a sports agent? I will discover new talent, point them in the direction of big sport, and get my share."

Everyone laughed.

"Féde!" Ernesto held out his hands to the young woman standing quietly beside her mother, waiting her turn. "So beautiful," he added, and hugged her tight. She did, indeed, look very lovely.

"Thank you, Ernesto," she blushed. "I'm so glad to see you."

Then Adriano appeared from the kitchen. "You've arrived," he exclaimed, rushing to Ernesto.

"Signor Marino!" Ernesto hugged Adriano, who already had tears in his eyes – and not because of the onions in his kitchen.

"Just one moment," Adriano said, running back to the kitchen. "Antonio, hurry up, he's here!" he shouted as he disappeared through the door.

Everyone sat down at a large table and began to ask Ernesto about his life in Milan; his trips elsewhere in Europe; the cities he visited; the people he met; and about his training and fights. Ernesto answered all their questions in detail and with pleasure. There was much laughter, many smiles, and more than a few happy tears.

Sitting among these people who loved him filled Ernesto with great joy. Before they all came into his life, only Grandma Ceci understood him, believed in him, rejoiced in him. But now, whatever happened, whatever might lie ahead, he would always have true friends, close people – his family.

At the table at the Chalet Martina that evening, only one person was missing: one who had encouraged him, supported him; had become his best friend. Yes, Mirella Esposito. Ernesto looked anxiously at the entrance: she had promised to come to dinner.

He checked his phone. One unread message: "Ernesto, I'm sorry, I can't come today. Mom is bad. I can't leave her alone. Let's meet tomorrow. Dévi will stay with her."

"Certainly! See you tomorrow," Ernesto wrote back, smiling sadly.

After Ernesto left Cupra, a great change had occurred in Mirella's life. One morning, she was woken by a telephone call; she looked at the screen; the number was unfamiliar to her.

"Hello?" she said.

"Good morning. Is that Mirella Esposito?"

"Yes, that's me."

"I'm Antonio Bugiardini. I am the lawyer for the Conte family."

"I don't want to hear anything about the Conte family!" Mirella had exclaimed indignantly – and hung up.

The phone rang again. Mirella did not answer, neither then, nor time after time when she saw that number on her screen.

Finally, she answered.

"Mirella, please listen," implored Antonio Bugiardini, "I'm calling on behalf of Patricia Conte!"

Mirella kept silent.

"Mirella, did you hear me?"

"You said you were from Patricia…."

"Yes, I speak for Patricia Conte."

"Conte? Is that right?"

"Yes, it is Conte. I need to speak to you about a very important matter. Please come to my office."

Again, Mirella kept silent.

"Mirella, can you hear me?"

"Yes," she answered uncertainly.

"So you will come? This is very important."

"Okay, give me your address."

Some hours later, Mirella was sitting in Signor Bugiardini's spacious office.

"Mirella, I have to give you some papers concerning yourself and Signora Conte. First, though, please read this letter. It's important." He gave her a sealed envelope, on which was written, in Patricia's thin handwriting: "To my dear Mirella."

Mirella looked at Signor Bugiardini in great surprise. He nodded his head in affirmation of this most unexpected address, then said that he would leave her alone to open and read the letter. He went out of the office.

Mirella opened the envelope, took out and unfolded the letter, and read:

My dear Mirella, my dear child. If you are reading this letter, then I am no longer with you. I couldn't tell you the whole truth personally – I didn't have the courage. But now, not having to answer your questions, or see the look in your eyes, I will reveal the whole terrible, dark secret of your birth.

You were born from a poor, unfortunate woman and a cruel, vicious man. Your father (my husband, Alberto Conte) dishonoured your mother, abused her – took advantage of her defencelessness. Alberto Conte has many sins in his soul, but perhaps none worse than this.

When I found you, you were very tiny, thin, and you were dying of hunger at the breast of your dead mother.

Only God knows how you survived. I took you in my arms and loved you as my own daughter. I loved you with all my heart.

Mirella, my dear daughter, forgive me if you can. Forgive me for selfishness, for weakness. I'm sorry for not daring to say – for hiding the truth from you – that you lived as an orphan but had a living father. But, believe me, it's better that you never knew him. And I'm sorry for not revealing my real name to you.

Daughter, I have always wished you happiness. I took care of you during my lifetime and will take care of you after. I bequeath to you everything that I have. That is only right, and fair.

I have a son; his name is Calisto. Someday you will meet him. He is a good, kind boy, although spoiled by his father. I want you to hold each other like brother and sister. Remember me, my dear Mirella, my dear daughter.

The letter was signed: "Your tenderly loving mother, Patricia Conte."

Having read the letter, Mirella wept. She felt nauseous and weak. She dropped the letter and covered her face with her hands.

And that is how Signor Bugiardini found her when he returned with a glass of water for her.

He gave her some time to recover, then began seriously: "Mirella, Patricia Conte is in trouble. She is ill; she needs care. And it has come about that you are the sole heir to the entire Conte fortune."

"And Patricia's husband, my…," Mirella stammered, shuddered, and fell silent.

"He died a few weeks ago," the lawyer replied dryly. "He shot himself in his office." Bugiardini took a deep breath and added: "Patricia's illness is not surprising, given the circumstances in which she lost both her son and her husband."

Mirella looked with horror at Signor Bugiardini. She was hurt and disgusted. However, she was a Conte, and Patricia needed help.

"Where is my mother?"

"Your mother? Do you mean Patricia Conte?" asked Bugiardini, surprised.

"Yes, I mean my mother, Patricia Conte."

"Ah, yes...." Bugiardini said thoughtfully. He tried to find a resemblance to Patricia Conte in Mirella's face, but could not. Her face resembled a different person.

"Mirella, we need your signature on some documents. Then I will take you to Ripatransone to see Patricia."

When Signor Bugiardini's car drove into the Conte courtyard, Mirella pressed herself deep into the seat. Certain that this was going to be difficult, she felt uncomfortable and scared.

Dévi, a beautiful girl in a simple black dress, was waiting for them. She smiled and waved her hand, and as Mirella got out of the car exclaimed happily: "Finally!"

"Hello, Dévi," said Signor Bugiardini in a business-like tone. "Where is Signora Conte?"

"She's in the garden, walking. I'll take you to her." Dévi led the way around the side of the house to the magnificent Conte garden.

When they found her, Patricia was no longer walking, but sitting in a garden chair beside a resplendent rose bush. When Mirella came close, Patricia looked at her for a long time and then, as if remembering something, beamed with joy and said: "Mirella, daughter! I didn't expect to see you here. I'm waiting for Calisto. He should be back from school soon."

Then Patricia turned to the maid: "Dévi, did you cook dinner for Calisto?"

"Of course, Signora Conte." Dévi caught Mirella's eye and winked.

"All the food he likes?"

"Yes, Signora Conte. Soup, salad, meatballs, everything."

"All right, Dévi. Alberto will be late today, so don't cook dinner for him."

"Very well, Signora Conte."

Patricia turned again to Mirella. "Mirella, my girl, come to me, I want to hug you." She held out her hand to Mirella, who walked over to Patricia and gently hugged her.

Patricia had lost her mind and her beauty, but she had not lost her ability to love. Her purity of soul, kindness of heart and true nobility remained intact.

From that day onwards, Mirella took care of Patricia. She fed her, bathed her, walked in the garden with her, put her to bed, read books to her: and every day listened to the same fantasies about Calisto and Alberto, who in Patricia's mind still lived, Calisto as a small boy. But Mirella was content: she had found comfort, a home and a mother.

On the day following his joyous return to the Chalet Martina, Ernesto walked happily through the streets of Cupra. It was so good to be back. In his hands he held a large bouquet of yellow roses, Grandma Ceci's favourite flowers.

He got on a bus to the cemetery: to his grandmother. There, among the flowers and candles, photographs and inscriptions, was a photograph of a young Ceci with the simple inscription: "Cecilia Bruno."

"Hello, Ceci," Ernesto said softly and leaned his face against the cold stone. "Please forgive me for not coming for so long. I was away ... a long way from here. I've seen so much: big cities, huge bridges, wide roads, and lots of beautiful houses. Do you remember how you and I arranged a competition for the most beautiful houses? I have found a winner. It is not in Cupra, but far away – in England. You would really like it. I would buy it for you. I can buy a lot of things now.

"Ceci, I'm going to America. I get scared when I think about it ... that I'll be there all alone, not knowing the language. But don't worry, Ceci. You said yourself that good people are everywhere. Now you can be calm: I am happy, I have friends, I have a dream … and you can still be proud of me."

A yellow butterfly with blue spots on its wings fluttered close to Ernesto and settled on his shoulder. He looked at it and smiled: it lightened and warmed his soul.

"Goodbye, Ceci. Don't be sad. I'll be back soon…."

ABOUT THE AUTHOR

Anastasiia Marsiz, a native of Zaporizhzhia, Ukraine, is a writer, journalist, and translator. Resident in Kyiv since 2006, she moved to Italy, with her school-age daughter, in March 2022, displaced by war. Fortunately, and as is magnificently attested to by her novel, *The Big Fellow*, she was already very familiar with people and places in certain parts of Italy.

In *The Big Fellow*, Anastasiia Marsiz raises the issues that concern her most: hypocrisy in society, betrayal, domestic violence, and racial and social inequality. In doing so, she demonstrates that faith, love, friendship and family are the values that truly matter, enabling resistance to evil and injustice. The book won the 2021 "Literary Ukraine" prize.

ABOUT THE TRANSLATORS

Andrew Sheppard is the editor of *East–West Review.* He provided the English translation of *War Poems* by Alexander Korotko (Glagoslav, 2022).

Michael Pursglove is a former Senior Lecturer in Modern Languages and is now a freelance translator. He has published translations of *Moon Boy* by Alexander Korotko and *Children of Grad* by Maria Miniailo. His latest translation of *Bera and Cucumber* by Alexander Korotko was published by Glagoslav in 2023.

ABSOLUTE ZERO

by Artem Chekh

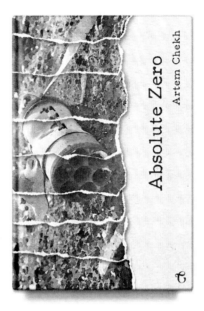

The book is a first person account of a soldier's journey, and is based on Artem Chekh's diary that he wrote while and after his service in the war in Donbas. One of the most important messages the book conveys is that war means pain. Chekh is not showing the reader any heroic combat, focusing instead on the quiet, mundane, and harsh soldier's life. Chekh masterfully selects the most poignant details of this kind of life.

Artem Chekh (1985) is a contemporary Ukrainian writer, author of more than ten books of fiction and essays. *Absolute Zero* (2017), an account of Chekh's service in the army in the war in Donbas, is one of his latest books, for which he became a recipient of several prestigious awards in Ukraine, such as the Joseph Conrad Prize (2019), the Gogol Prize (2018), the Voyin Svitla (2018), and the Litaktsent Prize (2017). This is his first book-length translation into English.

Buy it > www.glagoslav.com

THE FANTASTIC WORLDS OF YURI VYNNYCHUK

by Yuri Vynnychuk

Yuri Vynnychuk is a master storyteller and satirist, who emerged from the Western Ukrainian underground in Soviet times to become one of Ukraine's most prolific and most prominent writers of today. He is a chameleon who can adapt his narrative voice in a variety of ways and whose style at times is reminiscent of Borges. A master of the short story, he exhibits a great range from exquisite lyrical-philosophical works such as his masterpiece "An Embroidered World," written in the mode of magical realism; to intense psychological studies; to contemplative science fiction and horror tales; and to wicked black humor and satire such as his "Max and Me." Excerpts are also presented in this volume of his longer prose works, including his highly acclaimed novel of wartime Lviv *Tango of Death*, which received the 2012 BBC Ukrainian Book of the Year Award. The translations offered here allow the English-language reader to become acquainted with the many fantastic worlds and lyrical imagination of an extraordinarily versatile writer.

Buy it > www.glagoslav.com

Someone Else's Life

by Elena Dolgopyat

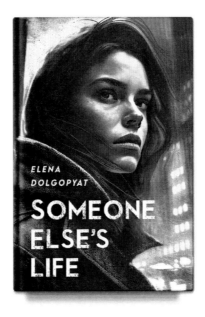

Elena Dolgopyat was born and raised in the USSR, trained as a computer programmer in a Soviet military facility, and retrained as a cinematographer post-perestroika. Fusing her diverse experiences with her own sensitivities and preoccupations, and weaving throughout a colourful thread of magic realism, she has produced an unsettling group of fifteen stories all concerned in some way with the theme of estrangement. Elena herself, in an interview given at the time of the book's launch, said, "Into each of these stories is woven the motif that one's life is 'alien'. It is as if you are separate from your own life and someone else is living it. You feel either that your own life is 'other', or you experience a yearning for a life you have not led, an envy for some other life." In his introduction to the collection, Leonid Yuzefovich writes, "Each of Elena Dolgopyat's stories … painfully stirs the soul with a sense of the fragility, the evanescence, even, of human existence … in her quiet voice, she is telling us of "the multicoloured underside of life". She is telling us of things that matter to us all."

Ravens before Noah

by Susanna Harutyunyan

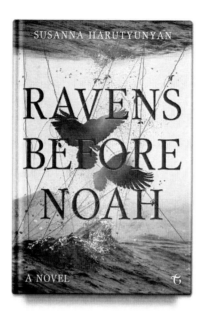

This novel is set in the Armenian mountains sometime in 1915-1960. An old man and a new born baby boy escape from the Hamidian massacres in Turkey in 1894 and hide themselves in the ruins of a demolished and abandoned village. The village soon becomes a shelter for many others, who flee from problems with the law, their families, or their past lives. The villagers survive in this secret shelter, cut off from the rest of the world, by selling or bartering their agricultural products in the villages beneath the mountain.

Years pass by, and the child saved by the old man grows into a young man, Harout. He falls for a beautiful girl who arrived in the village after being tortured by Turkish soldiers. She is pregnant and the old women of the village want to kill the twin baby girls as soon as they are born, to wash away the shame...

Buy it > www.glagoslav.com

Glagoslav Publications Catalogue

- *A History of Belarus* by Lubov Bazan
- *Children's Fashion of the Russian Empire* by Alexander Vasiliev
- *Empire of Corruption: The Russian National Pastime* by Vladimir Soloviev
- *Heroes of the 90s: People and Money. The Modern History of Russian Capitalism* by Alexander Solovev, Vladislav Dorofeev and Valeria Bashkirova
- *Fifty Highlights from the Russian Literature* (Dutch Edition) by Maarten Tengbergen
- *Bajesvolk* (Dutch Edition) by Michail Chodorkovsky
- *Dagboek van Keizerin Alexandra* (Dutch Edition)
- *Myths about Russia* by Vladimir Medinskiy
- *Boris Yeltsin: The Decade that Shook the World* by Boris Minaev
- *A Man Of Change: A study of the political life of Boris Yeltsin*
- *Sberbank: The Rebirth of Russia's Financial Giant* by Evgeny Karasyuk
- *To Get Ukraine* by Oleksandr Shyshko
- *Asystole* by Oleg Pavlov
- *Gnedich* by Maria Rybakova
- *Marina Tsvetaeva: The Essential Poetry*
- *Multiple Personalities* by Tatyana Shcherbina
- *The Investigator* by Margarita Khemlin
- *The Exile* by Zinaida Tulub
- *Leo Tolstoy: Flight from Paradise* by Pavel Basinsky
- *Moscow in the 1930* by Natalia Gromova
- *Laurus* (Dutch edition) by Evgenij Vodolazkin
- *Prisoner* by Anna Nemzer
- *The Crime of Chernobyl: The Nuclear Goulag* by Wladimir Tchertkoff
- *Alpine Ballad* by Vasil Bykau
- *The Complete Correspondence of Hryhory Skovoroda*
- *The Tale of Aypi* by Ak Welsapar
- *Selected Poems* by Lydia Grigorieva
- *The Fantastic Worlds of Yuri Vynnychuk*
- *The Garden of Divine Songs and Collected Poetry of Hryhory Skovoroda*
- *Adventures in the Slavic Kitchen: A Book of Essays with Recipes* by Igor Klekh
- *Seven Signs of the Lion* by Michael M. Naydan

- *Forefathers' Eve* by Adam Mickiewicz
- *One-Two* by Igor Eliseev
- *Girls, be Good* by Bojan Babić
- *Time of the Octopus* by Anatoly Kucherena
- *The Grand Harmony* by Bohdan Ihor Antonych
- *The Selected Lyric Poetry Of Maksym Rylsky*
- *The Shining Light* by Galymkair Mutanov
- *The Frontier: 28 Contemporary Ukrainian Poets - An Anthology*
- *Acropolis: The Wawel Plays* by Stanisław Wyspiański
- *Contours of the City* by Attyla Mohylny
- *Conversations Before Silence: The Selected Poetry of Oles Ilchenko*
- *The Secret History of my Sojourn in Russia* by Jaroslav Hašek
- *Mirror Sand: An Anthology of Russian Short Poems*
- *Maybe We're Leaving* by Jan Balaban
- *Death of the Snake Catcher* by Ak Welsapar
- *A Brown Man in Russia* by Vijay Menon
- *Hard Times* by Ostap Vyshnia
- *The Flying Dutchman* by Anatoly Kudryavitsky
- *Nikolai Gumilev's Africa* by Nikolai Gumilev
- *Combustions* by Srđan Srdić
- *The Sonnets* by Adam Mickiewicz
- *Dramatic Works* by Zygmunt Krasiński
- *Four Plays* by Juliusz Słowacki
- *Little Zinnobers* by Elena Chizhova
- *We Are Building Capitalism! Moscow in Transition 1992-1997* by Robert Stephenson
- *The Nuremberg Trials* by Alexander Zvyagintsev
- *The Hemingway Game* by Evgeni Grishkovets
- *A Flame Out at Sea* by Dmitry Novikov
- *Jesus' Cat* by Grig
- *Want a Baby and Other Plays* by Sergei Tretyakov
- *Mikhail Bulgakov: The Life and Times* by Marietta Chudakova
- *Leonardo's Handwriting* by Dina Rubina
- *A Burglar of the Better Sort* by Tytus Czyżewski
- *The Mouseiad and other Mock Epics* by Ignacy Krasicki

- *Ravens before Noah* by Susanna Harutyunyan
- *An English Queen and Stalingrad* by Natalia Kulishenko
- *Point Zero* by Narek Malian
- *Absolute Zero* by Artem Chekh
- *Olanda* by Rafał Wojasiński
- *Robinsons* by Aram Pachyan
- *The Monastery* by Zakhar Prilepin
- *The Selected Poetry of Bohdan Rubchak: Songs of Love, Songs of Death, Songs of the Moon*
- *Mebet* by Alexander Grigorenko
- *The Orchestra* by Vladimir Gonik
- *Everyday Stories* by Mima Mihajlović
- *Slavdom* by Ľudovít Štúr
- *The Code of Civilization* by Vyacheslav Nikonov
- *Where Was the Angel Going?* by Jan Balaban
- *De Zwarte Kip* (Dutch Edition) by Antoni Pogorelski
- *Głosy / Voices* by Jan Polkowski
- *Sergei Tretyakov: A Revolutionary Writer in Stalin's Russia* by Robert Leach
- *Opstand* (Dutch Edition) by Władysław Reymont
- *Dramatic Works* by Cyprian Kamil Norwid
- *Children's First Book of Chess* by Natalie Shevando and Matthew McMillion
- *Precursor* by Vasyl Shevchuk
- *The Vow: A Requiem for the Fifties* by Jiří Kratochvil
- *De Bibliothecaris* (Dutch edition) by Mikhail Jelizarov
- *Subterranean Fire* by Natalka Bilotserkivets
- *Vladimir Vysotsky: Selected Works*
- *Behind the Silk Curtain* by Gulistan Khamzayeva
- *The Village Teacher and Other Stories* by Theodore Odrach
- *Duel* by Borys Antonenko-Davydovych
- *War Poems* by Alexander Korotko
- *Ballads and Romances* by Adam Mickiewicz
- *The Revolt of the Animals* by Wladyslaw Reymont
- *Poems about my Psychiatrist* by Andrzej Kotański
- *Someone Else's Life* by Elena Dolgopyat
- *Selected Works: Poetry, Drama, Prose* by Jan Kochanowski

Printed by BoD™in Norderstedt, Germany